IN ORDER OF APPEARANCE: TRACIE MCBRIDE, MANDY BURKHEAD, MARK RIVETT, ALI ABBAS, W. T. PATERSON, K.A. FOX, J. WOOLSTON CARR, ROBERT B. READ JR., NILS NISSE VISSER, BRIANT LASLO, MERCURY, E. A. CATANIA

Gears, Ghouls, and Gauges

A Steampunk Short Story Anthology

Contents

Foreword

Of all the literary genres I know, Steampunk is the hardest to pin down. The definition and parameters vary from person to person, book to book. And in the case of this volume, from story to story. Within these pages, Steampunk and Gaslamp Fantasy fans will see many things they recognize, but there are also plenty of tantalizing tidbits that are fresh and new.

One of the cornerstones of Steampunk is the "airship." These retro-futuristic conveyances may feel familiar, like a blimp, or something completely new and gravity-defying in its own way. Six of our twelve tales include one of these crafts in some way, and yet they are all different in their role in the stories and in the lives of the characters. In *The Bronze Bomber* by Briant Laslo and *Jewels of the Deep* by Nils Nisse Visser, for instance, the airships serve as the backdrop for a thrilling climax, be it espionage or the threat of the supernatural. In *Divine* by E. A. Catania and *The Lady Defiance* by Mandy Burkhead, airships give women a chance to cut their own path in the world and build new families of their choosing. Whereas in *Fractured Moonlight* by W. T. Paterson, the airship is more akin to an escape, allowing its captain to soar above his sorrow and regret.

Another beloved mainstay of Steampunk fiction are automatons and other fantastical inventions. In real life, clockwork creations were mostly used for entertainment, such as a mechanical swan music box that appeared to eat fish. In the hands of a Steampunk author, they are so much more. Though many of our stories have a whimsical tone, they also carry their own weight. *The Steam Horses of Stem Park* by Paul Michael features talking animals, but also speaks to the entrenched fear that machines will one day replace us all. *The Grand Assault* by J. Woolston Carr sets a mechanical fencer against a human champion, using the spectacle to distract people from the true conspiracy happening under their noses. In *The Mechanist's Daughter*, which opens this collection, an automaton meant for protection malfunctions, and it's a race against the clock to figure out how to shut it down.

Other, even grander machines also come into play in our assembled stories, but lend themselves to a decidedly darker tone. Great war machines trundle across a war-torn wasteland overrun by the dead in Mark Rivett's *An Evening on Harbor Ridge*. The main character of *In the Cavern of the Sleepers* by Ali Abbas uses his all-terrain, mechanical centipede to explore a mysterious jungle, which brings him face to face with gods of old. In our space-western, *La Muerda* by Mercury, people can travel the stars but still end up in the gutter. *Basic Black* by K.A. Fox illustrates how an inventor's life can be anything but glamorous, especially with a deadly disease lurking around every corner.

We did our best to preserve the particular styles and international flavor of this collection by not demanding they all adhere to a single style sheet, so you will see both British and American English conventions. This anthology has been a delight to edit, and I hope you will delight in reading it. Whether this is your first time reading Steampunk or your fiftieth, you are sure to find something to love.

Phoebe Darqueling
 Editor

The Mechanist's Daughter by Tracie McBride

The doorbell rang three times, the third a long and insistent peal. Alice sighed and pushed her safety goggles up on top of her head. Whoever it was, they were evidently in sore need of her attention. She rubbed the worst of the grease off her hands and onto her workman's apron before opening the door.

At first glance, Alice took the child on her doorstep for a street urchin. She was certainly grubby enough to be one, and her clothes were a mishmash of colours and sizes, bespeaking a lack of adult care and supervision. Her golden hair had been inexpertly brushed, several snarls and tangles visible beneath the smooth outer strands. Then Alice observed the fine leather of her shoes, her well-fed form, and the healthy glow barely disguised by her grimy cheeks; if she was an urchin, she must be a beggar or pickpocket par excellence. A black box about the size and height of a bull terrier sat at her feet, steaming gently on a set of flexible treads.

The child and her mechanical companion made a curious sight. But then, Alice supposed, so must she, all smeared in grease, goggles askew, and the tools of her trade protruding every which way from her apron pockets.

"What do you have there?" Alice said, nodding towards the box.

"It's my bodyguard. It's not working properly. Nana says it's m…mal…mal-functioning," the girl said.

Alice folded her arms across her chest. A likely story—perhaps the child was a thief, and this was but a ruse to gain entrance to the house.

"It's a box," she said pointedly. "A box on treads. It's clearly not designed to 'guard' anything. Now, if you'll excuse me, I have important work to do."

"Ssshh!" the girl said, pressing a finger to her lips, her hazel eyes wide with alarm. "Don't raise your voice. That's part of the problem. Ebony's been too sensitive lately and attacking anything noisy. Just yesterday, it shot an entire murder of crows out of a tree just because they were cawing too loudly."

As if on cue, the box began to unfold. Within seconds, it turned from a squat and angular object into something vaguely humanoid, extruding rounded limbs and a sleek dome of a head, all in some glossy, black metal. The head swivelled silently, and its only distinct facial features, two red bulbs for eyes, protruded towards Alice on articulated stalks. A row of three small apertures opened across the machine's chest. Cold darts of air hit Alice in her face, neck, and breast, so sharp that she gasped and clutched at herself.

The child threw her arms up in exasperation. "You see what I mean?" she said. "You're lucky Ebony used up all its poison-tipped darts on the crows."

Alice gaped at the automaton for a few moments before finding her voice. "Get that thing out of here!" she hissed. "Don't you know the penalty for having an armed automaton? I could be sent to prison just for having it on my doorstep!" Alice knew this only too well; her mother had been accused of constructing just such a machine. She had been arrested and perished shortly afterwards in a fire in the prison. With her father having died when she was a toddler, this left Alice orphaned at the age of fifteen. Like her mother, she was determined to pursue the mechanist's craft, but vowed never to repeat the older woman's mistakes. So, she led a blameless life (a necessity, as the authorities closely scrutinized the output of her workshop for many years after her mother's arrest), and one without the complications of a spouse and offspring. At the age of twenty-four, she remained contentedly a spinster.

The girl's eyes welled with tears. "I had so hoped you could help me. I don't know how to turn it off, and now it won't always obey my commands. I'm worried it's going to hurt somebody it's not supposed to, or…or even turn on me. Besides…." She looked beseechingly up at Alice. "Nana said you're the best mechanist in the city. She gave me your address before she got really sick and said I should call on you if anything happened to her. She also said that you'd probably want to help on account of your per…po…professional curiosity."

The child was right about that; illegal or no, the automaton was the most beautiful piece of engineering she had ever seen, and she yearned with an almost palpable intensity to explore its innards. Besides, she'd never forgive herself if it did go on a malfunctioning rampage and hurt an innocent. At the very least, she could use that as her defence should the authorities find her in possession of the device. Then there was the not insignificant matter of the mysterious Nana's identity. Why, out of all the mechanists in the city, had she singled out Alice?

"All right," Alice huffed. "You'd better come in and tell me all about it."

The child's name was Tabitha. Despite her probing, Alice was unable to determine the precise nature of the relationship between Nana, the automaton's creator, and the child, nor the whereabouts of Tabitha's parents.

"Nana made Ebony to look after us," Tabitha explained, "but one day my parents went out without it, and they never came back. And now Nana is sick and forgets things a lot of the time, so she can't fix it."

Alice nodded. "So it's out of poison darts, you say," she said, eyeing Ebony nervously. "But what else can it do?"

Tabitha sang the first six notes of "Sing a Song of Sixpence" in a pure, clear soprano. Alice smiled; she had always loved music, despite being unable to carry a tune in a bucket, and the nursery rhyme was a childhood favourite of hers. In response to the tones, blades slid with a soft *snick* from the end of the automaton's fingertips. Alice leapt backward with a surprised yelp. The automaton whirled and drove the blades deep into the back of an upholstered armchair, sending stuffing floating through the air.

"Sorry about that," said Tabitha. "It was only meant to show its claws on that command, not actually use them."

Alice took another step backward, drawing Tabitha with her. "Anything else?" she said, her voice quavering.

"Well, there's—" Ebony went into a blur of motion, smashing the chair until it was little more than a pile of shredded fabric and kindling on the floor. "…That," finished Tabitha.

"And you don't know how to turn it off?" Alice asked, her voice suddenly hoarse with fear. Tabitha nodded miserably. "Well, that presents a…challenge. We could just wait it out. Stop fuelling it and wait for it to run out of steam, and keep out of its way in the meantime."

Tabitha shook her head. "It's self-feeding. If I don't fuel it, it will burn whatever is at hand." As if on cue, Ebony opened a hitherto invisible hatch in its belly, revealing a small, glowing furnace. The automaton scooped up remnants of the armchair and fed them through the hatch, then closed it.

"Water?" inquired Alice.

"It doesn't need much, and what it does need, it sucks out of the air. Mostly it runs with…" The girl's face contorted as she struggled to recall the right word. "Mer…make…mercury?"

Alice whistled, long and low. She'd heard of mercury-powered automatons, but thought them a theory only, as yet beyond the technical capabilities of the age. Absentmindedly, she tapped a forefinger against her chin, a habit she had inherited from her mother.

"First, we need to put Ebony somewhere safe. If we can't turn it off, we need to contain it where it can't hurt anybody. Then we need to talk to this Nana of yours—see if we can coax more information from her."

Tabitha looked doubtful. "Nana says I must never bring anyone to the house. Not anybody, not ever."

"But Nana trusts me, doesn't she? Isn't that why she gave you my address?" Tabitha nodded.

"Well then, let us proceed with the plan."

Many years previously, Alice's mother had built a steel-lined room in their basement, "in case of emergency," she had said, although what kind of emergency might necessitate such a room, she had never elaborated upon. It had sat, dusty and unused, until now.

"Ebony is responding intermittently to commands, so let's hope that it will obey this one," Alice said. "I want you to lead it into that room, and tell it to stay. Once you have left the room, I will lock the door."

Ebony followed them into the basement meekly enough, and when Tabitha, with another sung command ("Greensleeves," if Alice was not mistaken) ordered it to stay, it rolled into a corner and folded down into its "incognito" box shape. Even though the basement door was mounted on casters, Alice struggled to haul the heavy structure closed. The automaton seemed to sense the duplicity. It unfolded and rolled with frightening speed towards the slowly decreasing gap. The door slammed shut with barely a second to spare, and Alice spun the key in the lock.

Several heavy blows sent the door shuddering; the machine testing the resolve of the door, Alice guessed. Then came several moments of ominous silence, followed by a faint and peculiar noise.

"Tabitha," Alice said warningly, "is there something you forgot to tell me?"

"Oh, did I not mention Ebony's flame thingy?"

"'Flame thingy'?"

"Yes. For setting fire to things. And for cutting through metal."

Alice pressed her hand against the door. It was several inches thick, but already it had grown noticeably warmer.

"And there's another thing. Ebony thinks you're an enemy now. Once it gets out of that room, it will destroy you on sight."

Images rose unbidden to her mind—a dozen pierced and poisoned black crows, her armchair shredded on her parlour floor, Ebony on the other side of the door wielding flame with relentless determination. She shuddered and backed away.

Tabitha tugged at her sleeve. "I have an idea," she said. "See this steel door? My entire house is like this on the inside. Even the glass window panes have been replaced with steel. Ebony knows its way home, but if we lock it out, it will take a while for it to cut its way inside. Maybe that will give you time to figure out how to fix it."

With no better plan, Alice could only allow the child to lead her away.

Tabitha hailed a hansom cab and fished a fistful of coins from her pocket with which to pay for it, leaving Alice to ponder further. Who was this ragamuffin child who lived in a steel-lined house, who wandered the streets with gold-filled pockets and an illegal, lethal automaton for a chaperone?

They alighted from the cab in a nondescript street. Tabitha waited until the cab was out of sight, then set off at a brisk pace down a narrow walkway between houses. "I always get them to drop me outside a different address and walk the rest of the way. Then if they're questioned later, they can't tell anyone where I live," Tabitha explained. "My mama taught me that."

Several blocks later, they slowed outside a well-kept two storey building that, except for its closed curtains, looked nearly identical to its neighbours. Eschewing the front door, Tabitha led Alice down the side of the building. The child set her palm against what looked like a randomly selected brick and leaned upon it. A panel slid open, and Tabitha slipped through the opening. Alice hesitated. The clandestine device further piqued both her curiosity and her suspicion. What secrets would necessitate a concealed entrance such as this? But as always, curiosity won out, and she followed Tabitha into her house.

Whereas the exterior of the house had been almost drab, the inside looked like it had been furnished by a flock of giant, crazed magpies. Opulent fabrics in clashing colours draped the walls. Exquisitely sculpted statues dotted the foyer at random intervals, all of them adorned with glittering necklaces, earrings, and bracelets of inestimable value. Vases of considerable vintage and worth overflowed with pound notes. Light blazed from an excess of crystal chandeliers. And in amongst it all trundled several cleaning automatons, whirring softly on well-oiled treads and tirelessly dusting.

One wall was adorned in a floor-to-ceiling formal portrait of a young couple. The man, with his wavy golden hair and finely chiselled features, possessed considerable masculine beauty and a vapid expression. The woman posed at his side, one hand resting possessively on his shoulder. The artist had captured in her no-less-handsome visage a lively intelligence in her eyes and a hint of cruelty in her smile. Alice was sure she'd seen their likenesses somewhere before. The society gossip pages of the newspaper, perhaps? Or the crime news?

Their entrance must have triggered an alarm, for somewhere in the upper level of the house, a bell pealed.

"Who's there?" came a quavering voice from above.

"It's me, Nana. Tabitha."

"Who's Tabitha?"

Tabitha exchanged a significant glance with Alice. "You see?" she said. "Some days she recognizes me, some days she doesn't, but it's been getting more 'doesn't' than 'does' lately."

They went upstairs and entered a bedroom just off the landing. Unlike the scene below, the bedroom was dimly lit with a single gas lantern and the furnishings sparse. Bedclothes rustled, and a figure sat up in the bed. A faint odour of rotting fruit, mothballs, and human ordure arose from her.

"Maude? Maude, is that you?"

The name was familiar to Alice. She had a maternal aunt named Maude who had run away to Australia to escape an unwanted arranged marriage and who, by last account, was doing very well for herself as a clairvoyant of some renown. But it was not the name that froze Alice's heart in her chest.

The woman in the bed appeared much older than the nine year absence would warrant, yet still there was no mistaking her as Celeste Kathleen Nottingham.

Alice's mother.

Celeste peered at her through rheumy eyes. "You're not Maude," she said disappointedly, then tapped her forefinger against her chin. "Yet, I know you…. Don't I?" She looked intently at Alice for a second or two before pouting like a child denied a treat and throwing herself back down onto the bed and wailing. Tabitha rushed to her side, stroking the woman's grey hair and whispering soothingly to her.

"You're a good girl, Tabby," Celeste whispered back. "But who is this woman you've brought home? Is she a doctor? You know I said no doctors."

A surge of jealousy, hot and unwelcome, flooded Alice's belly. Her mother was alive; alive, and apparently more willing to live with a stranger's child than to return to her own flesh and blood. Alice clenched her fists at her sides and released them repeatedly. It would do none of them any good if she failed to wrestle herself into some semblance of clear-headedness.

"I'm Alice," she said, stepping closer to the bed. "I'm your daughter."

Tabitha and Celeste both looked at her with confusion.

"My daughter?" Celeste shook her head. "No, you can't be my daughter. Alice is only a child."

Alice tried another tack. "I'm here to fix your automaton," she said, slowly and loudly, as if speaking to a simpleton. "But first, I need to know how to deactivate it. How do you turn Ebony off?"

Celeste pouted again and turned herself towards the wall. "No!" she said, her voice muffled as she pulled the covers over her head. "I won't tell you my secrets! You just want to lock me up again, don't you?"

Alice sighed in exasperation. To Tabitha, she said, "Does Celeste, I mean, Nana, have a workshop? Maybe I'll find some clues in there."

"Yes, but it's locked," replied Tabitha. "I'm forbidden to go in there."

Alice took but a moment to savour the petty triumph. Her mother had not only allowed, but positively encouraged her to go into her workshop and tinker when she was a child, alongside her mother or on her own. Yet evidently that trust did not extend to Tabitha.

Then she set her pettiness aside; whatever had happened since her mother's disappearance, little Tabitha was blameless. And as a fellow orphan, the child deserved Alice's empathy and assistance far more than her antipathy.

"And the key?"

Tabitha pointed at Celeste. "Around her neck."

"Right." Alice pushed up her sleeves. "None of us are going to enjoy this, but needs must." With that, she set upon her mother.

Alice had no illusions that retrieving the key would be an easy task, yet still it took all of her strength and several scratches to her face and hands before she was able to accomplish it. As soon as she had it in her grasp, it was as if she had removed a magic talisman. Celeste transformed from a hissing, spitting wildcat to a hysterical, frail old woman. Breathing hard from her exertions, Alice turned to find a teary-eyed Tabitha pressed tightly into a corner of the room.

"It's OK," Alice said gently, extending her hand to the girl. "You see how she is. She'll forget soon enough that she ever had a workshop or a key to open it."

Just as Alice had anticipated, Celeste's workshop was neat and orderly. It was also immense, covering the entire basement level of the house and a second subterranean level which housed, amongst other things, several vats of mercury. Chronic exposure to the element had most likely caused Celeste's illness. Her mother had never been one for keeping written records, probably to reduce evidence of her less-than-legal activities, but in this secure environment, she had let her guard down. A bookshelf stretched along one wall, stacked with hundreds of journals filled with notations and diagrams in Celeste's meticulous hand. Alice eyed them with dismay; it could take months, even years, to find the answers they so sorely needed.

A cry of alarm came from the top of the stairs. "It's Ebony!" shouted Tabitha. "I can hear it at the window!"

Snatching up a claw hammer, Alice rushed up the stairs. She led the girl back to Celeste's room, shut the door, and barricaded it with an oak dresser. It would prove a flimsy defence against Ebony's mechanical might, but with luck it would buy them enough time for a last desperate attempt to extract the shutdown code from her mother.

A loud bang sounded from the foyer, making them all flinch.

"Who is it?" Celeste called, pawing at her coverlets in agitation.

Alice's mind raced. She pulled Tabitha close and whispered in her ear.

Tabitha frowned, but went to Celeste's bedside as instructed.

"Nan...I mean, Mama," she said softly. "It's me, Alice."

Celeste's features lit up. She drew Tabitha into a fierce embrace. "Oh, Alice, how I have missed you! I wanted to return for you, but I couldn't. The authorities were watching you too closely, and if they caught me, I would surely hang. But now you're here with me, and that's all that matters."

Alice choked back tears; in the darkest moments of her orphanhood, she had dared to comfort herself with fantasies of this very scene. And now here she was, all grown up, and listening to her gravely ill mother saying the words she had so longed to hear to another child who stood as her proxy.

Tabitha looked to her for reassurance. Alice nodded with a confidence she did not feel as she listened to the murderous automaton smash and crash throughout the house.

"I know it's not bedtime yet, Mama. But I wondered, could you sing me that song? You know, the one about a mother leaving her baby by the roadside while she goes to pick blackberries?"

"Highland Fairy Lullaby?" Celeste's brow furrowed in concentration. "Why of course, sweet child. It goes like this."

There was another almighty crash, and the bedroom door flew open, the heavy oak dresser pushed aside as if it were made of paper. Ebony rushed into the room, all blades and flames and glowing red eyes. Alice stepped between it and the pair on the bed, raised her hammer, and steeled herself for her inevitable demise—

—and Celeste's soprano rang out.

Ebony's flame extinguished, its eyes dimmed, and it sputtered to a halt. Overwhelmed with relief, Alice slid to the floor like a marionette with cut strings. She crawled toward Tabitha and Celeste, and the girl slid off the bed to join her, sobbing, on the floor. Alice turned to check on her mother.

And found her lifeless, staring at the ceiling, her lips forever set in a benevolent smile.

Over the next few days, Alice pored through Celeste's journals and other papers in the house. Using these, plus a fair amount of intelligent guesswork, she pieced together the details of her mother's final eleven years. Tabitha's parents, Samuel and Lily Beaumont, had been highly successful criminals and narcissistic ones at that, judging by the copious number of newspaper clippings they had kept in which their exploits were mentioned. Samuel was a conman who moved within high society circles, seducing money out of wealthy, lovelorn women. Lily had been the brains of the pair, increasing their financial and social influence through a combination of savvy investments and ruthless extortion until they ruled the city in all but name.

Lured with the promise of unlimited funds with which to conduct her research, Celeste came under their employ around the time that Tabitha was born. On the instructions of the Beaumonts, she created Ebony to be used as a mechanical assassin. In its sinister design, Celeste had evidently excelled. Although her employers were implicated in the deaths of several of their rivals, their cast iron alibis spared them from the hangman's noose.

Despite her prodigious engineering talent, Celeste was no criminal mastermind. Word of her work fell on the wrong ears, and she was arrested. Recognizing her immense worth to them, the Beaumonts arranged for her escape. A fire near Celeste's cell was lit, the body of some hapless pickpocket secured to take her place in the wreckage, and the authorities were none the wiser. Celeste lived with them, creating the fortifications of the house and a myriad of other useful devices. She also became close to baby Tabitha, perhaps as a substitute for the child she had been forced to abandon.

What became of the Beaumonts remained a mystery. Most likely, their life of crime finally caught up with them, and they were done away with. Left to raise Tabitha alone, Celeste reconfigured Ebony for a more defensive function. And so they might have continued in somewhat chaotic contentment, had Celeste not fallen ill.

All of this was of scant concern for Alice as she sat at her mother's workbench with Ebony laid open before her. She imagined turning over the automaton's plans to the military, imagined the country's foes laying down their arms in the face of a field of ebony metal warriors, imagined the reverence and acclamation that would be her rightful due from her peers. She pulled a length of vein-like tubing from Ebony's left arm and squeezed, watching thoughtfully as the mercury slipped away on either side of her fingertips.

No. That would never do. She would only be trading the swift and brutal deaths of her countrymen for the long and protracted deaths by gradual poisoning of the labourers who would be needed to manufacture the things.

With infinite care, Alice took the automaton apart and stored its components on the shelves. Job done, she ascended the stairs and found Tabitha in her playroom. The girl sat fondling the lace trim on the dress of a porcelain doll, her gaze distant and her sombre expression befitting someone of far greater years.

Poor little mite, Alice thought. What must it be like to be left all alone in the world at such a tender age?

But then, Alice knew exactly what that was like. And the power to rectify it lay solely in her hands.

"Come, Tabitha," she said. "I think it's time to do some redecorating. A style that is a little less ostentatious is called for, I think."

Tabitha wrinkled her nose. "Oss...osten...what?"

"You'll see," Alice replied, ruffling Tabitha's hair. "I'll remove the steel panels from the windows, too, while I'm at it. This place could do with some natural light. Then we might see about employing a governess for you, and after that.... Have you ever been to the circus?"

Tabitha shook her head, eyes wide with wonder.

"Then tonight is your lucky night."

About Tracie McBride

Tracie McBride is a New Zealander who lives in Melbourne, Australia. Her work has appeared in over 80 publications, including the Stoker Award-nominated anthologies *Horror for Good* and *Horror Library Volume 5*. Her collection *Ghosts Can Bleed* contains much of the work that earned her a Sir Julius Vogel Award, and has had several stories shortlisted for other national genre awards. She is an active member of the Horror Writers Association and a member of the Australasian Horror Writers Association. Visitors to her blog are welcome at http://traciemcbridewriter.wordpress.com/.

The Lady Defiance by Mandy Burkhead

"Harpies ahead, Captain," the first mate called out.

"How many?" Henrietta asked.

Khaleel adjusted the telescopic contraption that he had replaced his missing eye with, gaining a clearer view of the floating island in the distance. "Three on some rocks, two flying around—wait, there's another."

"At least six, and that's just on this side of the island," the captain mused. "That's practically a swarm."

Harpies—a human-like species sporting bird wings, talons, and feathers—were well-known predators. Like any birds of prey, they usually hunted solo or in pairs, and it was rare to see more than three together unless they were planning an attack or defending their nests. Henrietta, like any good airship captain, kept the known nesting islands marked on her map, and this was not one of them.

"We'd best give them a wide berth," the captain commanded. "No telling what they're up to."

"That'll put us off course," Khaleel warned. He reconfigured the telescopic eye to his normal vision and opened his other eye, blinking as it adjusted to the sunlight.

"*The Lady Defiance* is the fastest ship around," Henrietta said with a smirk. "Don't worry; we'll catch up to them."

Khaleel knew it to be true. After all, he'd invented the Aether engine himself. Most airships were still running on old technology. The magical Aether was required to keep the ships afloat in the air, but older airships were limited to just that. Those ships were still reliant on wind to fill the sails or airstreams in order to actually travel. Khaleel's engine could not only keep the ship afloat, it could also propel it, even when the winds were calm. That, paired with the small size of *The Lady Defiance*, made it an especially fast ship.

Khaleel's engine could have revolutionized airship travel if anyone at the Academy had taken him seriously. Khaleel was from Druij Skey, a nation whose people followed ancient traditions and who shunned any new technology. However, Khaleel, whose parents were travelling merchants, had taken him to numerous lands, and in the process, he'd fallen in love with tinkering with gadgets and engines. When he'd submitted his proposal to the Academy of Aetherscience, though, they'd laughed in his face. After all, what could a Druiji possibly know about engines?

Thankfully, Captain Henrietta was not one to judge by appearances. When she heard about Khaleel's skills, she paid him to repair the old engine on her ship. When he suggested building his theoretical prototype, she hired him on as her first mate, in charge of maintaining the new engine and any other gear on board. Khaleel tried to explain some of the workings to her, but the captain claimed that she didn't have the brain for such things. Her specialties were sailing and combat, not magical science.

They adjusted their course to avoid the floating island. Even so, some of the crew still plugged their ears with wax out of fear. Legend had it that a harpy's siren song could enthrall people or drive them insane. No point in risking it.

By nightfall, they'd caught up to their prey once more. The fat cargo ship that they'd been stalking, unimaginatively named *Prosperity*, could pay the crew for at least four months. But it was also well armed. The cargo ships had grown wise to the pirates' games, now boasting cannons, grappling hooks, and even spikes. They kept lookouts posted all hours of the day and night.

At the captain's command, the crew cut the lights on *The Lady Defiance*. It was a dangerous maneuver—their only guidance in the dark skies was now the ship in front of them—but it would allow them to sneak up on the ship. They approached from above and off their prey's starboard side, their cannons angled down at forty-five degrees. The captain held her hand in the air, waiting for the best moment. The wind stilled, as if holding its breath in anticipation, and she lowered her hand like an axe, striking the gong beside her wheel to alert her blinded crewmates to strike. Fire lit up the night, followed by the boom of cannons.

Screams and shouts erupted on board the merchant ship. As flames licked up its sails, the crew scurried about. Some went to the cannons, aiming blindly in the direction that the shots had come from, while others attempted to put out the fire.

"We took out two of their sails, Captain," Khaleel observed. "Another round should be all we need 'fore she's ours."

The captain hit the gong again. Moments later, the cannons burst once more, toppling the last sail and crippling *Prosperity's* movement. Their adversaries attempted to fire back, but the *Prosperity's* lower elevation left them at a disadvantage, and their cannonballs fell short. The battle was over before it had truly begun, which was exactly how the captain preferred it. She'd informed anyone who joined her crew that the goal was to minimize damage and loss of life. The former obviously meant that their stolen goods were less likely to be destroyed in battle. The latter was to appease the captain's personal moral compass.

Henrietta raised her lips to the voice projector. "If you surrender without a fight, your lives will be spared. We will take your cargo and nothing more."

There was silence from the cargo ship below for a few moments, as the crew likely conversed with the captain. Then they heard a battle cry, and *Prosperity* fired its cannons once more.

Henrietta sighed. "So be it."

Squall cursed to herself as the fighting started up again. When she'd heard the captain's terms, she had hoped that the crew would surrender and the fighting would end. Clearly, from the sound of things, that wasn't the case.

Another loud boom came, and the ship around her trembled. Squall yelped as she fell over, the sound muffled by the cloth wrapped around her mouth to gag her. At least the fighting had taken all of the men upstairs, so they no longer leered at her and encouraged one another to see if a harpy could satisfy them as good as a human woman. She didn't doubt that one of them would have worked up the courage to force himself on her given enough time.

The rope around her midsection bound her wings and arms tightly to her back. Her hands had long gone numb, and blood stung ankles chafed from the ropes around them. As she searched for some way to loosen or cut her bindings, she could hear the cargo ship being boarded, steel ringing on steel and guns firing.

Squall wriggled her way across the floorboards, trying to ignore the splinters that bit into her and the indignity of it all. She didn't know if the pirates attacking the ship would be any kinder than her captors, and she certainly wasn't going to sit here helplessly waiting to find out. Not to mention that if they destroyed the ship, she would go down with it. She had never felt so claustrophobic in her life, stuck belowdecks with her wings bound. The fear of the ship falling to the depths of the wasteland below the floating islands, cracking and breaking against the rocks, made her nauseous. She wondered that these wingless humans even dared to leave their islands in their flimsy ships.

With another bang, the nose of the ship began to dip. Crates and barrels came sliding toward her, and Squall barely managed to avoid being crushed by them. She fell back against one, hissing as something sharp sliced across her thigh. Glancing down, she spied a rusty piece of metal sticking up from the crate. Better than nothing. Squall knelt in front of the metal and began running the ropes over it.

As she worked at cutting herself free, the sounds of battle above her began to die down. She could hear voices speaking and footsteps moving around. Whether the pirates or her captors were the winners mattered not. She needed to free herself. As footsteps descended the stairs to her level, the ropes finally gave way.

The door swung wide. Silhouetted in the flames stood the slender figure of a young man. Metal glinted on his brown face, some strange contraption fitted over his eye, and he commanded, "All right mates, let's see what we've won."

Squall didn't wait another moment. Her feet and mouth still bound, she spread her newly freed wings and launched herself at the man.

Henrietta heard a scream from belowdecks. Keeping her pistol trained on *Prosperity's* captain, she yelled, "What's going on down there?"

There was the sound of a tussle as her crewmates fought with someone. She hadn't expected there to be more crew hidden belowdecks; all hands were needed on deck for a ship under siege. She was also surprised that she didn't hear gunshots. Within moments, the scuffling sound stopped, and Khaleel ascended the stairs, a struggling figure in his arms.

"A bit of a surprise belowdecks is all, Captain. She attacked us," Khaleel said. "But I'm guessing from the bindings that she isn't exactly on their side."

Henrietta narrowed her eyes at the figure. She wore a leather jerkin and skirt, both of which were tight against her skin and left her midriff exposed. Harpies weren't known for modesty, sometimes eschewing clothing altogether. Her figure was similar to that of a human woman, but instead of feet she had talons, and brilliant blue and black feathers sprouted from her head rather than hair. Her mouth and feet were bound, and judging by the rope burn on her arms and the broken feathers on her wings, it was clear that she had recently broken free of bindings around her midsection as well. She looked between the two captains, silently glaring daggers at them both.

"You took a harpy captive?" Henrietta demanded, turning on the recently defeated captain. "Are you insane, man?"

"She's not just any harpy," he growled. "She's what passes for a princess among their type. Daughter of a powerful chief. Either they'll pay a handsome ransom, or I'll fetch a high price for her on the slave market."

Henrietta spit on him, pressing the barrel of her pistol against his forehead. "I loathe slavers," she hissed. "Rotten scum, every one. I ought to put a bullet through your brain right now."

He glared back, no fear of death in him. "You don't have it in you. We've all heard about you, Henrietta, Queen of the Freaks. A softhearted bitch who can't stand the sight of a little blood. You and your crew are going to get eaten alive by real pirates one of these days." He leered, one gold tooth shining amongst the rotten ones. "I'd hoped I'd be the one to take you down meself."

Henrietta wavered, wondering if she should kill him. He wasn't completely wrong. She didn't hate the sight of blood, just needless death and suffering. Oftentimes, their prey were innocent merchants or travelers. But a kidnapper and slaver was another matter. She wouldn't lose any sleep over his death.

"Any of you lot forced into this slavery business against your will?" she asked. A few of them, the cook and ship's boys by the look of them, nodded. She beckoned them forward. "You may either join my crew or take the lifeboat and escape." Before they could move, she added, "But know that if I ever catch you slaving again, I'll kill you myself.

"As for the rest of you…" She pulled the gun back, cocking her head at the captain. "Y'know, in this case, you're right. Why bother soiling my hands when I can just let the harpies find you? Have you heard what they do to humans who attack their kin?" She grimaced. "Those talons are mighty dangerous things. They can just shred a man's guts to bits."

The captain before her went white, his eyes darting to the harpy's clawed feet.

"What should we do with her, Captain?" Khaleel asked, nodding to the harpy woman in his arms.

Henrietta approached her slowly, hands held up in placation. "We have no intention of hurting you. We will set you free if you promise not to attack my crew again."

The harpy glared at her for a moment before nodding.

Khaleel released her, pulling a dagger from his boot and cutting her remaining bindings. "You're injured," he noted, reaching out to touch her wing, which had a long gash running down it. The harpy darted away from him with a hiss.

"We have a doctor aboard our ship," Henrietta said. "You're welcome to join us. Your injuries are minor, though, so you'll have to wait until he's tended to those wounded in battle. Or you can stay here and stare at these ugly assholes on this broken ship until your kin find you. Your choice."

The harpy glanced up at the *The Lady Defiance* above, then at her surroundings. "I'll…I'll go with you, then," she decided.

Henrietta nodded, then began giving orders. "All right crew, load up anything of value from below. You three, tie up any survivors to the main mast. We'll leave them for the birds to feast on!"

Squall watched as the crew of *The Lady Defiance* began hauling crates and barrels of goods up from below. Although there were only twenty of them, they made quick work of it. A hatch opened in the underside of the pirate ship's hold, then a rope with a net on the end descended. They unhooked the net from the rope and stacked the goods on it. Attaching the net once more to the hook, the rope began to reel the goods back up into its hold.

Squall attempted to fly up to the ship, but she didn't get far before her injured wing began to throb in pain. She fell back to the deck of the ruined *Prosperity*.

The man who had first found Squall approached her. "Care for some help?" he asked.

She failed to hide a grimace. "Fine, then. How do you wingless humans get around?"

He gestured to the grappling hooks and ropes that kept the ships tethered to each other. "See the ropes here?" he asked, gesturing to one. She nodded. "Each one is shot from a special device, propelled forward into the wood of the enemy ship, where it hooks in and tethers us. We push this button to release the hook, and the pulley in the machine retracts the rope. All we have to do is grab hold of it, and it will pull us up."

Well, these humans certainly were clever. She supposed they had to be, to make up for the fact that they couldn't fly. "So you just grab this?" She indicated the loop of leather below the hook.

"Yep. It's best to actually put your wrist through the loop, then grab the rope above it, like so. That way, if you lose your grip, you hopefully won't plummet to your death. It can also be a bit difficult climbing over the ledge onto the ship once you get up there, especially since it's your first time. It would probably be easiest if you just held onto me." He held a hand out to her.

She stepped toward him tentatively, and he wrapped one arm around her waist, pulling her tight against him. He instructed her to push the button releasing the hook. They were lifted off the deck of the ship, zipping along over open air. Being a harpy, Squall had never feared heights before, but with one of her wings suddenly useless, she clung to him.

"I'm First Mate Khaleel, by the way," he said with a grin, his face just inches from her own. He lifted an eyebrow, clearly waiting for her to introduce herself.

"Squall," she replied curtly.

Within moments, they had reached *The Lady Defiance*. "Here you are then, Lady Squall," said Khaleel. "Up and over now." He gave her a boost, and she grabbed the railing, pulling herself onto the deck. He swung himself up beside her effortlessly.

"If you wish, I can escort you below to the bunk room so you can rest for a bit," Khaleel said, offering his hand once more. Was this some strange human custom, or was he just eager to touch her? She backed away from him reflexively.

"I'm fine here," she replied. The thought of being stuck belowdecks once more, without the open air around her, made her feel sick.

He shrugged. "As you wish. Just try not to get in the way."

The rest of the crew made their way up to the ship using the strange rope devices. Those who were injured were carried below, where Squall presumed the doctor awaited them. As each rope came free, *The Lady Defiance* seemed to strain, as if longing to get away from *Prosperity* and back into the open air. The captain was the last to arrive, and as her feet landed on deck, her crew cheered. Squall had to admit the captain was an impressive figure, with her coat flapping in the wind, pistol in one hand and cutlass at her hip.

She pulled off her tricorn hat and the goggles that kept the wind from her eyes, grinning at her crewmates. "All right freaks, let's get out of here fast, then we can drink to our victory!" the captain commanded.

Soon they were sailing once more, leaving the wreckage behind them. Squall retreated to the back of the ship, avoiding the sailors and their stares.

Khaleel found her anyway, a flagon in each hand. "Care for a drink?"

"No," she said. "Unless your doctor is ready to see me, we have no reason to speak."

She turned away from him, but jumped when he slammed the drink down on a barrel beside her.

"Hey, maybe try showing a little appreciation for what the captain has done for you, rescuing you and all," he said.

Squall turned back to him with a glare. "All my life, I have been warned to stay away from humans and their cruelty. And then, on my first hunting trip alone, I am kidnapped by those men who threatened to rape and enslave me. So while I am thankful for the rescue, forgive me if I don't trust any of you, especially considering that you're pirates who only found me by accident while attacking the ship I was on."

His anger deflated, at least towards her. "Those bastards! We may be pirates, but Captain Henrietta is very strict about her crew's behavior. Rape and slavery are never tolerated, and we always give the other ship a chance to surrender, to minimize the loss of life." He sighed. "I'm sorry for what you've been through. But you should give the captain a chance. We're pirates, yes, but she's a good person. She cares for those who…who don't fit anywhere else."

All her life, Squall had felt as if she didn't fit in with her people. All of the warnings she had been taught about humans as a child had only made her curious about them. What was it like to live without wings? How did they have the courage to take to the air in their ships, knowing full well that they could sink and die? Why did her people never attempt to make peace with them?

As her curiosity had grown, so too had her longing for adventure. She wanted to explore the world, to visit other islands, to fly down to the Wastelands below and see them with her own eyes. But as the chief's daughter, she was expected to someday be chief, which meant staying near her island and defending it from any foes. Oftentimes, she wished one of her sisters had been chosen instead.

"Those who don't fit…. What do you mean by that?" she asked.

Khaleel smiled. "Let me show you."

As they walked the deck, Khaleel pointed out different crewmates, telling their stories. They were all of them outcasts, unwanteds, freaks. On a ship this small, they all got to know one another intimately—where they came from and what they'd been through.

"See that woman over there, with the grey skin and white hair?" Khaleel asked. The harpy nodded. From the way she stared, it was clear that she was fascinated by the woman's strange skin color. "Her name is Ogechi. She came from below." He pointed down.

"You mean the Wastelands?" Squall asked in wonder. "People actually…live down there?"

He shrugged. "Some. It's a barren, lawless place, full of monsters and darkness, where the sun rarely reaches. But apparently some kingdoms send their unwanted people there. Those born with deformities or illnesses. And if a person lives down there long enough, their skin starts to turn grey from the lack of sunlight."

"Why…why did they send her down there?" Squall asked.

"She was born with an illness in her head," Khaleel answered. "She has visions of the future. When the visions came, she would have fits. Her entire body would start to shake. She would lose control of herself completely. Sometimes, the fits would last for hours. So, as a child, she was sent below. She grew up there. But apparently slavers recently have become brave. They've realized that they can easily snatch people up from below and sell them as cheap labor. The captain took down one of these slave ships. The people on it, they wanted to go back. Below. As dangerous as it is down there, they felt it was the only place they could be free. None of them wanted to go home to the people who had gotten rid of them."

"But Ogechi, she stayed with the captain?" Squall asked.

He nodded. "The ship's doctor, Doctor Satoru, he said that he could give her medicine that would control the fits. But she has to take it every day, so she has to stick with him."

"And the visions?" the harpy asked. "Does she still have them?"

"Of course. Only now, they don't hurt her." Khaleel glanced over at the door that led below, where a crewmate was waving at him. "Ahh. It would appear that the doctor can see you now."

He led her down below to the doctor's surgery room. An operating table sat in the middle, recently cleaned from the smell of the room. Against one wall was a wooden cabinet with numerous drawers, each etched with the name of the tools kept inside. Another table held beakers, flasks, tubes, and other equipment for brewing medicines. The doctor finished washing his hands and turned to them with a smile.

"So, this is the lovely songbird I've been hearing about from all my patients," he said. "I apologize for the wait, but there were stab wounds to stitch up and bullets to remove first. Please, come sit and let's take a look."

Khaleel leaned against the wall, watching the doctor work. He cleaned her rope burns and applied salve to them first, stating that they would heal in a few days. Then he turned to her wing. "Please forgive me, but this will be my first time treating a feathered appendage. It isn't really taught in medical school."

Squall nodded. "I understand. Just do your best, please."

He poked and prodded at the wing, stretching it this way and that. Khaleel could see that this caused the harpy pain, but she was strong, only allowing herself the occasional grimace or hiss. He considered offering to let her squeeze his hand, but she seemed especially averse to being touched.

"Well, it does not appear that any bones are broken," said Doctor Satoru, "but you do have a nasty cut that goes deep into the muscle here. I will stitch it up, but you will need to give it time to heal before attempting to fly."

"How long?" she asked.

The doctor shrugged. "For a human, I would say such a cut into the muscle might take a month or two before regular use is restored; but as you are not human, I can't be certain how quickly your body heals from such wounds. We will simply have to keep a close eye on it and see." He began stitching the wound closed. "I have never had the chance to actually speak with a harpy before. May I ask you some questions about your kind?"

She frowned, thinking over the request. After a moment, she nodded. "Yes, you may. If you answer one of mine first." The doctor nodded his assent. "Why are you an outcast?"

Doctor Satoru smiled, his eyes crinkling behind his spectacles. "That would be because the Royal Medical Society feels that men of my…inclination…are not appropriate to practice medicine."

"Inclination?"

"It means he buggers men," Khaleel explained.

It seemed to take her a moment to understand his slang, but when she did her eyebrows lifted. "How would that make you less capable of healing the wounded?" she asked the doctor.

He shrugged. "There are some who feel I would be distracted by the sight of a nude masculine patient and would…take advantage of the situation. Of course, that doesn't stop them from practicing medicine on female patients."

"That's idiotic," Squall stated bluntly.

"Yes, well, thankfully the captain agrees with you and saw fit to employ me on her airship."

The doctor then proceeded to ask her numerous questions about her people. What did they eat? How much? How far could they fly before tiring? Were they prone to any particular illnesses? How did their vision compare to humans?

As Doctor Satoru asked questions and Squall answered, he continued stitching up the wound. When he'd finished, he put his tools in a bucket for cleaning. "Well, that is all that I believe I can do for you," he said. "I do have one final question, but it is…ahh…well, if it is too personal, you can simply say so."

"Of course," the harpy replied.

"Well, yes. I have always rather wondered…do you lay eggs or have live births? After all, birds lay eggs, but you have breasts, which would imply mammary glands, so…" The doctor blushed.

"That is quite inappropriate, and she does *not* have to answer," Henrietta interjected as she strode into the room. "Doctor, you should be ashamed of yourself. She is a guest on this ship, not a research subject."

"Ahh, I apologize, Captain," said the doctor. "I did not see you there." He began nervously cleaning his glasses.

"You should apologize to Squall," Henrietta said.

Squall held up a hand before he could. "No, it's quite all right. I understand that humans have certain rules of propriety, but the same is not true for harpies. Sex is not something that we are shy about. And besides, I've already learned that the doctor does not have any inclinations toward me in that respect. To answer your question, Doctor, we do not lay eggs. While we have nests, so to speak, they are for raising our babies once they are born."

"Fascinating!" the doctor exclaimed, ignoring the captain's presence in his excitement to learn more. "And tell me, are there male harpies? It's just that we've never seen them before. Only females."

"Doctor—" Henrietta growled.

"Well, that's because they're human," Squall replied. They all stared at her in shock. "Oh, you didn't know this? Only female harpies can fly. Male harpies are physically no different from male humans: no wings or feathers or talons. Thus, they stay in the nest and raise the children."

"You mate with human men, then?" Khaleel asked, raising an eyebrow at the intriguing thought. "Then why all the animosity between humans and harpies?"

"Yes. Well, no," said Squall. "They are no different from human men, but they are harpies still. They are part of our society and culture. We fight with humans because your technology and expansion threaten our society. We are only seeking to protect ourselves."

"So that's why we've never seen male harpies," Henrietta noted. "Interesting. Your captor called you a princess. Is it true that your father is a chieftain?"

Squall shook her head. "You misunderstand again. My mother is the chieftain. Though I'm not anyone particularly important. Every island has a chieftain, and there are hundreds of islands that we inhabit."

"Ahh, then you're a matrilineal society?" the doctor asked.

"If you mean that the women are in charge, yes," said Squall. "As I said, the men take care of raising the children and tending to the home. The women are warriors and leaders."

"Now that's a society I could get behind," Henrietta said.

Over the next few days, Squall adjusted to life aboard the airship. Khaleel became like her shadow, at her side almost every waking moment. He was entertaining at least, always teaching her something new about the airship and how it worked. While he had plenty of stories to tell about the other crewmates, she found that they were more than happy to tell their life stories themselves. The only person whose history she had yet to hear about was the mysterious captain.

She was surprised to learn that, apparently, where Captain Henrietta came from, women did not lead. In fact, their women were treated like little more than property, their homes like cages. Thus the airship captain was an anomaly of sorts among her people, having become a feared and respected leader.

The more Squall learned about humans and their strange customs, the more she realized how little she actually knew—and, inevitably, the more curious she became. Despite her mistreatment at the hands of the other humans and her earlier uncertainty, she found herself warming to the crew of *The Lady Defiance*.

There were some human customs that she couldn't grow used to, however. For example, the constant touching, especially from the young man Khaleel.

Henrietta laughed when Squall mentioned this as they sat together in the captain's chamber, sharing a drink. "That's because he fancies you, birdbrain," Henrietta chuckled.

Squall ignored the jibe. She had quickly learned that the captain had a personal insulting nickname for every one of her crew, and that this was apparently a sign of affection. "Fancies?" Squall asked. While she could speak their language, there were certain colloquialisms that she had difficulty understanding.

"How can I put this so you'll understand…." the captain mused, stroking her chin. "He wants to build a nest with you and make lots of little feathered babies."

Squall blushed. "So these are mating rituals?"

Henrietta snorted. "If that's what you want to call him following you around like a lovesick puppy dog."

Squall was surprised. She knew some of the humans on the airship found her wings and talons unsettling, though they were too polite or too scared to say anything to her face. And yet Khaleel apparently found them alluring. How very odd. "How should I respond?" she asked. "I mean, how do your mating rituals work in your society?"

"Well, if you want him to stop, tell him so," the captain replied. "If he doesn't, punch him in the face."

Squall blushed. "I don't necessarily wish to dissuade him…."

The captain laughed, then shrugged. "I couldn't really help you then, lass. I don't particularly care for the whole marriage business, myself."

Squall could hear a change in the other woman's voice, a bitterness or darkness that wasn't usually there. "You know, I've learned everyone's story on board this ship except yours," she said. "How did you come to be the Queen of the Freaks?"

Henrietta was quiet for so long that Squall thought she wouldn't answer. When she spoke, she sounded far away, as if lost in her memory. "I was married once. An arranged marriage. He was twice my age and prone to cruelty whenever he didn't get his way in life, which was often."

"He would hurt you? Why didn't you just leave?" Squall asked.

The captain shook her head. "It wasn't that easy. Women have no power in my society. A woman alone is vulnerable. We're the property of our husbands. And even if I'd reported it to the authorities, they wouldn't have done anything." She took a long gulp of her whiskey. "We had a baby girl. She was the light of my life. I could tolerate anything he did to me as long as I had her. And he wasn't around much. He was an airship captain, often gone for months on end. But then…she got sick. She was just two years old. And after I lost her, something in me broke. A rage consumed me. The next time he lifted his hand to me ended up being the last."

Silence stretched between them for a moment. "How did you become a pirate captain?" Squall asked her.

Henrietta laughed, though it sounded hollow. "Well, there I was, suddenly a widow. If I'd stayed, they would have hanged me for murder. So, scared as I was to be all alone, I took all the money we had and escaped in his airship. Thankfully, I'd gone on enough outings with him that I'd picked up the basics of sailing. After that, I pretty much lucked into finding my crewmates. And over the years, I've found a strength in me that I never knew I had."

"And you have no desire to mate again? To make another baby?" Squall asked.

Henrietta shook her head. "I've never felt the need to take a lover. I have all the family I need right here on this ship."

They were suddenly interrupted by a loud and all too familiar shriek. Squall knew it to be a harpy's war cry.

The captain and Squall both jumped to their feet. "Bloody hell," Henrietta cursed. "We're under attack!"

The harpies descended suddenly, striking under cover of darkness. Arrows rained down from above, and screams erupted on deck as the crew descended into chaos in the sudden ambush.

Three harpies hovered above the deck, bows trained on the crew. "Humans!" their leader shouted. "We know you have taken one of our own captive! You will die for your mistake!"

"Stop!" Squall screamed as she burst forth from the captain's chamber. She rushed forward, wings spread, hoping they would block any stray arrows.

"Sister!" Flitter cried, swooping to embrace her. "We found the ship that took you captive and questioned their captain. They said that they'd been attacked by pirates, who took you as a slave, and gave us a description of this ship."

"I knew I should have killed that damn slaver when I had the chance," Captain Henrietta cursed.

"You've been misled," said Squall. "Please, lower your weapons! These people saved me from my captors. Look, they stitched up my wing. I've been travelling with them because it's too damaged for me to fly." She breathed a sigh of relief as the other two harpies slowly lowered their bows, though they still eyed the humans suspiciously.

Flitter looked her over, making sure that she was not hurt in any other way. "Come, we should be able to carry you between us," she said. "Mother will be so happy to have you return to the nest."

Squall bit her lip, glancing around the airship and its crew. Captain Henrietta, Khaleel, Doctor Satoru, Ogechi, and all the others. Her heart ached at the thought of leaving them. Would she ever see them again? How would she be able to contact them in this big world of floating islands and airships to the horizon? She hadn't realized just how much she had come to care for them in such a short time.

And suddenly, she knew she couldn't do it. Squall turned back to her sister, hugging her once more, though this one was to say goodbye. "Flitter...take my feather back to mother. Tell her that I'm safe and happy where I am."

Flitter stared at her, eyes filled with wonder and hurt. "You don't wish to come home?"

"It's not that. I wish to travel the world, to see other lands. To meet more humans. Who knows? Maybe I can become an ambassador for human-harpy relations." Squall laughed, though tears sprung to her eyes. "I'll come back.

Just not yet."

Flitter stared at her for a few more moments before nodding slowly. "If this is really what you wish," she said. "We'll inform the other harpies that this ship is not to be attacked under any circumstances. You've always been an odd bird, sister."

They embraced once more, and Squall plucked a feather to send back to her mother. Her sister and the other two harpies alighted at once, desperate to return to her mother with news of her safety.

Squall took a deep breath and turned to her captain and crewmates.

Henrietta grinned. "Welcome to the ranks, freak."

More from Mandy Burkhead

The Black Lily

Courtesan. Spy. Assassin.

Across the Kingdom of Arestea, the shadowy league of professional killers known simply as the Guild has long since earned its terrifying reputation. And none of its current members are more infamous than the Black Lily.

Now Lily is about to discover if her reputation has been inflated or not, for she has just been assigned the most daunting mission of her career: infiltrate the royal palace and eliminate the entire Arestean line of succession to make room for the Guild's puppet ruler.

But when unplanned circumstances take the king from his country to help secure the front lines in his latest war of expansion, Lily is left trapped in her assumed persona behind the palace walls and forced to stall for time. And when a particularly bad stroke of luck reveals her cover to the king's brother, Crown Prince Adrian, Lily finds herself ensnared in her own web, forced to use all her skills of subterfuge and manipulation if she is to stay one step ahead of the naïve but righteous young man and finish her mission — or die trying.

You can follow Mandy Burkhead on Facebook, Twitter, and Instagram @Burkshelf. To purchase *The Black Lily*, visit her website at www.burkshelf.com.

An Evening on Harbor Ridge by Mark Rivett

The morning sun, obscured behind an endless ocean of clouds, cast the world in a pallid grey hue. A thin frost had been left by the night's cold. Silence ruled the trenches. Soldiers bundled beneath filthy longcoats for warmth – napping, keeping watch, tending their gear, or contemplating their lot in life.

Andrew sat with his back against the slatted wooden wall of the trench. He held a small, scratched mirror between his knees. With careful strokes of his razor, he brushed away white shaving cream and brown whiskers. After each stroke, he rattled his blade in a tin can of water to clean it.

A voice, muffled by a gas mask, broke the stillness. "Is that smart?"

Andrew looked around for the source of the voice, but he could not distinguish between a half-dozen expressionless masks. It was easy to tell the new recruits and recent draftees from the veterans. Rookies always wore their gas masks. Whether he was sleeping, playing cards, or sitting behind a musket, life carried the stink of a rookie's own breath and was viewed through two round and foggy eyeholes.

Andrew gave up trying to identify who had addressed him. "You need to shave, or your mask won't keep its seal."

"What if there's a gas attack?"

This time Andrew was able to attribute the voice to one of two soldiers sitting across from him. Four black, glass eyes stared forward, but it was impossible to determine which soldier had spoken.

"Gas attacks don't happen during the day." His work complete, Andrew inspected his face in the mirror, dumped his can of water onto a ragged cloth, and cleaned his face.

"Bullshit! In training, they said we should expect gas attacks at any time," a different voice retorted.

"Yep," Andrew replied curtly.

He leaned his head back against the trench wall and closed his eyes. The trenches didn't offer much, but what they did offer was abundant time between short intervals of excitement. Because of unpredictable sleep schedules, naps were encouraged when not on duty. When something significant happened, watchmen from all over the perimeter would sound an alarm.

"Why?" The first voice came back again.

Andrew was annoyed, but he opened his eyes. He was once again met with the same four black glass staring back at him. "Why what?"

"Why don't gas attacks happen during the day?"

The rhythmic turning sound of distant gears caught Andrew's attention. He searched through the grey backpack at his side.

"All the Ire Sea Conclave officers are undead; vampires and liches, mostly…" Andrew began.

"So what?"

Andrew pulled five metal rods from his pack and screwed them together end-to-end to form the shaft of his trench-pike. He affixed the rods above the barrel of his standard-issue musket, before attaching a sinister looking serrated blade at its head. The shaft of his trench-pike stretched six feet in length.

"Whelp, the undead commanders don't trust their human thralls to handle chemical weapons. They need their humans for labor…and food. A misfired canister or change of the wind—even a rogue or suicidal slave—and suddenly you've wiped out an entire stable of people. People you need for war production and to protect you during the day. Hell, even Ghoulherders are human. Barely."

Andrew preferred blades to unreliable black powder firearms, but the anxiety of hand-to-hand combat began to itch at the back of his mind. Other veterans had their pikes assembled as well, but many of the recruits looked on in confusion.

The two rookies across from Andrew looked at each other and hesitated, then removed their masks.

"Why did you assemble your pike? Was there an order?" one of the soldiers asked. He was a young man—no more than fifteen—and certainly possessed no need to shave.

"There will be," Andrew replied.

He glanced up and at the walls of the fortress city behind him. Old Castle was a brick and steel bastion of might that guarded the northwestern border of Sylvania. Its ten-story walls were scarred by centuries of conflict. Narrow embrasures lined with steel armor plates housed powerful cannons that could fire at targets well out of view of the soldiers within the trenches. Atop Old Castle's battlements, commanding officers could survey the battle alongside archers and snipers.

The implacable structure sat at the eastern edge of a vast wasteland between Sylvanian and Conclave territory. The no-man's land was an enormous graveyard of countless battles. Ancient, labyrinthine trenches stretched for miles. Disabled war machines—cannons, artillery, and steam-powered land ships—sat scattered about the battlefield in rusted ruin. Most prevalent, however, were the corpses of innumerable warriors who lay where they had fallen for weeks, years, decades, and centuries. For this reason, Old Castle had been ominously dubbed Tombstone by the warriors who defended its walls.

"Bullshit!" challenged the other soldier, slightly older but equally green.

"What's bullshit?" Andrew got to his feet, hefted his backpack over his shoulders, and fished some binoculars out of his shirt pocket.

"How do you know there will be an order to assemble pikes?" the younger soldier asked.

"Pikes!" An order from some distant trench echoed over the cold wasteland. The order was taken up by other commanders and repeated over and over again until it made its way along the entire trench line.

The two young soldiers, along with every recruit in the trenches, began to assemble their pikes. Andrew considered asking them their names, but thought better of it. Like most recruits, their chances in the trenches were slim – and learning their names was bad luck. These boys were not the sons of wealthy or connected Sylvanian businessmen or politicians. Like Andrew, they were the sons of poor farmers or blacksmiths. They were unable to buy the relative protection of Old Castle's walls or afford the cost of officer school. They had been sent to man the trenches, and they would have to learn quickly or die. If they survived their first day, as Andrew had, then he would learn their names.

"I'm Gerald." The younger soldier nodded toward his older companion. "This is Peter."

"Damn." Andrew sighed at the jinx that Gerald had just unwittingly invoked. He pushed himself to his feet and climbed to the edge of the trench wall. Andrew spoke to the youths while he looked through his binoculars over the frigid terrain before him. "Hear that clicking?"

"Yeah?"

"That's the sound of the elevator chains that Tombstone uses to haul ammunition up from the holds to the cannons. They keep the gun rooms stocked with incendiary shells for zombie legion and vampire attacks. They keep the anti-personnel shells in the holds."

"So, we'll be fighting the living," Gerald concluded. "Why pikes then? Why not a gun line? Just mow them down when they try to cross no-man's land?"

"Basic training says bullets kill living, blades are for ghouls, and fire is for vampires." Peter spoke with the defiant confidence of a scholastic overachiever with no real-world experience. "We should form a two-row gun line."

A high-pitched whistle ended with a deafening explosion. A thin trail of smoke streaked from no-man's land over the trench. It terminated in a billowing cloud of debris and ash against the wall of Old Castle. More artillery bombardments followed the first. Murmurs of excitement and fear rolled through the soldiers. The artillery barrage would come in waves for the duration of the battle. The vast majority of shells would explode harmlessly off the impenetrable walls of the fortress city, and each one would be a small victory to the soldiers below. A very few would find their mark within the artillery embrasures and knock out a cannon, killing the crew. Those would feel like soul-crushing defeats to the men in the trenches.

Old Castle opened up with its own response. A coordinated series of booms thundered out from the artillery embrasures, followed by billowing white smoke that wafted up the walls of the fortress. Vapor trails streaked out toward some target beyond the horizon. Distant explosions echoed back.

Andrew would have been inclined to ignore Peter, but considered that a little advice might help to stave off the bad luck of having learned their names. "The Conclave wants to soften us up with waves of mindless undead first. The real threat is the live soldiers behind the zombies – fanatics, cavalry, stitches, assassins, dogs, maybe werewolves. Tombstone is countering by firing over the vanguard into the rear ranks to soften *them* up. That means there will be more zombies for us to deal with." Andrew placed his binoculars in his pocket. He ran his finger over the serrated blade of his pike to test its edge. "A lot more. So, yeah, pikes."

"Werewolves?" Gerald gasped.

"Look on the bright side." Andrew shrugged. "No gas attacks."

"How… What *is* that?" Gerald had grown quiet in his fear, but he summoned the will to ask yet another question.

Peter hid his own terror by rebuking his companion. "It's smoke, dumbass."

The younger soldier continued to gape at the wall of mist that was slowly rolling toward the trench.

"Dammit," Andrew sighed at having to give yet another explanation to the young soldiers. He was wasting his breath on dead men, but Andrew spoke anyway. "The zombies at the front of the vanguard are called 'Thurifers' by the Conclave. We call them 'Smokers.' They're equipped with thuribles.

Incense pours out of their thuribles as they shamble. Their job is to bless the battlefield with smoke. They call upon the fallen to rise up and join the fight on behalf of the Conclave. Mostly, it just provides cover for the Ghoulherders and turns these trenches into a foggy mess."

"And it looks creepy as all hell," Gerald answered.

"Smokers!" An alarm rang up from the trenches.

Andrew looked into the smoke and saw the first silhouettes approaching the trench line. Rotten corpses trudged forward at the behest of their masters. They were dressed in white robes and wore heavy iron collars. Thuribles swung from chains attached to those collars, vomiting fetid fumes. Specially designed caps discharged incense into the shape of ghostly, howling faces. To the uninitiated, the approaching legions appeared to be bolstered by spectral apparitions. The scene was mesmerizing, until Andrew was startled by the pounding rattle of a crank gun.

The sound was met by a cacophony of moans from beyond the mist. Meandering shadows of the approaching undead host slowly materialized through the smoke. Rotten, stitched-together corpses limped as a single, undulating wall of death. They carried all manner of rusty and jagged weapons – picks, axes, clubs, and hammers. Here and there, one of the innumerable leering faces would vanish and fall to the ground as the crank guns found their mark. Most of the weapons' firepower, however, punched harmlessly through bodies that did not bleed.

As the multitude got even closer to the trench, explosions erupted through their ranks. Sylvanian soldiers hurled grenades into the vanguard. Huge swathes were blasted through the attackers' formations. Rotten bodies exploded into chunks of putrid gore. Some stayed down. Many continued crawling toward the trenches on shattered and mutilated limbs.

It couldn't hurt to remind his two rookie companions, "Remember, try to find the Ghoulherders and kill *them*. The zombies are mostly mindless. Each Ghoulherder commands dozens of zombies that will wander off without them. Ghoulherders are human. They die just like anyone else."

"I don't see any!" Gerald was on the verge of panic. He had, no doubt, imagined that the Ghoulherders would be easy to pick out among the mindless hordes.

"They're out there," Andrew assured him. "They look and act like zombies, but if you search hard enough, you can spot them. Look." Andrew gestured at one of the approaching packs of ghouls. "Tell me what you see."

Peter blinked out at the enemy. "Just…just a bunch of walking cadavers."

"Look closer." Andrew took hold of the soldiers, directing their gazes. Among the throngs of lumbering undead, there was a single figure who wore a pistol. His clothes had been torn and his skin had been caked with mud, but his eyes held something unique among his comrades – life. "Do you see the ghoul with the matchlock pistol on his hip?"

Gerald nodded. "I see him." "That's a Ghoulherder. Zombies can't use guns." Andrew set his pike against the trench wall, and drew his own matchlock sidearm. "And that guy probably thought that pistol would come in handy once he and his herd were fighting us in the trenches. Once you learn to look for details like that, it's easy to pick them out." Andrew took careful aim and fired. His target fell instantly, and he casually reloaded his pistol. "See? Now we have a dozen or so fewer ghouls to deal with."

Andrew's companions smiled nervously. Andrew also grinned, though he knew that his claim wasn't entirely accurate. When a Ghoulherder fell, his herd would disperse mindlessly, but other Ghoulherders could easily draw them into their own ranks to replace the fallen. Despite that fact, the notion that Andrew had struck a vital blow with a single shot was still very appealing.

"Phalanx!" the voices of the commanding officers ordered. Instantly, the soldiers in the trenches who had been hurling grenades and picking off Ghoulherders with their pistols joined in formation with their pikes. A wall of blades lined the edge of the trench from end to end. Andrew, Gerald, and Peter joined the phalanx with their own pikes. The wall of serrated blades looked as impenetrable as it was vicious. It would be insane for any attacker to throw themselves upon the steel wall. But still they came.

Within moments, a multitude of dead had thrust themselves bodily upon the vast line of trench pikes. Andrew caught the first approaching ghoul in the chest and drove his serrated blade up and forward with a sickening crunch. Zombies did not bleed, but often oozed viscous bile that stank of rot.

"Cut it apart!" Andrew ordered. He expected that the rookies' basic training had covered that concept, but its reinforcement could only help. Peter and Gerald violently hacked at the beast, severing its arms and eventually driving a pike through its face. As quickly as they dispatched the first attacker, a second crawled over its mutilated body.

Peter did as Andrew had done and drove his pike up and forward. This creature, however, held a broken spear in one hand. Despite being immobilized and impaled, it jabbed after whatever victim it could. Gerald caught the creature's weapon arm with his own pike and severed it at the elbow. By this time, Andrew had extracted his pike from the first attacker's corpse, and positioned himself to dispatch the spear-wielding ghoul.

"Do it quick, like this!" Andrew shouted as he drove his pike into the throat of the monster. Black gore sprayed from the wound, and Andrew twisted hard. The blade of his weapon did as it was designed to do, and the creature's rotten head flopped off. The ghoul's shoulders slouched, and its arms fell lifeless to its side.

"Again!" As soon as the third attacker emerged, Andrew thrust his pike into its chest. His comrades immediately took to the task of carving the monster apart.

The entire trench had erupted into a violent melee. Soldiers worked in teams of twos and threes to impale and dismember zombies as efficiently as possible. Occasionally, a ghoul would get a lucky swing in with an axe or a pick, and a Sylvanian warrior would go down. Some teams were not able to deal with their attackers quickly enough, and rotten corpses would flood into the trench. Soldiers and zombies tangled into deadly brawls.

"Keep at it, boys!" Andrew felt a sense of guarded pride in his two new protégés. They were learning quickly, and their section of trench was holding against the onslaught. Dismembered limbs piled high around them, and the earth ran slick with ichor. Together they were a machine – an engine of war that broke the Conclave attack with a determination that eclipsed even that of the fearless undead.

"Grenade!" someone screamed.

The world slid out of time. Andrew turned from the fray, searching for any clue as to where the deadly explosive might be. Ghoulherders were the lowest-level soldiers of the Conclave, and they rarely brought sophisticated weapons to war. Whether the grenade had come from a Ghoulherder or a clumsy Sylvanian soldier was ultimately of little consequence.

Unable to discern from which direction the danger would come, Andrew acted on instinct. With each hand he gripped the back of Peter and Gerald's long coats, tore them from the carnage of defending the trench, threw them to the ground, and dove atop them.

The explosion slammed into Andrew's body, threw him into the trench wall, and knocked the wind from his lungs. Everything went dark.

"Sew them bits... Sew, sew, sew... Sew the bits..."

Andrew awoke to the sound of raspy muttering and the sweet smell of tobacco smoke. He opened his eyes, but the blackness remained – save for a patch of light behind the silhouette of a crouching figure.

"Shh...." A gentle hand slid over Andrew's mouth.

Andrew's eyes adjusted to the darkness, and found the faces of Gerald and Peter. His head and ribs ached, but he felt otherwise uninjured. They were in what seemed to be a small cave. The sounds of battle had died away, leaving only the murmuring creature at the mouth of the cavern. Andrew looked around for his pack and weapon, but found only the pistol on his belt.

"Sew them bits... Sew, sew, sew... Sew the bits..."

The gaunt creature rolled a cigarette from one side of its mouth to the other as it sang. Its flesh was caked in mud, and dirty rags hung over its waist. Grey dreadlocks hung shoulder length from the creature's head, concealing its face. Filthy black fingers clutched a needle and thread that passed through the flesh of a dead Sylvanian soldier. Methodically, the monster sewed a new arm to a corpse that had lost its original in battle. Despite all appearances to the contrary, the creature was human – a Conclave Ghoulherder.

"Sew them bits… Sew, sew, sew… Sew the bits…"

"What do we do?" Peter whispered.

"Sew them bi—"

The Ghoulherder stopped his work and turned his head to gaze into the cave. Dark eyes scanned the gloom as a puff of smoke exited cracked lips. With one bloody hand, the Ghoulherder reached into a pouch that hung on his waist and extracted a pinch of tobacco. He set his stitch work down and retrieved a small slip of paper with his other hand. Adept fingers that dripped with the gore of his work rolled a fresh cigarette, placed it in his mouth, lit it off the first, and tossed the butt on the ground. Finally, the Ghoulherder turned his attention back toward his work. "Sew…them…bits… Sew, sew, sew… Sew the bits."

Andrew, Peter, and Gerald let out a sigh of relief.

Andrew carefully pushed himself into a seated position and leaned toward his companions. Peter held the broken head of his trench pike, and Gerald hugged his musket, but they too had lost their packs.

"Where are we?" Andrew asked under his breath.

"The grenade ripped a hole in the trench wall. It's a cave!" Gerald answered in a tone almost imperceptibly quiet. "When we saw that we were going to be overrun, we hid in here."

Andrew mulled the information over. If a Ghoulherder occupied the trench outside, it was held by the Conclave. He looked at the muttering creature, then gazed past the two young soldiers to be confronted by the dank blackness of a narrowing tunnel. There was no telling how far it went.

"How long have I been out?" Andrew cast his glance back at the Ghoulherder. The thin figure was stitching together a new zombie from the corpses of those that had fallen in battle. It did not matter for which side of the conflict the dead had fought. They would soon rise to join the Conclave.

"A while. Hours," Peter replied.

"Follow me!" Andrew pushed past Peter and Gerald to crawl deeper into the cave. "Hurry!"

The tunnel was barely wide enough to squeeze through in some places. Cold earth threatened to press in around them, and their very presence seemed to invite collapse. Every few yards, rotten and worm-eaten logs supported the structure, but none inspired confidence in the cave's stability.

Peter whispered, gasping in the stuffy cavern air. "Why do we have to hurry? What's going on?" Andrew continued to crawl on elbows and knees into the blackness. The outside light was obscured, and Andrew fished around in his pocket for a brass lighter. "Don't you think we have a contingency plan in the event that the outer trench is taken by the Conclave?"

The impotent flame of Andrew's lighter revealed only the dirt hole that lay before him. How it had come to be, and how it had not collapsed beneath the ruckus of a thousand battles, was beyond Andrew's guess.

"To Old Castle, we're dead men. Any second now, the trench will be doused with oil. Frankly, I'm surprised it hasn't already. They probably didn't tell you that in basic training, did they?"

The soldiers crawled until their muscles burned. Eventually, they arrived at a section of tunnel that was large enough for the three of them to sit up. As determined as Andrew was to put as much distance between himself and the trenches as possible, he needed a rest. He closed his lighter and plunged them all into blackness.

Gerald broke the silence. "Are we far enough from the oil?"

"The oil? Far enough from the oil, but we can't go back. Our best bet is to continue on, hope it opens somewhere in no-man's land, and make our way back to Old Castle above ground." Andrew replied.

"That's suicide!" Peter interrupted. "We should just wait and head back after the Conclave is burnt alive."

Andrew sighed. "Go ahead. I'm going forward."

Silence reigned for a few moments. Peter was proud, but smart enough to trust in the veteran's knowledge. Instead, he waited for Gerald to probe for more information.

"Once the trench is clear, wouldn't it be safe for us to go back?"

Gerald's curiosity originated from a desire to learn rather than a desire to be seen as someone who had all the answers, and Andrew decided he would indulge the boy. He resumed the crawl, guided by his lighter.

"The Conclave isn't stupid. They know that Tombstone has a plan for when the trench is taken, so they'll let their zombies and Ghoulherders eat the burning oil. Then, the living soldiers – the ones we were shelling earlier – will just take the trench. You can bet one or two will find this cave and get curious." Andrew groaned as he struggled through a particularly narrow section of tunnel. "So, we can't go back, and if this tunnel has no way out, we're screwed."

Cold but refreshing surface air carried the muffled clamor of battle with it. Andrew and his companions had crawled for hours, redoubling their efforts when sounds and smells hinted at an exit. The mouth of the cave was hidden beneath the hull of a hollowed-out landship. The ancient, wheeled war machine lay in a rusted heap, its mechanical innards obliterated by the shell that had killed it. It was once the proud invention of some long-forgotten artificer with dreams of ending the war. Now, the vehicle was just another ruin in no-man's land.

Andrew helped Gerald and Peter from the tunnel and sat down to rest. Night had fallen, and stars lit the sky beyond the brittle, broken ribs of the landship's metal frame. Distant explosions and cracks of gunfire echoed through the nocturnal wasteland. A cold wind carried the smell of smoke.

The three soldiers gathered themselves and then surreptitiously assessed their surroundings. A light frost hung on tufts of grass that sprouted from the broken and blasted terrain. Old Castle was south and east of their position. Its walls were lit by an orange fire that consumed the trench at its base. Conclave artillery was bombarding the fortress south and west of their position. A wooded, northern rise that ran east to west seemed the safest location to better assess their next move.

"This area is crawling with Conclave patrols, so when we move, stay low—" Andrew began.

"We should run!" Peter interrupted. "The longer we're out here, the more likely we'll be spotted."

"Ok, you run. I'm going to crawl."

Andrew looked around one final time, saw that the area was clear, and pulled himself along on hands and knees. Gerald followed.

Peter stayed behind, glowering at having been contradicted yet again. He glanced around for any sign of the Conclave, took a deep breath, and launched himself into a sprint toward the northern ridge.

"Dammit!" Andrew hunkered down in anticipation of a barrage of musket fire.

In seconds, Peter passed Andrew and Gerald, and dove behind the nearest tree for cover. After a few moments, there was no indication that he had been spotted. He gestured for his fellow soldiers to join him.

Andrew eventually arrived at Peter's position with Gerald in tow.

"That was stupid. If you get spotted out here, there's nowhere to run, and the Conclave has quite a few nasty things it can send after you. Wolves, werewolves, undead werewolves…"

"We're fine." Peter smiled, his confidence in himself and his training renewed. "Where to now?"

"We move up the rise, *slowly* and *quietly*. If it looks clear, we move eastward. I think this is Harbor Ridge, and that means Broken River is on the other side. That will take us straight back to Old Castle."

Andrew hadn't studied his maps intensely, but he had seen Harbor Ridge through his binoculars many times.

The soldiers moved from tree to tree up the rise. Periodically, they stopped to assess their surroundings. As their elevation increased, so too did their vantage of the battle below. While the walls of Old Castle seemed impenetrable, the assaulting Conclave forces seemed limitless. Steam-powered engines of war designed to scale or penetrate the fortress lumbered into combat. Oceans of troops advanced in broken formations under Sylvanian artillery. The flames of war illuminated the battle in a beautiful but terrible glow.

A female voice pierced the night. "Why do the Sylvanians not rise up and overthrow their own rulers?" The Sylvanians dove for cover and searched for the origin of the question.

"Their rulers have them convinced that it is better to stay dead than to have the opportunity to rise into undeath," a male voice answered. "Barbarians."

Not far away, a noble-looking man and woman sat upon a blanket. The woman was dressed in a light blue, embroidered evening gown. She wore a matching, wide-brimmed hat atop braided, blonde hair. In her gloved hands she held a set of long-handled opera glasses that she used to observe the battle. Next to her, the man wore a long-tailed tuxedo with a blue vest and matching cravat. A thick, twirled mustache adorned his upper lip. He wore a top hat and held a wine glass. Behind them, a corpse hung upside down, suspended from a tree branch. Its arms dangled about a foot from the ground, and a metal tap had been inserted into its neck.

"That is so terribly sad." The woman stood, sweeping up a long-stemmed wine glass of her own. She stepped to the corpse and turned the handle on the tap. A steady stream of blood filled her glass. "Everyone deserves a chance at immortality. It is unspeakable that such ignorance exists in this modern, civilized era! Don't you agree, Raphael?"

"They just do not understand our way of life, Evelynn. They have to be made to learn, but right now they are convinced that eternal death is better than even unlife as a zombie. Backward, sad little fools. Do not fret, my love. The Conclave needs but a foothold, and our way of life will spread like wildfire through that backward kingdom."

Raphael drained his glass and handed it to Evelynn. She handed her full glass to him and filled the empty one from the hanging corpse.

"Vampires?" Peter whispered.

Andrew nodded. Vampires were not uncommon on the battlefield, but Andrew had never seen vampire aristocracy. The contrast was not as extreme as he had imagined. The vampiric warriors of The Conclave were proud and flamboyant. They charged into battle clad in expensive armor, brandishing the most advanced weaponry, upon enormous steeds protected by heavy barding. They carried the banners of their bloodline with them, determined to bring fame and glory to their house. It did not surprise Andrew that the "civilian" vampires were a pretentious and ignorant lot.

"Shh… Move quietly," Andrew ordered. "A vampire's eyes and ears are sharp." He took several cautious steps to put distance between himself and the aristocrats. "We'll circle around."

"I do so love it here, Raphael. When the war is over, I want to fill in those unsightly trenches and build a summer home in the valley," Evelynn continued.

"This area *is* prime real estate. It'll go cheap after the war. We should start an investment plan. All the new blood will be itching to stake claim, and we can bleed them dry." Raphael started to chuckle. "We could even dress the chattel up in Sylvanian uniforms and have annual reenactments."

"What a fantastic idea!" Evelynn confirmed.

"Is that what you think you're going to do?" Peter bellowed.

Andrew whirled around to see the young soldier brandishing his broken pike-head like a dagger and storming toward the vampires. The soldier in Andrew wanted to join his young and foolish companion, but the veteran in him urged restraint. He grabbed Gerald by the shoulder and wrenched him behind a tree.

"Stay back, Evelynn! I'll deal with this brigand!" Raphael sprang to his feet and raised his fists.

"Oh, you poor thing!" Evelynn cooed. "You are filthy! Put the blade down and come with us."

"You think this is a game? You think this is entertainment?" Peter growled. "People are dying down there!"

"What's he doing?" Gerald gasped.

Whether it was the trauma of battle or overwhelming outrage that motivated Peter, Andrew could not say. In disbelief, he gripped Gerald's arm and pulled him away.

"Get back, rapscallion!" Raphael backed away from Peter with Evelynn behind him. He kept his fists raised, but appeared fearful of the armed Sylvanian. "I am quite capable of defending myself!"

Evelynn seemed oblivious to the dangerous situation. "Oh, Raphael, he is just scared. Look at him! He must be lost. Let us keep him!"

"Come here, corpse! That vamp tux will fetch a month's hooch where I come from," Peter growled as he advanced with his blade. "Let's see if you can find investors to pay for a new head."

"Oh shit!" Gerald gasped.

Andrew looked up from the scene unfolding before him. Dozens of silhouettes emerged from the dark woodlands of Harbor Ridge. Dressed in finely tailored tuxedos and elaborate evening gowns, a host of vampiric nobles had been drawn to the commotion. They looked on with the curiosity of a social group anxious to witness the day's gossip. "He's a dead man! Come on! We have to go!" Andrew whispered as he crawled further up the ridge.

"We have to help him!" Gerald quietly protested. "They'll kill him!"

A gunshot rang out, and Peter stopped in his tracks. His shoulders slouched and the blade slid from his grasp. He dropped to his knees, then fell face-first onto the ground.

"No!" Gerald shouted. He pulled himself away from Andrew, leveled his musket at Raphael, and fired. The vampire took the shot square in the chest and tumbled backward.

"My love!" Evelynn squealed.

Andrew scurried up to the ridge and found some cover. The young soldier below was hurriedly reloading his weapon while the group of vampire lords and ladies swelled. A few of the vampires had pistols drawn and trained on Gerald's position. Evelyn helped Raphael off the ground.

"Raphael, old chap!" a voice mocked. "Have you not learned to never leave home without your dueling pistols? Or at least a penny to bribe the beggars?"

Raphael inspected the wound that stained his blue vest and smiled. "Lord Vandergrift, I thought that if I had to defend *my* honor, I could borrow *your* irons. I knew you would not be needing them, as you have no honor to defend."

Laughter rolled through the assembly of vampires. Peter was dead, and Gerald was certain to be next. For the undead, however, the evening's events were no more than an unexpectedly exciting social outing.

Lord Vandergrift called out a challenge to the armed men in the crowd.

"A thousand coins to the vampire that drops the scoundrel!"

Andrew's hand went to his pistol. He wanted to help Gerald, but a lead ball fired from his pistol would result in nothing but giving away his position.

Gerald had managed to reload and took a shot at the gathering. The crowd of vampires gasped. Some ducked in fear while others giggled nonchalantly. Those who had their pistols out took the opportunity to return fire.

Andrew watched with a broken heart as his young companion convulsed from the impact of several shots. Gerald dropped his weapon and crumpled to the ground.

"Does the blood of a soldier taste different than slave blood?" a female voice asked.

"I believe it does," someone answered. "I have heard it is smoky with a bitter finish."

Andrew did not stop to hear the rest of the conversation. It had already taken all his will to keep from firing into the crowd. If he had to stand by while they discussed drinking the blood of Peter and Gerald, he would be unable to resist. Instead, he darted from tree to tree, stopping briefly to assess his surroundings. He guessed that most of the vampires in the area had gone to investigate the earlier commotion, but evidence of their infestation remained. Picnic blankets lay scattered through the forest, and dead slaves hung from trees, twisting in the moonlight. Elegant, horse-drawn carriages stood parked at the top of the ridge. Andrew considered stealing a horse, but thought better of it. If Conclave aristocrats were anything like Sylvanian aristocrats, some would employ drivers. Those drivers would sound an alarm if he were spotted.

Eventually, Andrew made his way to Broken River. The shattered remnants of a dozen stone bridges gave the waterway its name. The natural border had defended Sylvania for centuries – and if there was a way across, the Conclave would have found it long ago. It was well guarded and passed through Old Castle itself. If Andrew could follow it southward and avoid being mistaken for the enemy, he would return home.

When a Sylvanian patrol finally stumbled upon Andrew, they almost shot him. After a few minutes of explaining, however, he was able to convince the commanding officer to send a boat across the river. On his return trip, he dwelt upon the deaths of his companions. To Tombstone, they had died for duty. To the Conclave, they had died for amusement. To Andrew, they had died for nothing.

They had sealed their fates when they had told him their names. Poor farm boys died in this war every day, but perhaps this day – Andrew thought – they did not have to die alone. The seed of an idea had taken root in Andrew's mind.

As he sailed beneath the stone archway that stood over Broken River and led into the bowels of Old Castle, Andrew recalled the noble vampires. They were not unlike the well-to-do aristocrats of Sylvania – woefully naïve on the subject of war. If the battle turned in some unforeseen direction, these vampiric voyeurs would drink from their wine glasses and engage in inane chit chat right up until the violence landed at their feet.

The cranking of the Old Castle elevator chains echoed through the stone dungeon, and the seed in Andrew's mind was growing into a wonderful, terrible idea. "I have information that might be useful to Command."

"Yeah? What kind of information?" The patrol officer appraised Andrew with the same indifference most officers had when addressing grunts. There was never a shortage of soldiers willing to trade some "vital" tidbit of intelligence for a few days light duty. Still, Andrew had escaped no-man's land, and there was the possibility that he had something valuable to share. If so, the officer wanted to be the one to share that information with Command. "I can make sure the right people are informed."

"I'd prefer to speak with an officer in the Artillery Corps," Andrew replied.

The patrol officer licked his teeth while he considered using his rank to extract the information. He decided not to bother and escorted Andrew further into Old Castle. The fortress was enormous, and the lower levels were a cold and moldy labyrinth of corridors, designed as much for structure as they were for defense. Soldiers rushed about the business of moving supplies. The wails of wounded men and women echoed through the passages. Andrew imagined that life in a firelit dungeon was much different than a muddy trench, but there were likely some unfortunate similarities.

The officer addressed one of the soldiers that had retrieved Andrew from the wrong side of Broken River. "Take him to Artillery …and come back with two casks of ale. Next patrol starts at dawn."

The soldier nodded, gestured for Andrew to follow, and bounded up a set of stone stairs. Andrew did as instructed. As they approached the exterior walls, the sound of battle could be heard echoing through the chambers of Tombstone. The Conclave was throwing everything at Old Castle, and yet Andrew was filled with a lack of concern for its outcome. Tombstone would hold, and The Conclave forces would exhaust themselves. After all the carnage, there would be a long period of calm while The Conclave regrouped. Then, it would begin again. Andrew had no illusions of changing that endless cycle.

"Here you are." The soldier who had escorted Andrew gestured at a door and bounded off to fulfill the second part of his orders.

Andrew pushed the heavy wooden door open and beheld a room unlike any he had ever seen. Long tables were covered with maps. Various objects that represented Conclave and Sylvanian forces sat upon the maps. The far wall was a chalk inventory of each artillery battery, its ammunition supply, the number of cannons within, and the crew. Two entire batteries had large, black X's scrawled over them, and Andrew did not need to guess what that meant. Amidst the elaborate collection of tactical information were dozens of officers arguing and shouting at one another while plotting the most efficient target for their cannons.

A calm, uniformed man stood appraising the soldiers under his command. He casually strode among the tables, pausing periodically to issue orders. It was this man that Andrew wanted to speak with, and he marched into the room.

In sharp contrast to their calm superior, panicked officers screamed various orders to their subordinates as Andrew made his way to the Commander.

"Ghoulherders are trying to scale the wall into battery three! We need barrels of oil and two security squads to defend if they make it over. And do not fire those cannons until that oil is used!"

A courier dashed off to deliver his commander's orders.

"We have reports of werewolves moving in to reinforce the southern trench line. Get enough silver from the holds for six volleys, take it to battery eight, and pound the shit out of these coordinates!"

Another courier vanished out the door past Andrew.

"There's a team of fanatics trying to pull a land ship out of the mud. Send these coordinates up to battery two and see if our anti-personnel shells can't change their mind."

Yet a third courier hurried to deliver his charge.

"Sir?" Andrew approached the calm officer supervising the activity within the room.

The officer turned to Andrew with a neutral look. He was tall and wore a peaked service cap. A horrid scar began below the brim of the hat and covered the right side of the man's face. A black eyepatch covered his right eye. "Yes, soldier?"

"I was in the trenches when they were overrun."

"Then I am speaking to a dead man." The commander's lips curled. While the scarred side remained inert, the unscarred side arched upward into what Andrew assumed was a smile. "Only the Conclave sends the dead back into battle after they've fallen." He laughed a deep, unsettling laugh that spoke of a sharp, yet slightly unhinged mind. "I suppose you would like to go home and a fancy funeral to send you off?"

Andrew had known many commanders to be somewhat disturbed. Front line soldiers' minds were quickly eroded by the horrors of war, but commanders, whose careers spanned decades, were often cracked and broken. They were held together by an inhuman resolve that, in a way, made them as alien as the undead monsters that clawed at the walls outside.

Andrew rattled off a quick explanation of how he had survived the trenches and where he had been. When he began to explain the deaths of his companions, he altered the truth. "As we made our way up Harbor Ridge, we stumbled upon a nest of spotters. We moved to engage, but they were vampires, and we were not equipped to fight them. My companions died heroically so I could escape and share what I've learned with Old Castle."

"Spotters, eh?" The commander waltzed over to the map that depicted Harbor Ridge in thorough detail. The topographical map was devoid of any significant representation of Conclave forces, and seemed vacant and irrelevant to the battle.

"Yes, sir. Maybe a hundred of them hidden among the trees," Andrew continued the lie.

"This is where I might put spotters if I were working for the enemy, but why should I trust the word of a dead man, eh?" The commander glanced up to Andrew with a twisted grin. "If you can't trust the dead, who can you trust?" The commander stared at Andrew for a moment as if he expected a genuine answer, and then abruptly turned back toward the maps. "I never did like all those trees. Officer Logan!"

"Yes, sir?" A soldier who was poring over the chart with a compass snapped to attention.

The commander placed an index finger on Harbor Ridge. "I want batteries six, five, and one to send a synchronized volley into this hill. Then, I want them to do it again. Then one more time for good measure."

"Yes, sir!" Logan nodded. "Anti-personnel? Explosive?"

"Incendiary! Let's give those vampire spotters some light to see by." The commander broke into a bizarre laugh that unsettled everyone in the room.

Logan did as instructed, and Andrew followed one of the couriers that was sent to execute the order. After snaking their way through numerous corridors and a handful of stops at ammunition holds, they arrived at artillery battery one. The room overlooked the firelit, nighttime battlefield. Snipers fired at targets below, while crews loaded a six-barreled cannon with the incendiary ammunition that had been requisitioned.

After the cannon was loaded and wheeled into position, its coordinates were adjusted with a series of gears and levers with functions far beyond

Andrew's comprehension. He looked over the barrel of the cannon and felt a giddy sense of satisfaction rise within him at the thought of delivering fiery death to the vampires that had killed his friends. If vampires wanted to make war a social event, he would make it one to remember.

"Fire!" the artillery crew chief ordered.

The deadly ordinance launched skyward toward its target in synchronicity with batteries six and five, and the shells found their marks. Andrew grinned at the notion that a dozen rich vampires were now writhing in flame. He watched the cannon pull back, reload, and send a second volley toward Harbor Ridge. With a deep sense of satisfaction, he watched the third volley vanish into the bright orange fire that engulfed the wooded hill.

The battle raged through the night, but by dawn the Conclave forces had retreated. A sea of dead and dying blanketed the smoldering hellscape of no-man's land beneath a dusting of fresh frost. New engines of war lay in ruin about the battlefield, and black craters dotted the earth like a pox.

Through smudged binoculars, Andrew scanned the devastation of Harbor Ridge. Black stumps smoked, and scorched earth cradled dying flames that had consumed all they touched. But here and there, he would catch sight of a charred patch of fine tuxedo or evening gown that drifted like ash on a chill wind.

Andrew's smile faded.

Daybreak had banished the excitement and horror of battle, but also inflicted a stillness that could only be filled by reflection. Andrew turned from the morning light and headed towards the dark passageway leading into the depths of Tombstone.

One of the artilleryman called after him. "Where you goin'?"

Andrew met the artilleryman's gaze. "Back to the trenches."

About Mark Rivett

Mark Rivett has professional experience as an educator, digital artist, and application developer. Mark began living in Pittsburgh, Pennsylvania in 1997, but now resides in Ann Arbor, Michigan. In addition to a background in digital technology, Mark is fascinated by the macabre and his writing is inspired by the horror and suspense genre.

54

In the Cavern of the Sleepers by Ali Abbas

Asif gripped his knife, the leather handle sweat-slick in his hand. The jungle was momentarily silent but for a twig snap. Someone was approaching. He let out his breath when the lanky form of his servant appeared.

"Are we still being followed?"

Prakash grimaced. "It's not like we're hard to track, and the ANT makes it tricky to see who else is on our trail." Asif raised an eyebrow, waiting for the actual answer. If Prakash was being obtuse there was probably little danger. Prakash shrugged. "If I had to guess, we're being trailed by children, or fat monkeys."

"Fat monkeys?"

"Go see for yourself, Sahib. The occasional footprints aren't large enough to be adult." He yawned and stretched, still shaking off last night's sleep.

"You think it's children from that village?" There had been a heavy air in the small collection of huts with its derelict shrine. The few people were lethargic and dull-witted. The place left Asif feeling distinctly uneasy, talking to people only half awake, caught between delirium and unfettered honesty. He'd been looking over his shoulder for two days since they had left it behind.

"They were odd people, but this is tiger country. I don't think they'd allow children to follow us." Prakash considered their wide trail. "There is something out there though. The ANT is a tempting target for dacoits, even fat monkey dacoits." The smile that accompanied this last quip faded. "I don't like this, Sahib. This area has a bad reputation—people going missing, nightmares and monsters."

Asif tried to stall the argument he knew was coming. "We can't go back. Whatever it is, we keep going."

"Be honest, Sahib. We could. We could ride the ANT. It will keep us safe, and we will be out of the jungle in days. If you insist on going on, we should go back and hire some guards."

Asif turned a quelling gaze on his servant. The smouldering defiance in Prakash's eyes was betrayed by several sleepy blinks. He turned away, knowing better than to push the subject, for now.

They broke camp with practiced ease and sent the All-terraiN Transport ahead. Its 18-foot-long, sinuous form slowly arranged itself into line, the six legs extended. Razor sharp blades swung out of the front. and it set off, clearing a path through the dense foliage. Brass scales glinted in the infrequent shafts of sunlight before it disappeared into the gloom.

They lingered a little longer than usual with Asif lost in thought. Years of travel in search of a cure for his condition had brought them here, on the strength of a crudely drawn map. He hated to admit it, but Prakash was right to be sceptical.

"You trust that scrap of paper?" Prakash asked, reading his master's thoughts.

"Do you?"

"I trust you figuring this out in your lab rather than chasing 'round the country searching for witch doctors and legends." Prakash turned back to making tea as his words settled in the small clearing, adding to his master's uncertainty.

Asif's mother called his illness talking with angels, reconciled to his difference by making it something special. When her son gently faded out of consciousness, it was not terrifying or shameful. It was no surprise that he could not remember the conversations; he was no prophet after all.

His father was more practical. He went so far as to pay a physician with the East India Company for a diagnosis. The new word "narcolepsy" gave Asif the spur to study medicine and search for a cure.

"No, Prakash." Asif stood and tapped his cartridge, the small box strapped to his spine. "I'm taking stronger and stronger doses of the formula, and still my episodes are getting more frequent. Besides, if the map is correct, we're nearly there."

Prakash handed Asif his tea, a weary acceptance in his eyes. This was the moment for Asif to say something motivating, but the world greyed at the edges. The silver handle of the glass slipped from his fingers.

The cartridge clicked, there was a jab by his spine, and he sneezed. The world came sharply back into focus as the blend of stimulants and histamines surged through his bloodstream. Prakash was at his side, the tea glass nimbly caught. He set it down and hopped away, blowing on his fingers.

"If I didn't know you better, Sahib, I'd say you did that on purpose."

There was a wet patch on the ground where some of the tea had spilled. A handful of ants were quartering the distance, lured by the promise of sugar. Asif watched them for a while, then retrieved his glass. The smell turned his stomach. He poured it out and tossed the glass to Prakash. "I can't live like this." He strode off along the narrow trail the ANT had left.

They caught up with the ANT an hour earlier than expected.

"Did you set the battery to charge last night?" Asif asked.

"Of course."

"Are you sure? You don't quite seem yourself."

The set of Prakash's shoulders declared he had taken offence. He stalked over to the ANT and briskly unclipped one of its domed rear sections. "It smells hot."

Asif joined him. "You're right." A bead of sweat dropped from his forehead onto the metal casing. It sizzled. "Something has strained it. Check the legs."

Prakash dropped into a squat as Asif unclipped another domed section. An oily steam rose out of the gear train chamber.

"Fat monkeys?" Prakash offered. It was not an absurd suggestion. The urbanised monkeys of their hometown Agra were fascinated by machines. It was not unusual for them to hitch a ride on a clockwork cart or steamcycle.

"We'll need to let it cool. I'll get the battery back on to charge; you take a look around. Stay in shouting distance."

Asif took the depleted battery and his portable water wheel. The route they were taking followed the river north through the wilds of Assam. He weaved through the undergrowth accompanied by the distant chatter of birds. He set the battery on the bank and took off his sandals, rolling his billowy shalwar trousers up to his knees. The water was cold. He hopped across the gravelly bed and staked the water wheel in mid-stream. Encouraging flicks of his fingers got the wheel spinning.

The birds fell silent. His hand drifted to the curved dagger at his side. He scanned the nearer bank. The foliage was completely still. He turned slowly on the spot, his toes churning mud under the gravel. Mid-stream was a long jump for a tiger, but not impossible.

Nothing moved. Sweat pricked at the back of his neck and ran down his spine. He turned to the opposite bank. Between the thick leaves there was something else. He stilled, eyes fixed on the spot. The shadows resolved, slowly at first, then suddenly swept into focus. A face stared back at him, dark-skinned and round.

The darkness around the face spread outwards. Asif's knees weakened. The box fixed to his back clicked once, twice, sensing the changes in his body. There was no stab of a needle, there was no sneeze. In his anger that morning he had forgotten to replenish his medication.

His body crumpled into the cool, welcoming darkness.

A drop fell on his shoulder. He felt it despite his sodden clothes. Another drop. His head throbbed. He remembered the river. The burning in his chest suggested he had fallen face first and tried to breathe water.

He took stock as his senses revived. He was propped up on a rough, solid surface. A closeness in the air suggested he was underground. He had not been allowed to die. His hands were tied and his legs immobile, so it wasn't Prakash that had saved him. His conscience stabbed that Prakash's safety had not been his first thought.

Asif opened his eyes a fraction. Light might turn the pain in his head into agony, but he needed more data.

It made no difference, it was pitch dark.

Another drop. The intervals were maddeningly uneven. He shifted his shoulders. Something was missing. He swore. His medication cartridge was gone. The wires into his spine were very fine, he was unlikely to bleed out, but the procedures for placing it were delicate. It had taken days to train Prakash in the art.

"I'm glad you are awake."

Asif's breath caught. He had no sense of anyone else in the dark, but the voice was close by, feminine and light. Silence fell again.

"It's difficult to tell in the dark."

"I mean you no harm Asif *mian*." The voice was unaccented, it could have been from anywhere in India. As she had applied a polite honorific to his name, he guessed he had not fallen to a jungle tribe or local dacoit.

Asif lifted his hands before remembering the gesture was futile. Somehow, his captor understood. "I'm sorry, my assistants were over cautious." Swift hands loosened the bonds at his wrists, and someone else relieved his ankles.

"A little light would go a long way to building trust," he suggested.

A match flared, glowing between a pair of palms, settling on a lamp wick. A figure shuffled out of the small circle of light before Asif could make it out. Another splash on his shoulder reminded him to move. He bit his lip to stifle a cry. Pain flooded his hands and feet as blood rushed back. The woman waited until he stopped writhing.

"Tell me about this."

His cartridge clattered into the pool of light. He caught a momentary glimpse of delicate fingers, tipped with sharp nails.

"I have an illness. It strikes with little warning. That box senses when my body is failing me and injects my medicine." As he spoke, he rubbed life back into his hands and tried to pierce the darkness. The third person had given no sign of their presence since loosening his bonds.

"Medicine?"

"It's not perfect, but keeps me awake. I'm still searching for something to help me sleep deeply."

"You fall asleep but cannot achieve true rest?"

"It is a cruel ailment; I can't control my waking, and I can't get a restful sleep."

Something in the movement of the air suggested the woman edged closer as her curiosity was piqued.

"It sounds more like an affliction of the soul, not the body."

"So far treating my body has worked."

Swift hands swept up the cartridge into the darkness.

"Is the enormous metal centipede also of your devising?"

"It is." If she knew of the ANT, she knew about Prakash. "Do you hold my companion?"

"If by companion you mean servant, and by hold you mean have I extended my hospitality to him, the answer to your question is yes." There was a wry note to her voice. Despite his uncertain position, Asif found himself warming to her.

"Can I see him?"

"Of course, but he's sleeping."

"Prakash usually sleeps very lightly."

There was a snort, as though someone had suppressed a sneeze or a laugh. One set of footsteps padded off in the direction he was facing. Asif lurched to his feet and grabbed the lamp. The soft slap of skin on stone told him the woman was also barefoot. He hobbled, hurrying to catch her, but she stayed out of the pool of light, pale flashes of her heels guided his path.

The walls to either side were narrow and damp. They glistened with multicoloured deposits, staining the uneven surface. Passages opened off to both sides. The woman chose turnings as though navigating a maze.

"Here."

The footsteps ahead of him stopped. He cast the lamp from side to side, but there was no sign of the woman. A door was set into the tunnel wall, made of a dense, dark wood. He cautiously pushed it open. Prakash was asleep inside.

A light shaking did not wake him. His body slumped back as soon as Asif let go of him. Asif shook him with increasing alarm. "What have you done to him?"

"I have done nothing." The voice was behind him, but when he turned there was nothing to see in the swaying lamplight. "He sleeps. Everyone who comes here sleeps. Except you."

"And you."

"And me."

"Who are you?"

"A servant. My name is Padma."

"And whom do you serve?"

"You will meet them soon enough."

"And when will I meet you?"

Silence. Asif waited, his hand on Prakash's shoulder.

She was short, slightly built and seemed to be dressed only in her silvery hair. It curtained around her body, maintaining her modesty, but not hiding her most salient feature. Her skin had a blue cast, and beneath her open arms a second pair was held out in front of her, holding his cartridge. There was an expectant look in her eyes, a premonition of hurt.

Asif's eyes widened, he had seen statues of four-armed women in many temples, but he had thought the avatars of Kali were a myth. It was impossible to judge her age. From moment to moment in the dancing light she seemed young, then infused with wisdom that only comes with age. He smiled, hoping to seem accepting and encouraging, but the glow of the lamplight closed around the edges of his vision. He had no means to stall it. "Oh no," he managed to croak before the narcolepsy stole his consciousness.

She was hovering over him when his senses returned. A nervous smile played on her lips.

"I thought the sleep had claimed you as well."

"My medicine usually stops that happening." He pushed himself up onto his elbows, missing Prakash as bruises blossomed. His servant's uncanny reflexes had been catching Asif since childhood.

"I'm sorry I took off your machine."

"The medicine has run out. There's more in the ANT."

"My BalishDeo dragged it into the cavern. It was very heavy, and I fear they were not gentle with it." She led him to another chamber. This time she stayed in the light, her long hair falling to above her calves.

The ANT was a mess of twisted metal, legs bent and control arms snapped. He popped the catches on a rearward section. Glass shards and spilled powders littered the banded wooden base.

Asif picked his way through the debris, locating a door built into the side of the mobile laboratory. There were four vials inside. All of his remaining stimulant formula. Another cabinet revealed a spare cartridge and fresh pack of needles.

"Is there a way to wake Prakash? He knows how to attach my equipment."

"He'll sleep as long as he is in this cavern."

"Let's go then. If your BalishDeo can drag the ANT they can lift one old man."

"It's not that simple."

"Why?"

"You can't leave."

Asif grabbed Padma by one arm. "Prakash can't wake, and we can't leave. You said you weren't a captor!" His heart sank with a sickening lurch. Kali was both creator and destroyer, Divine mother and the dark one. Which aspect was in this Padma avatar?

"I'm trapped here too."

Her voice was small and caught with a sorrow that pierced his anger. He noticed the cool smoothness of her skin in his hard grip. Asif let her go as though scalded. She stepped back a little, out of the light, hurt by his reaction. Silence filled the awkward space between them. Asif heard Padma take a deep breath in, then release it slowly.

"Tell me why you came here," she asked.

"Please, just get us out of here."

"Answer my question. I think it could be important."

The urgency and uncertainty in her tone startled him, suggesting she was indeed not his captor. "There's a temple in the jungle. I've been chasing rumours of it for months now."

"You are a Muslim; what is there for you in a Hindu temple?"

"A cure. I've been seeking out healers and holy men for so long now I don't remember doing anything else. I heard there was a temple where everyone sleeps." The words came out in a rush. "The hardest part of my condition is not sleeping deeply, with dreams. It's getting worse. I guessed there was some local plant or atmospheric condition that I could replicate."

"This cavern is that temple. I don't know why, but you are immune to the sleep that affects those who come here."

"A side effect of my condition, perhaps?"

"Perhaps." She bit her lip unconsciously as she thought about what he had said. "No one has been able to break the enchantment before."

"Enchantment?"

"There's something that needs to happen here. Until it does, no human can leave. The BalishDeo aren't human, but they can't carry anyone with them." Asif raised an eyebrow at that. Padma gave a complex shrug in reply, four arms moving upwards. "Despite appearances, I am human, mostly."

Asif frowned. He was a man of learning and science. He knew there was knowledge in the ancient faiths of India, but his studies so far had shown it was grounded in cause and effect that had become shrouded in myth and mystery.

"My masters are the Nagas of the East." She paused before going on with slow, deliberate words that seemed difficult to say. "They should slumber for years at a time, guiding their followers through dreams. But they made a mistake, now they doze fitfully. The ordinary human mind cannot cope with their unease and takes refuge in sleep."

Asif shook his head. "Superstitious rubbish. Show me the way out. It must be close; no one would drag the ANT farther than they had to."

Her laugh broke the tension that had been building between them. "Your people have hard words for non-believers. Well, I will make you believe."

There was a large set of double doors at the end of the next tunnel. Asif hauled on the iron handles, but the doors did not budge. "A little help, please?"

She snapped the fingers of all four hands in a rapid pattern. Dark, short shapes emerged from the shadows. They seemed roughly humanoid, with the chubby faces of children, but their arms and legs were massively muscular. A multitude boiled out of the darkness and melted away again. These were Prakash's fat monkeys that had been spying on them in the jungle. In their wake, the double doors were thrown wide open.

Asif gave Padma a smirk and strode towards the open air. Evening was settling in outside, but there was still enough light to see by. The sounds of the jungle replaced the silence. Between one step and the next Asif slowed. The air thickened, solidifying around his limbs. He pressed forward. His body froze, one foot in the air. He had not made it two yards beyond the threshold. Forcing his head down he saw the ground ahead was twisted and uneven. What he had taken to be the roots of trees were clusters of moss-covered bones.

Asif inched in reverse, wincing as something crunched beneath his feet. His muscles strained and tore. He dropped to the ground, gasping when the air relinquished its grip. He could not rise, so he came back to Padma on his hands and knees, penitent. His old cartridge was still in her hands. At his gesture she passed it to him.

He clambered to his feet with the help of one of her arms, then pivoted to hurl the cartridge through the door. It sailed into the night and landed on a protruding femur. The casing smashed, littering the undergrowth with broken pieces.

"This was once a famous temple, served by a dozen villages. It drew pilgrims from as far as China and Lanka. When my masters...." She paused, the words seemed difficult for her to say. "When they made their mistake there were months of chaos. Some pilgrims fell asleep, never to wake. Some realised something was wrong and tried to flee. A few made it out and must have warned others away. Then my masters fell into their half sleep, and the enchantment was sealed. No one comes here now."

Night fell over the desperate remains of previous prisoners. Years of searching had brought Asif here, only to end in a captivity that would lead to death. When it was fully dark outside, he turned back. Padma was waiting in the glow of the lamp, expectant, perhaps even hopeful. There may be truths in what she had said, but he needed more evidence. "Show me."

She stayed much closer this time, in the pool of light, only half a step ahead, taking him deeper into the cavern system. Their walk became a trudge as it grew hotter. When Asif stopped to wipe his brow, Padma turned. Her hair was darkened with sweat, gathering in thicker strands, giving tantalising glimpses of her skin underneath.

He blushed. It deepened when she laughed again, a throaty, richer laugh. She pulled a little further away, affecting more of a sway in her gait. Asif swallowed hard. The mullahs in Agra had lambasted him for frequenting temples and visiting Hindu mystics; lustful thoughts about Padma would condemn him once and for all. He kept his eyes fixed downwards and so missed when the tunnel opened out into a broad space. Padma's hand on his arm made him look up. She took the lamp and lit a series of torches. Mirrors reflected the light upwards.

The statues of three Nagas reared above him. Vast, snake-headed spirits, rendered in sandstone. Cobra hoods flared out from around their heads. Two male Nags stood on either side of the hugely pregnant Nagin. Her hands were cupped in front of her distended belly, holding something with great care.

As he watched, the figures shifted minutely, sending dust falling from the heights to settle on them. "Where is the mechanism?" he asked in hushed tones, awed by the size of the figures.

"They are the Nagas of the East; there is no mechanism."

"Right."

"Stay a while; watch them move. They rest uneasily. Like you."

"Why?"

"My mistress holds an artefact from the Buddha. An earring. The Nags thought to use its power to make their child into one of the great Gods. But the earring was not theirs to take, and the child balks at being born into wrongdoing. Its unborn cries keep the Nags and the Nagin from sleep."

"What is your role in this?"

"I'm the midwife."

Asif failed to restrain the bitter mockery in his own laugh. "You're here to help a statue give birth, which it can't because the baby feels guilty?"

"You bash your head before a God you cannot see or hear; which of us is the fool?"

There was a groan from the tons of masonry, and more dust drifted down. The frank look Padma gave him was a challenge.

"Real or not, what is it that you need from me?" he asked.

"I cannot go against the wishes of my masters, but I can guide someone else to."

"You want me to steal from your gods." Asif was caught somewhere between scoffing and incredulity.

Padma nodded. "For their own good."

Would Prakash have used underhand means to turn Asif around, had he known the peril of their journey? He thought back to childhood days when swift hands had caught him and gentle counsel stopped him testing his ailment recklessly. It was loyalty to his companion that swayed Asif.

"If I do this, can Prakash and I leave?"

"Once they lose hold of the earring the spirit can be born. The interdiction on humans leaving will be lifted. Your companion will wake up, and you can both leave."

"What about you?"

"I have to wait until the spirit is born. Then my task is done, and I can take the earring back to the monastery where it belongs." She looked at her arms. "Although I'm not sure how I feel about leaving this sanctuary."

He stared at the strange blue woman. There was a bitter truth glistening in her eyes. "There is no cure for me here, is there?"

She shook her head gently, setting her damp hair swaying about her body.

"I can't even offer you the rest that others have enjoyed, before it killed them."

"It sounds like I have nothing to lose."

She tilted her head to examine his features more closely. It took a moment for her to realise he was agreeing to the task.

"Thank you."

"I can't do it without my medication."

Padma put up four palms. "I'm good with my hands."

There was a tremor in Padma's whisper. "Their skin is not very sensitive, but their hearing is good." The statues soared overhead. In shared nervousness, Padma's hands wrapped double around Asif's sweaty palm.

She went up first, her many hands and lithe form finding a path up the body of a Nag. Asif followed less gracefully, hauling on the rope she secured for him. His knuckles scraped on the rough stone, and the thin cotton of his shalwar tore at the knees, drawing small beads of blood.

They paused halfway up to catch their breath. The left hand of a male statue jutted out several yards from its midriff, and it shifted as Padma crawled along the fingers. Asif stayed by the wrist, his back pressed into the heel of the palm. He tore his eyes from the plunging depth, but that meant looking at Padma, with her hair in disarray. His sense of balance fled.

The long drop yawned beneath him, suddenly elastic. His point of view narrowed, clouding at the edges. The newly positioned cartridge clicked once as a dose of his medicine was pumped into his body.

Asif sneezed. The world lurched back into focus. He grinned over at Padma. Her surgery had worked.

The horror on her face stole his good humour. The statue moved.

Padma fell, grabbing a finger with her two upper hands as the lower pair flailed. Asif leapt forward, sprawling full length on the statue's index finger. Her lower arms grabbed at him as the statue lurched again.

He dragged her halfway up, then she urged him away. "Quick. They know you are here now."

The statue shifted again, this time throwing Asif back into its midriff. He took hold of the loin cloth and hauled himself up. The belly and chest of the statue were bare but for a crossed pair of belts which stood a little proud of the skin, giving Asif room to wedge in his fingers and claw his way upwards.

The statue lived. A titanic, slow heartbeat pulsed. It moved. The stone belt flexed in, crushing Asif's fingers. His scream of pain drew the Nag's attention. The cobra-hooded head turned and dipped, tons of stone dropping with controlled momentum. Asif clung on with his right hand, sobbing with pain over the crushed fingers of his left.

"Hurry!"

The vast head continued swinging round to focus on Padma. Asif lost his grip and slid down. He kicked hard on the belt and landed in the crook of the Nag's opposite elbow. The male and female statues stood arm to arm. Squeezing his left wrist to numb the pain, Asif leapt from one forearm to the other, teetering on the curved surface.

An ominous rumble through his feet made him risk another leap to land in the cupped hands of the Nagin. A wooden chest, a foot high and several feet in length, rested against her fingers. The lid was open, and inside lay the thick gold earring of the Buddha. His one good hand fumbling, Asif looped a rope around one of her fingers and threw it over the side. He slammed the box closed and pressed it to his waist with his left wrist, spinning the rope around his waist.

The world closed in again, shutting down his senses as pain washed through him, his narcolepsy struggling to own him against the agony raging up his left arm. He sneezed. The Nagin's fingers curled. He hurled himself off into the air.

The rope burned through his palm, stripping flesh as he clattered into the huge belly of the female. The box fell, disappearing into a cloud of stone dust.

"Asif!"

The desperate cry brought his attention back to Padma. Asif kicked against the stomach, dropping further down the rope. His arc took him beneath Padma. She dropped onto his back, four strong hands wrapping round the rope, and her legs taking his weight as his right hand failed at last, spraying blood beneath them.

On the ground once more, Asif dropped onto his knees and elbows, holding his ruined hands in the air while searching for the earring.

The box had landed on the female statue's foot. A huge palm swung down from the darkness above. With a final, desperate roll, Asif kicked the box away. The hand stopped as a loud crack of splitting stone reverberated around the cavern. Asif and Padma lay in a sprawl of limbs amid a drifting haze of dust.

The heavens fell on them. A scalding, viscous downpour replaced the dust with a wall of fluid. The female goddess's water had broken.

They lurched out of the path of the fluid, slipping and hauling each other, choking and spluttering.

The blood was gone from Asif's hands, his fingers were straight and whole, healed by the Nagin's life-giving power. Padma's hair fell in two thick ropes at her sides. He doubled over with a yell. The painstakingly placed cartridge sprang off his back and shattered on the floor. He stared at his hands, then at Padma. "Do you think?"

She took his face in her upper hands to search his eyes and gave another of her complex shrugs. "Perhaps." Stone groaned above them. "How do you feel about helping birth a God?" she asked, lower fists clenched with excitement.

"If it's anything like humans, we still have a little time."

"Why?"

Asif slumped to the floor and leaned against a flat rock, weary, but strangely at ease. "I don't know about you, but I could really do with a nap."

More from Ali Abbas

Like Clockwork

Commander Raymond Burntwood of the Royal Navy has returned to England where he meets the reclusive heiress Lady Ariana Grayhart. After the scandal of a night spent dancing together, Ariana returns home to Northumberland. Raymond's superiors—seeking information about Ariana's father—dispatch the commander under the cover of courting the heiress.

All is not as it seems in the Grayhart household. Captain Grayhart is an invalid, the servants maintain a monkish silence, and secrets are layered upon secrets. Everyone has their own agenda, from Raymond's friend and confidante Du Bois, to the family lawyer Sir Berwick, and Ariana herself.

In the midst of it all, Raymond must unravel the truth of Captain Grayhart's decline and save Ariana's reputation and fortune. In doing so, he learns dark secrets about himself that could tear his world apart.

Fractured Moonlight by W.T. Paterson

The first time I saw Dr. Oculus drinking by himself, I realized he was a broken old man. At one point, he was my father's best friend, which meant he was my sworn enemy. Most people would have felt sorry for the old fool, but not me. I could see the past written across his face.

Too many nights in a war balloon dropping bombs onto sparsely inhabited islands under the orders of a long gone General.

Too many hits off the helium pipe to steady his nerves.

Too many nights alone in the altitude freezing his lungs with the last bits of oxygen that our world could hold onto. I didn't have to kill him; he was well on his way.

When I drew the courage to sidle up to his lonely table, he spoke as if we were already acquainted.

"You don't have to believe in ghosts," he whispered, thick salt and pepper mutton chops outlining his jaw. "But you'd be foolish to believe in finality."

We were drinking in a bar called the Raven's Widow. It was late spring in the warm climate of the American Southwest. The steam engines had yet to bring in the tourists looking for red rocks and turquoise, despite the heat of the summer.

"Ghosts," I grunted, taking a sip of Fortune's Ale, a locally brewed delicacy. "Sure."

"You doubt kaleidoscopic perspective?" he asked. "Multiple outcomes for the same event?"

"What I'm saying is that…you're old. You were a war pilot by the looks. Up there, things get scrambled in your brain."

"Easy, boy," Oculus said, his venomous tone a warning not to press. "The only reason I'm not jumping over this table and strangling you to death is because your father was a good man. Don't make me think otherwise, 'cause I'll wind you up good."

He *did* know me. If not by my reputation as a traitor, then by my looks. Though I hated to admit it, I looked just like my father, Jonathan Pure, the great war hero.

For years, I had thought of him as the ultimate hero, too. Brilliant inventor, a mind like a stallion stampede, and the first man to harness lightning to charge a pulse cannon. What was there not to love? Many credit him with inventing the weapon that took back the Rio Grande expansion. The sheer devastation of being able to shoot lightning from a cannon had been enough to give pause to our enemies. The Low Southerners, the Air Raiders, the Bandits, they'd all backed off.

The best memory I had of my father was being in our garage as he tinkered and played with small metal scraps. He welded me a toy man with moving joints and wind-up features.

"If you wind him this way, his arms move. If you wind him down here, his legs move. If you wind them together, he dances!"

This was back when he wasn't *everyone's* hero, it was back when he was just *my* hero. Later that night, he'd shown me how to modify the coils and winders so the toy could do different dances, throw punches, or bow like a gentleman. Even then I realized that he was showing me through a toy how to be a man. With the right twists and coils, we could be made to do anything.

Even leave.

How many nights had my mother cried herself to sleep, and in my youthful ignorance, had I believed it was because she was proud? How many birthdays, holidays, graduations had he missed because our country needed him more? All was forgiven because *everyone* else *loved* him so much.

Then came the handwritten letter delivered by courier. A man with a blue suit, white smile, and triangular hat handed me the letter with a whistle and left me to read it alone on our porch. My father would not be at my 16th birthday. He apologized for breaking a promise and then promised to make it up to me. Break a promise; make another – a trend I was quickly starting to decode with him.

I caught wind that the reason he could not come was because he had been invited to another family's house to a birthday party for *their* son. They had offered to pay him a great deal of money to make an appearance, but he turned it down and showed up for free. He was *that* guy. Public favor meant more to him than his own family. It was in the newspapers. How he'd thought I wouldn't see it only made my disdain grow.

So when I turned 16, I told my mother I proposed that we change our names. I didn't want to carry his anymore. She nodded and agreed.

"What should we call ourselves, then?" she'd asked.

"Anything, as long as I'm not Jonathan Pure, Jr.," I'd snarled. "Maybe it would upset him the most if we took the name of one of our great enemies, one of the Low Southerners."

"You are most certainly my son," my mother had said.

Her dresses were usually light pink or yellow, perfect for evening strolls under the lace umbrellas that could barely shelter her from the murderous heat. She always wore her hair up in a tight bun that wrapped her head like a sleeping cap. However, that night she took a knife and hacked off what she could, leaving only jagged bangs and a light trail of uneven edges in the back. I started to comb my hair back and lifted railroad spikes to make my arms strong so that the day my father did come home, he would hardly recognize me.

"I want to be Horatio Diablos," I'd said, "and I want you to be Katirin." I drew out the word so it became *kat-her-een.*

"Why stop there?"

Two weeks later, we had sold our home in the Midwest to move to the Southwest. I had just received my small craft license and was able to scrape together enough to buy an old, used blimp. We packed everything we could into small wicker baskets, strung them to the side of our ship, and sailed off. Neither of us has ever looked back.

"You look just like him," Oculus said that night in the Raven's Widow.

"Ghosts..."

"I'm not him," I said, and clenched my fists under the bar.

"That much is clear," he said, laughing. He nodded at my top hat with dyed feathers sticking out from the top. "Yellow with black stripes – you hold no allegiance. Red – you've spilled blood for your cause, whatever that may be. And blue – a deep blue. You fly best by nightfall, under the stars." He slowly waved his callused hands over his face like the whole thing was a showcase. Though he was not wrong, I didn't like that he knew me better than my father did.

"Where is he?" I asked.

"Do you believe in ghosts?" he mumbled.

"So he's dead?" I replied, perhaps too eager to hear a positive confirmation. Dr. Oculus merely sighed and pushed his drink away from his mouth. He stared into the dissipating white froth, a cumulus cloud losing itself to the wind. He shook his head, but he didn't mean no. I didn't know what he meant.

"Have you ever been so close to the moon that you've swallowed the stars?" he asked to no one.

"Old fool," I spat, standing up with such force that I knocked the wooden stool over.

A man with a monocle (non-prescription, it didn't catch the light properly) and well-groomed mustache began to protest at the noise. His suit was finely pressed, and the woman he was with barely looked old enough to be in the Raven's Widow, the curls in her hair like perfect tubes falling to her shoulders, and she wore a low cut dress that allowed her white lace undergarments to peek out.

"I demand you apologize," the short man said, standing up and stomping his cane to the ground. His rotund belly was pushing against a pressed white shirt beneath a dress coat with a purple square handkerchief stuffed neatly into the front breast pocket.

Politicians, they think they own the world.

"For what?" I laughed, pointing to his table where no drinks had been spilled.

"Apologize for disturbing my night and startling this beautiful young lady."

"How about I disturb this beautiful young lady by pulling your pants down and showing her the size of your pecker?"

The lady held a hand up to her mouth to stifle laughter.

"I know who you are, Diablos," he threatened.

"Then do something about it," I told him, walking to the swinging saloon doors. "And if I see her with as much as a bruise because she laughed at your pecker, I'll hang you from your ankles off of my air ship stark naked."

My ten-year mean streak had never tempered with age. It only grew into something that I found funny. Most people were all talk and no action. Those that were no talk and all action were the ones to watch out for. After chipped teeth, a few broken noses, busted lips, and black eyes, I learned who I could and could not win fights against. It's not that I *wouldn't* fight those people, I just preferred not to. Anyone else was fair game.

Like most other nights, I came home to my mother yelling at her boyfriend to stop stealing our steam supply.

"We built our own pipes! Keep your damn hands away from the valves!"

"Come on, baby, just let me fill this sack and you'll never know it was gone."

"Listen to the lady," I said, taking off my hat and letting the suspenders fall from my shoulders. "Because I won't ask you to stop. I'll just break your fingers."

"What type of man still lives with his mother and isn't out getting some mid-air strange at your age?"

God Damn Billy Klepper. Thought he was a hotshot bandit because he robbed the last car of a broken down steam engine. "Got away clean," he liked to brag. What's worse is that people believed him, including my mother up until she realized he was full of it.

"What type of man robs $200 worth of pocket watches from an engine train heading *north?* Did you not realize the caboose is for the staff who don't carry any riches beyond what they are given?"

He made a play like he was going to come at me, almost like he wanted my mother to hold him back. When she didn't, he stopped himself and mumbled about his knee hurting. That's why he wasn't going to pummel me, his knee happened to be acting up.

My mother had short hair dyed black. She kept a belt of bullets around her waist with a six-shooter hanging low off the left side. Her dress was black and dark blue, a hand-painted skull with horns across the front in white. She never shot the gun, never even loaded it. But that's the thing about a weapon. If you have one, most people assume you know how to use it – even if you don't. Me, on the other hand, I didn't believe in guns. If you couldn't hurt someone with your hands, then what was the point? Chalk it up to another rebellion against my father and his war machines. I'd much rather feel the fight than be taken out of it in a blinding flash.

"I'm gonna go lie down," Billy said, and then he limped towards the bedroom that my mother slept in.

"Why do you put up with him?" I asked for the hundredth time.

"Because deep inside, he's a scared little boy. That's what keeps him loyal, even if he's a talker."

"I found Oculus," I mentioned, pulling out my notebook and scribbling down the last thing he'd said to me. *Have you ever been so close to the moon that you've swallowed the stars?*

"You need to stop doing this to yourself," she said. Her hands were callused by the desert sun, but they felt so much more tender than the pale hands stained by tears in my youth.

"I need to know," I said.

"It won't make the pain stop."

"Who says I want it to?"

I slammed my notebook shut and walked over to a steam valve. With a quick turn, a massive hiss outside let me know that my cruiser ship was filling with propellant.

"One of these nights, you're going to fly too high and I'll never see you again, Horatio."

I kissed her on top of the head.

"That's the plan," I told her. "And when that day comes, I'll send for you."

"You sound like your father." She frowned, then stood up to check on Billy.

From the hand-carved wooden chair with a scorpion etched on each arm, I smiled to myself as I heard my mother slap her boyfriend silly. She threatened that if he ever tried to steal our steam again or take a run at me, she'd be in good mind to shoot him dead and collect on the bounty. Billy let out weepy apologies and swore up and down he wouldn't do it again.

"I'm just like *you*," I happily whispered, lacing up my boots before grabbing a fork-tailed jacket and goggles.

I sailed for hours that night above the clouds in the cold winds, the stars poking holes through more and more of the darkness as I climbed. I don't know what I was looking for, but it felt right to be in the air. Something about the coldness that comes with altitude, the way the lungs wanted to shut down but couldn't, the realization that everything on the ground was just a tiny cosmic dust storm put me at ease. Who would ever want to capture the majesty of lightning and weaponize it? To what end could it hold?

As soon as I landed and the sun started erasing the stars with gold and blue, I decided to sleep for a spell. Billy was passed out on the couch, nursing a big bruise on his forehead. Mouth dangling open, gut falling through the bottom of his shirt, he was no train bandit. Not by a long shot.

My eyelids grew heavy in the dense air at the bottom of the world, and my lungs were able to properly expand. It put me right to sleep.

I dreamt that my father was a wind-up ghost wandering the world looking for people to turn him in different directions. I saw me as a boy standing next to me as a man. We were winding up the different parts of him. Near his jaw, I turned the pin and programmed him to say, "Be anyone but me, son. Save more lives than you take." Then I wound him up again, and instead of saying what I wanted him to, he said, "Lightning still fears the stars." His mechanical mouth malfunctioned and fell off.

The younger version of myself and the current version of myself both reeled back in horror. That's when the younger me reached for my hand and felt it was made of cold steel and valves. Instead of being afraid, he looked me up and down, and found that I, too, had grown to be a wind-up toy. He twisted knobs and tightened my coils. My arms moved, my legs flailed. Young me laughed with excitement at the clumsy dance. Then he pulled a string from my back and waited to hear what I would say.

"You'll spend so much time hating him that by the time you're me, you will be nothing but a shell of a man built to dance, incapable of dancing for the joy of it."

"I forgive you," young me said, then pushed me over a ledge of my air cruiser. For a moment, I floated against the fractured moonlight that could only reflect the sun and reveal tiny bits of the world below. When I looked back, my ship was on fire.

It woke me up with a harsh breath, and my stomach twisted into broken cogs.

I went back to see Oculus that night, and the night after, and every night that I could.

"Why do you want to find him so badly?" Oculus asked, putting up with my company rather than welcoming it. "What comes for you then? Redemption? Reunion?"

"Respect," I answered in a drunken stupor. "For me. I want him to see that I took the name of his enemies and became my own man."

"Ha. Enemies. As if he held such things. You know nothing of the war, of what we were made to do, what obligations we were made to uphold."

"Enlighten me," I said. My eyes were half closed, and the women behind the bar seemed to glow.

Oculus slid his drink away and lifted his hat. Beneath it was a silver feather – the highest honor among those who serve. It was light; perfectly delicate and wonderfully strong.

"My brain isn't what it used to be, I'll give you that. The air up there makes a man go mad. But your father, he saved me. Not from a battle or an air raid, but from the depths of suicide. Our mission was to cross into enemy territory and scout a geothermal when a fierce wind blew us miles off course. Everything below was dry and sandy. Couldn't touch down without the fear of capture, so we had to stay in the air. In order to avoid detection, we climbed further up into the atmosphere."

"I've heard the story," I groaned.

"So you must have heard that on the fifth day of no food, barely any water, and light air, I tried to hang myself with the rope from a sandbag? Your father wouldn't let me, he wrestled me to the floor and with his…cunning mind helped me hold onto sanity. He built these little wind-up toys that could move, dance, fight, bow, and after a while I believed they could love. He would wind them up, and my mind would focus on only them, not my starvation, and how these little wind-up men and women were falling in love, betraying one another, forging friendships, making amends. I found in them the life I wished I had lived. Through them, I was able to live a life where I didn't become a doctor who dropped bombs from the sky. Your father gave me that little bit extra to hold onto."

It hurt to hear. I knew the feeling well, and that is why it hurt. In the toys he made me as a child, I saw myself as an adult. Sturdy, obedient, made from nothing into something.

"Then you were rescued?"

"Aye, but I never saw your father again. I thought you were his ghost when you first walked through that door. I shoulda known he had a son. Only makes sense. A brain like his, he knew what they'd do to him, so he wanted to pass it on."

Clanking glasses and steam whistles fell to white noise as I stared at Dr. Oculus. Though my body was warm with ale and my woozy breathing a dead giveaway to my condition, something was becoming clear.

"Do what to him?" I asked.

"They wouldn't let him go home. He was their moneyman. Wherever they could send him, he had to go. People funded the war because they thought he would win it with his cannon. They weren't wrong, but I could see the classified pictures of him standing and smiling with hollow eyes. Presidents, politicians, picture stars—they all wanted part of Jonathan Pure, and once they met him, they all wanted one of his wind-up toys. There were rumors, mumblings that if you put all the toys and parts together, and wound them, it would reveal the true nature of God."

"You old idiot," I spat. "You cowardly fool. Don't sit there and feed me garbage." The alcohol was speaking louder than my rational mind. The younger me was horrified at what the older me had become. "I changed my name to Diablos, and you speak of God!"

The doctor motioned for a glass of water and leaned forward onto the bar as though I weren't even talking to him. He started humming an old folk song about sailing the mountain winds.

"He died three years ago, but he's not dead," the man said when he finally spoke. Then, he placed his head down onto the bar top and ran a stubby finger along the edge. "He was their wind-up man, just as you are his wind-up son. This was his." Oculus handed me the silver feather. "Wear it when you see fit."

Then he belched in a sad way that showed just how much he had given up on life.

"They don't give these to cowards who abandon their families!" I barked, clamping the silver feather in my hand.

Suddenly, the man came roaring to life and grabbed me by the throat. His eyes were red with fury. He had killed before and would do it again. Over and over, he slammed my shoulders and head onto the table behind me until there was a pool of blood. When I thought the last bit of air was going to be choked out of me and the warm cut behind my ear would pour forever, he stopped and tossed me to the floor.

"And you call *me* the fool. The wind-up son bleeds, he feels, he hates because he loves. Yes, yes, I'm the fool. I am betrayal, I am friendship, I am the world you never got to see. I am your wind-up toy."

Then he slunk back to his seat with a heavy thud as the bartender yelled for me to leave at once and never come back. After the scene, I doubted I ever would.

Someone sent for my mother and Billy. Billy showed up and kept telling people he was *the* Billy Klepper. No one cared. My mother's gun was pushing into my ribs when I put my arm around her shoulder to stay steady. The gun she never used, it was only for show. She was trying to be someone she wasn't, a wind-up mother playing her role.

A bartender with a curled mustache mechanically washing glasses with a rag.

A piano player mechanically playing music.

Patrons mechanically sipping their drinks and putting them down.

Billy, looking for respect and never finding it.

A father who believed a lightning cannon would end a war because people…people were predictable. You just had to wind them up and let them go. They'd cling to habits, they'd exist within routines. How many times had I been dragged bloody and beaten out of a pub?

A wind-up son that couldn't think beyond his own pain.

It took three days before I was able to get out of bed without the spins. When I did, I took to the night sky. Silhouetted against the moon, I imagined my ship to be a specter of sails and sacks, the top far larger than my wooden steering port beneath it. Why had I always come to the sky for answers? What made the night so important to me?

Again, as I'd seen a thousand times before, the fractured moonlight of a half-split crescent illuminated the world below in sweeping shades of blue and silver. Like a painter's stroke, I could see towns and buildings, roads and trees, lakes and mountains, but only in places where the light could tread. It looked so peaceful.

And that's when a thought occurred to me: what if my father was trying to teach me something different entirely? It wasn't about building toys for his son, or showing him how to be a man, it was about taking the scraps of whatever you are given and building the world you want to see. Inside of those wind-up toys, sprung with gears and coils, I lived out all of my dreams and stories. As I looked down again, I saw no explosions, no fire in the clouds. The world was peaceful – at least for now. My father hadn't built a machine of death, but rather had created the ultimate sacrifice for peace. He built the world that he wanted me to grow up in, and it was one where the battles fought were short-lived and ill-planned.

My neck and shoulders still throbbed, but elevating my machine higher and higher, the chilly night air crept into my lungs and I closed my eyes to feel their icy sparkle.

Fly close to the moon and swallow the stars.

Whatever Oculus had lost up here, whatever world he fought for, all the times my father never came home, it was all for this. It was all for the idea that a greater life existed on a grand scheme, and a tiny one. Perhaps my father had died, but he lived on through the wind-up worlds of imagination, and those imaginings turned into realities.

Dr. Oculus may have just been a crazy old man, but he was correct in telling me that it would be foolish to believe in finality.

I kept elevating my ship, feeling ice begin to form around my glass goggles and fingers. The open air was a dangerous mistress, but one that I had always loved. The oxygen was running out at this altitude, and I could feel my knees give way. It knocked loose my descender valve and the ship began to sink towards safer heights. Whether or not I would change my ways didn't seem to matter, because I was wound up and coiled inside of a life that I thought would be better. I was living out a fantasy to get back at my father, when really he had given me the tools to survive it. I plucked two feathers from my cap, leaving only the blue one. The red and yellow feathers danced away into the clouds.

I steered the ship homeward and passed through a lightning storm. With my body aching, the name of our enemy as my own, returning to a world where the only love I felt was misguided hatred towards my father and an unwavering loyalty to my mother, a lightning bolt cracked the sky.

For a moment, I could have sworn it said my name. My true name. Jonathan Pure, Jr. And in that moment, I felt the coils inside of me tighten and wind in a way that I hadn't felt since I was a child.

And so I slid the silver feather into my hat and let the wind blow cold across my eyes.

About W.T. Paterson

W.T. Paterson is the author of the novels *Dark Satellites* and *WOTNA*. A Pushcart Prize nominee, his work has appeared in over 40 publications worldwide include Fiction Magazine, The Gateway Review, and a number of Anthologies. He is a current MFA student at the University of New Hampshire. Send him a tweet @WTPaterson.

Basic Black by K. A. Fox

I waited in line, dancing from one foot to another, anything to keep the blood flowing. I was grateful for the gloves I'd thought to grab as I left the house. The worn, rust brown fabric was soft and little protection against the bitter wind biting through to my skin, but better to have that than nothing. The temperature had dropped overnight as rain fell, the sun rising on a city clean and gleaming, encased in ice. Beautiful. But already the shine was dimmed by a tinge of gray clinging to the crystals that had been so bright just hours earlier. The soot in the air tainted everything.

Someone coughed behind me, and I tried not to flinch. The wheezing sound of Creeping Black was sadly familiar here. Basic Black, the Families called it, up on the hill in their shining homes. Once the coughing began, it was only a matter of time before you were cleaning up dark clots of blood. Few lasted long once The Black took hold. I hunched deeper into my coat, my arms wrapped tight to keep it closed where the buttons had been lost seasons ago. Buttons were luxury items now, too expensive to replace.

The doors ahead swung open twenty minutes late, quieting the angry murmurs of the crowd. We all had places to be. Time was money. Never enough of either, it seemed. Knowing the drill, each person entering the office stepped to the lane assigned by their last name, never straying over the red lines marked on the cracked floor. I took my place behind a young woman holding a baby, appreciating the warmth. I thought of the people still waiting outside in the cold. "Early birds eat their fill," my father liked to remind me when I didn't want to get out of bed.

A man I didn't recognize took a seat facing the line I stood in. He didn't hurry, settling himself and checking all his drawers before finally gesturing to the person at the head of our group. I hardly listened as people filed up to his window, handing their Vouchers through. Instead, I turned my thoughts to the math problems I'd been working on all night in preparation for today's exams. Twisting them around in my head, I closed my eyes and visualized the numbers hanging in front of me in the darkness. I kept my focus on the calculations, my feet moving me forward in step with everyone else. The brass gear charms my younger sister had woven into my braids for good luck swung with each step I took. The shining metal in my dark hair and the bright blue of my uniform shirt told everyone all they needed to know about me. Candidate. Engineering. Earning her way.

The woman in front of me stepped to the window, soothing the baby that had started to whimper.

"You know the rules. Only one person at a time." The man's voice was cold and grating, the scorn in it barely disguised.

"But I didn't have anywhere to take him. He's sick."

He shook his head. "Come back tomorrow. Alone."

"Please. I need my Basic today. Bills are due." The frantic note in her voice was unmistakable. We'd all been there.

"Tomorrow." Eyes hard, the man waved his hand dismissively at her.

Without thinking, I stepped forward and his eyes flicked to me. Narrowed.

I reached out to the woman. "I'll hold this one." She hesitated at my offer, but I gave her a smile. "I've held babies with sniffs worse than this little guy. I don't mind."

She looked between me and the man at the window, my smile and his angry jaw at odds with each other. She finally nodded and handed the baby to me. I stepped back to my place at the front of the line, balancing his weight on one hip. He grabbed at my shirt collar, pulling it toward his mouth to chew on. I unwound his fingers carefully, distracting him with math problems whispered in his ear. My shirt had years of wear on it, the collar carefully mended time and again, but I knew it was scrupulous clean. I needed to keep it that way. Basic we might be, but my family had a reputation to maintain. Everyone knew the Quinn name.

The baby's mother finished, her allowance for the month disappearing into her bag. She turned to me and held her hands out. The little boy leaned toward her, and she gathered him into her arms, a quiet thank you mouthed to me as she walked by.

My turn. I stepped forward again, tugging off my gloves as I approached the window. I pulled the Voucher from my inner pocket, sliding it through the small opening. The filtered air on the other side of the glass pushed out at me, the paper fluttering in my grip. I could hear the unhealthy whine of the air handler through the divider. It needed maintenance or it would die soon. Then the clerks would have to breathe the same air we all did.

The man grabbed my Voucher, glancing at it before shoving it back to me. "You can come back tomorrow."

"Why? This is the first day of the month. The Voucher says it can be collected today."

"You stepped out of line. You come back tomorrow."

"I can't come tomorrow." I kept my voice low and even, not allowing a hint of my frustration to show.

He grinned cruelly, his perfect white teeth telling me plenty about him. A child of the Families, but distant enough that no one had bought out the time he had to serve at the Basic Office. His answer was loud, drawing the attention of those around us. "Come back tomorrow."

"No. You can't refuse to honor the Voucher. I know the rules." His eyes roved over me, and I stiffened at the scrutiny.

He pointed up to the wall where a framed copy of the Basic Commandments hung behind glass that had long ago become opaque as layers of soot had collected on its surface. "If you know the rules, you know that when you took that Baser's brat, you stepped out of line. You lost your place." People were turning, staring at us now.

I refused to back down and shook my head. "I'll talk to a supervisor instead." My voice was polite, but firm.

He bared his teeth. "Supervisor isn't here. Big meeting at the Assembly. You can sit over by the door if you want to wait. No telling how long they'll be."

I bit my lip, worried about time. The office opening late had already set me back, and I still had to get across the city to campus. Professors didn't tolerate tardy students. Exam day meant the doors were shut once testing started. Missing one exam could mean the end of a candidate's career. Not worth the risk. I grabbed the Voucher and stuffed it back into the pocket my mother had sewn inside this coat, hidden from thieving fingers.

I stepped away from the window. Only one day. We could get by. As I turned to go, the man in the window laughed, the sound acid in my ears. "See you tomorrow, Baser." My hands shook, anger tinged with panic writhing in my stomach. The others still in line shot sympathetic glances my way, but stayed quiet as I passed them. I refused to swipe at the tears building up in my eyes, not wanting anyone to notice.

The doors opened just as I shoved into them, and I stumbled out into the cold. Large hands steadied me, saving me from a fall down the steep stone stairs.

"Whoa, slow down there, Cam. Don't want ya hurtin' yourself." Bran's voice was as warm as his hands, his soft brown eyes concerned as he looked down at me. He was tall, his hair even darker than mine. The angles of his face hadn't changed, still exactly as I'd memorized them. The same as the ones I saw every night in that weak moment between asleep and awake. "You all right?"

I shook my head. "Can't talk now." I caught the hurt twisting his lips. "Exams. Don't wanna be late." I started down the stairs, but turned back, a heavy exhale leaving me. "Thanks, Bran. I'll see ya."

I hurried toward the stop, whispering hopes that I hadn't missed the bus to campus. It was a long way, and I was already later than I could afford. I jogged, my bag of books slapping against my back in time with my feet hitting the pavement. The cold air stung my lungs, but I kept on. Just a little bit farther.

I was almost to the stop when I heard my name. Turning, I saw Bran racing to catch up with me. I stopped and waited, looking back over my shoulder to check for the bus. Not yet.

Bran slowed and tried to catch his breath. "You're faster than I remember."

I laughed. "You haven't chased me since we were kids. I've grown a lot since then."

"I noticed." He grinned and reached into his pocket. "Found this in the lobby back there. Thought it looked familiar." He handed me a lone glove, the mate to the one my fingers went to in my pocket.

"Oh, thank you. I didn't even know I'd dropped it."

The bus pulled up, belching black fumes as it stopped at the bench behind me. Bran started to say something, but I backed away. "Gotta go. Thanks again."

I rolled up the gloves, holding them tight when the door opened. Warm air rushed over me as I stepped inside. Dropping into the seat, I shrugged off the heavy bag, and relief rolled over me in a wave.

I glanced out the window just as the bus lurched, throwing me forward. The charms in my hair pinged as they hit the glass. Bran stood where I'd left him, and when my eyes met his, he waved goodbye.

By the end of the day, I was exhausted and hungry, my stomach growling angrily. Exams were done and I'd been able to bargain for some extra time in the lab. My latest design wasn't due for a few weeks, but I felt every second of that time running out. As I peered at the mechanism I'd laid out under the glass shield, pride surged up in me at the intricate connections of gears. With the risk of corrosive contamination high, every prototype was assembled in the sterile environment of the labs. The historians pointed out in their lessons to the Candidates that we treated our gears the way society had once treated babies not yet ready for the world. Precious, fragile things that required extra protection.

As I looked through the magnifying sphere, I manipulated the parts in minute increments. My hands were sure on the sticks as I moved them carefully to guide the claws inside the sealed case. Just one more adjustment was all I needed. My stomach growled again, but I ignored it. I pulled the claws back and flipped the power inside the case on. A motor beneath my feet grumbled to life, even as I made sure the gauge stayed steady at the lowest level. I watched as the steam began to flow, my smile growing as the gears started to turn, each one working in perfect harmony with the next. They spun together a few seconds more before I eased the switch to its off position, the vibrations beneath my feet slowly ebbing away. Then, I marked the progress I'd made in my chart and closed down the file. I unlatched the base from where I'd locked it into place when I started working, rolled it over to my station, and slid it smoothly into my locker space. After keying in the code, the light above flashed red, and the clamps locked my work desk into place, safe and sound until I came back. I grinned, satisfaction spinning through me as I gathered my bag and left the lab behind for now.

As I neared the exit, the arched atrium windows rose up over me. It was dark outside, later than I thought it would be. I groaned, already hating the long walk ahead of me.

Bran's solid form stepped out of the shadows as soon as he spotted me through the glass doors. I shivered, wondering how long he'd been out there waiting. Only Professors and Candidates were allowed inside. I took a moment, drinking in the sight of him before I steeled myself to leave my haven behind.

"Figured you'd still be here."

"New design due soon. Don't want to fall behind."

He reached out to my braids, his fingers gliding along the charms that shone in the yellow light. "Fall behind? You've earned more of these than any other Candidate in the time you've been here. No one can keep up with you."

I shrugged. "The sooner I'm done, the sooner I can patent designs under my own name. Get some money coming in."

"Thinking of the future finally. Any other plans?"

The braid slipped from his fingers as I shook my head. "Getting through day by day is hard enough. You know that."

I expected him to argue, but instead he reached into his bag, falling in step with me as I started the trek toward the stop.

"I brought dinner," he said. "Guessing you forgot to eat today?" He offered me a wrapped square.

I wanted to refuse, but my stomach clenched as the smell of fresh bread and hot ham wafted over to me. I accepted with a nod, and he pulled a second one from his bag, unwrapping it for himself. I bit my lip, but couldn't keep myself from tearing into my own sandwich. The bread was soft against my tongue, and the ham had a wonderful bite of salt. With my mouth full, I relaxed a fraction, savoring the flavors.

"You need to be thinking, Cam. Has anyone offered for you yet?" Bran asked.

I choked, the lump of meat and bread sticking in my throat at that question. I didn't want to think of what an offer would mean. Marital contracts were all too common as Families fought to keep their influence strong. Engineers could bring prestige and, more importantly, a steady stream of income if their designs were good enough. More patents equaled more money. Offers on Candidates were rare, hard to turn down, and even harder to break once accepted. The Scholars took their contracts seriously. I forced myself to chew the mouthful of meat into miniscule pieces before I swallowed it down. "Nobody wants me. I'm just a Candidate. No guarantee I'll finish. Too much risk."

Bran laughed, a free sound that warmed me inside even though I forced myself to ignore how good it felt. "You've already had five patents released under the school's banner. You're beating out all the other Candidates. I bet you'll graduate in less than a year keeping this pace."

I swatted at him, trying to force some distance between us, even though we kept drifting toward each other as we walked. "How does anyone even know that stuff?"

"People talk. Especially about Engineers." He leaned in, the spicy smell of him layering over the smells of the food I'd gulped down shameful quick. I couldn't help but breathe him in. His voice dropped, softer now. "Especially you."

I stopped and stepped back from him even though everything inside me wanted to draw up close, to touch him. "Please don't."

There was enough light on the path that I saw the change, the flecks of honey in his eyes growing brighter as he lost his grin. "We weren't responsible for his choices, Cam. He's not our burden to carry."

I couldn't breathe, pain welling up through the heart of me. Because I knew the truth. We were the reason. We'd broken him. Best friend. Brother. Broken him and wrecked my family beyond repair.

"I can't talk about this." My voice grated, the threat of tears already audible.

Bran wrapped his warm hands around my shivering fingers. He raised them to his lips, kissing the tips gently. "Devlin chose his way. Nothing we can change about that."

I shook, standing there on the path, oily soot from the air falling around us like snow. Even this far away from the fires that kept everything running, soot still found us. Stained us. Just like the day I'd walked into Bran's apartment and heard him arguing with my brother. That memory stained me still.

"I love you, Bran." Dev's words lashed out, his hurt a harsh note beneath the anger. "I've loved you for years."

Bran was sitting, face in his hands, and I remember I was surprised to see him trembling. I should have left then. Maybe they could have salvaged something. But Bran looked up and said, "I'm in love with someone else."

At those words, the air flooded out of me. I don't know if I gasped, but something made them both turn to where I stood. Bran's face softened when he saw me. And Devlin knew, in that moment, what I'd stolen from him.

I'd cried after Dev departed, Bran holding me until there were no more tears left. Soft kisses on my hair and cheeks, kind and gentle. I hadn't realized what I was feeling, how it happened between us, until it was too late to go back.

When I got home that night, Devlin was gone. The few engineering charms he'd earned as a Candidate were scattered across the floor, his dreams left behind. He didn't say goodbye. Not even a kiss for our mother who'd watched him from her bed, unable to catch her breath long enough to stand.

Dev opted in for Basic within days. Bran saw his name on the roll, watched from his desk as my brother cashed in his Voucher and left without a look toward his lifelong friend. He lived off his Basic, letting the Drift take him, breathing in the haze until it washed him away.

It took some time, but I finally tracked him to a sad building where single rooms were rented out on day-by-day basis. I'd pounded on his door, begging him to open up, not caring if others heard. I pleaded for forgiveness, asked him to come home until my voice was raw. It was hours before I got any response. I'd collapsed against the rough wood of the door, the filthy floor sticky beneath me, when Devlin finally spoke. As if we were sitting back to back again, like when we were younger.

"I could've made him love me. If it weren't for you." Glass shattered on the other side of the door. Then nothing but silence. I waited, wondering if he was talking about Bran. Or if it had been our father he was referring to. Devlin never said another word.

When the landlord grew concerned about the smell, they found his body three days later.

We wore white to his funeral. Me. My family. Bran, who carried my mother to the grave so she could be there. All we had to offer him in the end. White clothes, stained black. Ruined, just like us.

Knowing how much the memory hurt, Bran walked with me, fingers cradling mine. When we got to the stop, he refused to leave. "I aim to see you home," was all he said.

When the bus arrived, he grabbed my bag and followed me up the steps. I didn't argue. With so much weight on me every day, it was a relief to let him share a bit of it.

I chose seats in the back. Bran sat next to me. His arm pressed into my side, his thigh against mine. With anyone else I'd have felt trapped, suffocated. Bran just felt like home.

He pulled a thick pouch from his bag and slid it into mine. When I shot him a questioning look, he whispered, "Your family's allowance. I talked to Graves when he came in. He told me to cash the Voucher today. Just have to turn it in tomorrow."

My eyes filled, surprising me. "How'd you know?" I asked, gratitude thickening my voice.

"That scene between you and the new guy was the gossip today. I had it all within minutes of walking in the door."

"Why were you even there? You're off on Tuesdays."

"Ah, so you have been avoiding me." He didn't say the words in anger, just recognition. He'd seen the distance I'd tried to force between us. "Graves had to be at the Assembly this morning. He asked me to come in for a bit, help out until he got there."

"What was so important?" I asked.

He sighed. "Cost of living's going up again. Next month."

I rested my head on the seat back, weariness hitting me at those words. Everything was going to cost more. "And no increase in Basic's been approved yet," I guessed.

He nodded. "You know how it is. Allowance increases have to be reviewed, voted on by the Council and the Families. That takes time."

I did know. It was always like this. Just when I thought I might be able to catch my breath. That we could get by a little bit longer.

"You gonna be all right?" Bran asked, his arm along the back of our seat, his body shifted so he could see my face.

"Yeah." I fought the tightness in my chest, made myself breathe slowly to tamp down some of the panic threatening to overwhelm me. "We'll find a way to get by. It's just that it keeps happening. This system, it doesn't work."

The fatigue in his voice was tangible. "It's what we've got, Cam. Without it, so many people would be hurting more than they already are." He saw those people every day. I remembered the woman in line. Bills to pay.

"I'm not saying it's a bad idea. Where would my family be without it right now?" We both knew the answer. I wouldn't be in school. No design future for me. "It's like Professor Sikorsky says to us. Grand plans, poor execution. People fall behind in the uneven times, they can't catch up."

"I know." Bran's voice was soft, sad, but there was nothing else to say. He didn't move as I laid my head on his shoulder and closed my eyes, trusting him to wake me if I fell asleep. He was solid beside me. Like always.

I crouched under the air handler in the back room of our small house. My father had found it in a disposal a few months after we moved. An early model, but he had it working again in a few hours. Dev and I had helped, listening as he explained the workings of this precious machine, the one that would buy our mother more time.

Now, it was my responsibility. I kept it as clean as I could, tending to the connections with careful swipes of a static-free cloth I stored in a sealed jar. A new one was expensive. This one had to last.

My fingers ran over the metal plate on the back, lingering on the embossed words – QUINN DESIGNS. This handler had been the first design my father released under his own name when he'd been declared an Engineer. His future had been so clear.

I pictured his wedding to my mother, paid for by the royalties from that one patent. Radiant smiles on both of them, the bright red of her dress unmarred by soot. She'd carried flowers, fragrant and freshly cut.

How completely things had changed. I wondered how it might have been different, if mother had just gotten ill at home, instead of a quiet cough that suddenly turned violent at a Family ball. The rose pink handkerchief she'd had to match her dress unable to hide the dark stains as she coughed into it. The Black had crept into their safe haven, a reminder that even the Family was not immune. She was cast out, us with her. Shunned.

My father spent all our money on this small home and medicines, hoping something would slow the disease that devoured the woman he loved. He never gave up, always working and selling designs as soon as he finished them for too little. We were tainted.

I thought of the last morning my father had kissed us all goodbye. Had his fingers lingered in my hair? Had he smiled a few extra times at my mother? Quiet moments, happy in spite of everything, a wave to us as he walked out the door. He'd agreed to repair a boiler that day, telling us it was the extra money we needed, a way to stay off Basic a little longer.

The explosion left nothing behind.

My sister Bella's shoes scuffed into view as she called to me. "Ma says you have to come now." I crawled out from below the handler, wiping my hands on the rag I always carried. We had dirt enough to deal with. No one wanted to clean up grease smears left behind because I'd been careless.

"What's she need?" I asked, curious and worried. Mother didn't pull me away from work very often.

Bella looked down, shoulders slumping. "You just better come."

I followed her, swallowing against the lump in my throat, afraid of what I'd find. Bella led me to the front of the house, a room of random chairs we'd collected. Mother was propped up between my youngest siblings. A man and a woman sat across from her.

The woman wore a deep brown dress, the hem buttoned up to keep it off the ground when she walked. Her hands were covered by matching gloves and a hat rested on her upswept black hair, the brim a current fashion that served to keep soot off your face when you were out. I caught the glint of a fine copper chain resting against her cheek, beautiful but more than jewelry. She wore a portable air handler, fine filters that covered your nose and purified the air as you breathed it in. A design my father had created. One he'd sold off for much less than it was worth. Another Quinn patent with someone else's name on it.

As I turned my attention to the man beside her, I realized I recognized him. He was the new clerk at the Basic Office. By the smirk on his face, he knew me, too. He sported his own handler, this one with a silver chain.

"Ah, so here she is." The woman's voice was clipped, proper in a way that I often heard from Family classmates. "Finally."

My mother coughed quietly into a black cloth before whispering, "They've come with an offer."

The woman smiled tightly, her lips pressed together. She nodded at my mother before turning to me. "It's a fair offer." Distaste dripped from her voice, her nose flaring like she'd smelled something bad. "You're just a Candidate at this point. We're taking a risk."

The words I'd said to Bran just days ago whirled through my head. *"Too much risk."*

He'd warned me to be prepared, and I hadn't listened.

She turned to the young man, her hand on his arm as she introduced him. "My son, Cooper. He's willing to be a party to this contract. Ten years, extensions required if there are children. Our name will of course be on any patents you sell. Family names inspire confidence in products, you know." She gave me another tight smile, her eyes hard.

Silence fell in the small room as I cleared my throat. If I accepted, this was my future. I'd be selling myself to this Family, tied to them until I served out my contract. Marriage to the man sneering at me. The Quinn name would never be on any of the machines I designed. I remembered dancing my fingers over those letters just bare minutes before, the painful hope welling up in me as I dreamed of bolting that name plate onto everything I created.

I took the pages I was offered, my eyes skirting over words I already knew. A contract that would change the life of a Baser girl and her family, starting the moment I signed my name to it. If I didn't, there was a risk no other offer would come. That I might not qualify as an Engineer. That my mother would die here, my siblings unable to attend school. I could gamble on the future I wanted. Or choose the one guaranteed to help my family.

"I don't understand your hesitation. It's a good offer." The woman spoke again, anger in every punctuated word. "Could be the only one you get, with your family's history."

Heat flashed through me, and I wanted to throw the pristine pages of the contract onto the ground in front of her. But I looked to my mother. She only watched me, shaking her head, telling me this was my decision to make.

"She has another offer." A voice behind me echoed, and I turned, shocked to see Bran standing just inside our door. Paper was clenched in his hand, the imprints of his fingers visible.

"Bran—"

He held up a hand to stop me. "A contract that puts no limits on design release. No extension requirements. She doesn't have to take my name. Quinn will be on all the patents."

"That's a fool's offer," spat Cooper, standing up and marching over to me. He grabbed my arm, spinning me around to face him. "He can't give you or your family anything like what we can. Everyone would use the things you create with our name on them."

I shook free of his painful grip. Hope that had been doused blazed back to life inside me. Even if I didn't accept Bran's offer, the fact that there was another one on the table gave me an out. He'd known, somehow. He always knew.

Bran handed the papers to me, and I was surprised to see they were notarized by the Contract School. This wasn't a draft or a ploy. This was a very real offer. For me.

I turned to face Cooper and his mother. "I'm afraid I must decline. Thank you. I trust you'll find your way out."

Cooper's face reddened as his mother gathered herself and stood. They marched out without a backward look at us.

My mother stood slowly, my siblings steadying her carefully. She gave me a gentle, knowing smile. "It's about time." Then she stepped into her bedroom, the door closing, leaving Bran and me alone.

I flung myself forward, wrapping my arms around him. "How'd you know?" It was no coincidence, his appearance with an offer at the exact time someone else attempted to negotiate a contract.

"I told you before. The office, always full of gossip. Tell one person, might as well tell everyone. New guy hasn't caught on to that yet."

I nodded. "I won't hold you to this, you know." He opened his mouth to speak, but I pressed on. "I appreciate it. But I didn't need you to rescue me."

He grinned at those words, shaking his head. "I didn't do it to rescue you. I did it for myself, Cam. I need you. If you took that contract, I don't know how I'd have gone on." Bran cupped my face gently, his fingers stroking over a smudge of grease. He brought his lips to mine and kissed me.

I let the kiss fill me as the truth of his words settled deep within, taking root. This was more than a contract. He was offering me a life.

More from K. A. Fox

The Devil's Own

Delaney Murphy has always known she's the Devil's daughter. And although the title itself is a burden, she never expects to inherit all her father's infernal abilities. When her newfound magic begins to poison the people closest to her, Laney must make a choice. To protect the world from the worst she can do, she leaves everyone she loves behind and builds a new life for herself, alone, in a place where she can control the urge to give in to the magic living within her.

But when she recognizes a familiar pattern in a string of murders, Laney leaves her peaceful, isolated life behind and goes on the hunt, unleashing a threat she never dreamed possible. Confronting this menacing specter could mean giving in to temptation and becoming the one thing she fears most. Will she use her magic to do the right thing, even if it means hurting the ones she loves?

Find out more at https://www.imkafox.com

The Grand Assault by J. Woolston Carr

Ephraim Noble dressed in clothes typical of a young gentleman, yet his appearance was distinct from his friends because his trousers fit fashionably tighter, his collar was starched more stiffly, and his cravat meticulously tied. He always wore his jacket, which was tailored to a lean physique. While his friends preferred going to watch scenes at the mechanical optical theater and riding dandy steam horses, Ephraim was earnest in his studies.

Children often inherit the opinions and interests of their parents. In this case, Ephraim Noble Sr. had the opposite effect on his son. Mr. Noble was known for his vices, which Ephraim Jr. despised, and so the boy became obsessed with virtue. Up till now, he had maintained a particularly proper and uninteresting life. But his sense of honor would change all that, starting with the proceeding events.

Ephraim's head was lowered deep into his book, his face hidden by Caesar's Commentaries. He was studious, but this particular posture had nothing to do with education. When his father happened to take notice, the Roman army of Gaul was unable to protect him.

"Ephraim, what are you doing? It is a Saturday, my dull boy, why on earth are you reading?"

Ephraim had hoped Mr. Noble would pass by without observing him, which was often the case, but he was never so impertinent as to directly ignore his father.

"Studying, sir," and he raised his eyes, unable to hide the fact that one of them was black and purplish, as if a plum had grown on his cheek.

"What the blazes, Ephraim? Were you in a fight?"

"Yes, sir."

"Well… Does the other boy look worse than you?"

Ephraim was not proud of his conflicts, usually the result of a bully's insult about his father, but he answered truthfully. "Yes, sir."

"Good. I am sure I will hear from some irate parent," said Mr. Noble, conceding to an unavoidable consequence. "Don't you have some activity on Saturday?"

"Yes, Father. I have my fencing lesson."

"Of course. Perhaps I should enroll you with the boxing teacher instead, eh?"

Ephraim startled. He was diligent in his books, but he delighted in the fencing classes. "No, Father, please!"

"Very well."

His father looked at him with a pale seriousness. Ephraim wondered if he was drunk this early in the day. "You know, Ephraim, the world is not a just place, and you cannot right every wrong. It is not wise to be too good. If you must live your life like Jesus, at least do not become martyred like Christ."

Ephraim nodded. It was not easy being at loggerheads with one's own parent, but such statements only confirmed for him the role he would take in life. He could see things in black and white, even when his father's vision was clouded grey by cigar smoke and liquor.

Ephraim walked to the Knickerbocker Fencing Club. It was located on John Street along a row of opulent brownstone buildings of three or four stories, all decorated with cigar-shaped, granite pillars. For the purposes of educating duelists, it was situated where it would get the most business, among lawyers and newspaper journalists.

New York City was a vibrant and brash metropolis in its youth, quickly growing equal to any capital in the world. The sidewalks of Broadway Avenue were a gathering of bobbing top hats and bonnets on well-dressed shoppers. Bankers and speculators negotiated financial deals on Wall Street. Steam livery carriages of the wealthy puffed along the cobbled streets amidst the nickering of the laboring horses of the working class. Fulton's steam ships had nudged their way into a crowded harbor full of rope and canvas from across the Atlantic. Goods from all over the world were welcomed in New York's harbor, bringing in a flood of Dutch and English textiles, rum and sugar from the Indies, wool from Australia, and steel machines from Germany.

It was the premiere city of commerce in the United States of America and growing at a rapid pace that much of the world envied and some of the locals feared, arguing that it was already losing its Republican simplicity to greed and ostentation. But to a boy like Ephraim, it was a world of enterprise and diversions.

The entrance to the club rested above half a dozen granite steps. Inside, the virile smell of leather and sweat lingered. The blustering rattle of fencing swords amid the shuffling and stamping of feet was occasionally interrupted by a cry of *"A Moi!"* or *"Touché!"* A poster on the wall caught his attention before he entered the spacious fencing room, for it displayed the name of the man Ephraim most respected in the world.

A Grand Assault at the Park Theater

Mr. Armstrong of the Knickerbocker Fencing Club will fight a match with the latest in steam mechanics for the art of fencing, the schermitore a vapore, or the steam fencer. This man-sized automaton was developed by the acclaimed Italian inventor, Doctor Cosimo Cervello, who is the creator of the Cervello Steam Boat that was used effectively in the naval bombardment of Algiers. Dr. Cervello claims that the steam fencer, a machine of speed and precision, can defeat any opponent. It has been educated in the use of arms by Count Enrico Strattofenza, the undefeated

Champion of the Italian Kingdom of Naples, who will accompany the schermitore a vapore as its manager and trainer.

They will be using the latest technology in the art of fencing, the Fioretto di pressione, or the Pressure Foil, also created by the eminent Dr. Cervello, who will attend the match in service of his new allegiance to the United States.

Inserted in the bottom corner of the poster was a picture of the Italian professor, proudly standing next to an American flag.

A mechanical fencer? It roused Ephraim's boyish curiosity in this age of growing technological wonders. Ephraim was familiar with the Pressure Foil. He knew it allowed for the scoring of hits mechanically rather than by the decision of human judges, and therefore rendered a true account of the touch in fencing. It was controversial among classically trained fencers, who felt it did not encourage the proper form.

Mr. Armstrong was the finest blade in the Club, the man Ephraim tried to emulate. His bearing was cultured and polished, his actions chivalrous on and off the fencing strip, even if his manner was sometimes loud and brash. Ephraim wondered if he could best a fencing automaton from Italy, a country known for its skill with the sword both in the fencing hall and on the dueling ground.

The boy hurried in to find his friend, unmistakable in his wavy locks of blonde hair and long bushy sideburns. He found him surrounded by a group of men dressed in the white canvass of fencing attire, all questioning him animatedly.

"What do you think of this fencing automaton?"

Mr. Armstrong smiled daringly. "It is called the *art* of fencing for a reason. No machine can match the manners and creative spirit of a bona fide gentleman fencer."

"How do you expect the Pressure Foil to differ, my man? Will it handle like a real foil?" another one of them asked.

"The skill is in the man, not the tool. Give me a broom handle, and I will fence any Italian champion, man or machine."

There was a round of hurrahs at Mr. Armstrong's statement, and Ephraim felt pride for his friend and his country.

The boy startled at the maitre's voice. "Ephraim, are you here for your lesson? Eh? Eh? Or to eavesdrop on others' conversations, *mon fils?*"

Ephraim turned to the compact man, his moustache and goatee tidily groomed, glaring at him. His bald pate glittered with sweat from his previous lesson.

Ephraim's face grew red. "No, sir. I mean, yes, sir. I mean…"

Maitre Grincheaux waved at him with his instructor's foil, a gesture meaning he should quit talking and get to the lesson strip. Their lesson commenced and would have seemed unremarkable to the uneducated eye. Blades whispered in the air so precisely that there appeared almost no movement, in concert as the student followed his teacher back and forth. However, several of the older fencers paused to observe the lesson with an envious eye, desirous of the skill displayed by a boy barely out of short pants.

At the end of the lesson, the master and pupil removed their masks and saluted.

"Do you think Mr. Armstrong will prevail?" Ephraim was eager for his master's opinion because the Frenchman was familiar with the European schools of fencing.

"Pah. Italians are overrated. I believe you, Monsieur Noble, could triumph in the match."

"Really?"

Maitre Grincheaux eyed him intently, then grunted. "Possibly."

It was a true compliment from a man who gave praise grudgingly, but Ephraim already knew he could defeat any man in the club except for Mr. Armstrong. This often presented a problem to the youth. He was eager to test anyone, but often found the others reluctant. If there was one virtue Ephraim lacked, it was humility in his ability as a fencer. It never occurred to him to let them win, or even score, and he was such a juggernaut on the fencing strip that few men were willing to suffer the ignominy of being thrashed by a child of fourteen.

Ephraim's thoughts were interrupted by a strong, clear voice. "Time for *my* lesson, lad! Ye gods, there is a pretty plum."

"Mr. Armstrong!" Ephraim touched the bruise on his face, having forgotten about it. "It's nothing, really. You will fence with me?"

Mr. Armstrong's eyes twinkled, and his face bore a broad, friendly grin, his wide chin marked by a deep dimple. "I am sore in need of the competition. I am in training, after all."

Ephraim questioned imploringly, "What do you think? Does this Strattofenza have a first-rate reputation?"

"Of course, he is Italian, after all. But as us New Yorkers say, a great reputation elsewhere is only one of a thousand in our city."

They engaged in a short match, after which they shook hands, and Mr. Armstrong gave him a comradely wink.

"Grand, Ephraim, grand. I shall have to surrender, now. You have pricked my ego too much, I am afraid. Tomorrow again? I am off for an appointment."

"Of course, sir."

As Mr. Armstrong departed, Ephraim noticed a trio of men watching them. They mulled about with their hands thrust in the pockets of their frock coats, glaring darkly from square faces beneath flat caps of soft cotton and a hard brim that gave them a foreign air. Ephraim decided to approach them, but when they recognized this they turned to leave. He heard one of them speak to a companion in a foreign language he did not understand.

Emphraim found the maitre sitting on a bench between lessons, smoking a thin cigarette.

"I think the Italians were spying on Mr. Armstrong." Ephraim's voice was filled with concern.

"It does not surprise me. They are a devious people."

"I heard one of them speak. What does *Lost ones gain* mean?" asked Ephraim.

"Eh? I don't know. Was it *'lass uns gehen'*?"

"Yes, that's it."

"Aha, even worse. It is German. Probably Austrians. They are always sticking their noses where they do not belong."

This confused Ephraim. He knew Austria had been a major power involved in the defeat of Napoleon. Were they now allied with the Italians in an effort to spy upon Mr. Armstrong? This chafed Ephraim's sense of honor, and he decided that if he saw them again, he would discover their intentions.

The Austrians were indeed in the club the following day, unsociably huddled away towards the back, whispering to each other with nods and brief gestures. Again, they left after Mr. Armstrong had departed, and Ephraim was determined to track them this time. They strode briskly up John Street, turning sharply north onto Broadway. Nervously, Ephraim hurried after them, but hidden within the mass of people, and they did not notice his pursuit. The air was chill and so gave him the excuse to pull his jacket up over his cheeks, hiding his face behind the smartly pressed collar. They continued walking for several miles until they reached New York's Vauxhall Garden, a small, enclosed park just north of the Bowery. He continued to give chase as they passed through an arched entrance to the park, but lost them in the square coves of trees and bushes separated by gravel paths. He wandered haphazardly, but only encountered a man relieving himself, who ignored him as Ephraim stumbled away, embarrassed. Ephraim backed into a mass of cloth, ribbons, and fur.

"Pardon…me…" Ephraim fumbled with his words as he turned to the woman. She was beautiful, with lush ebony hair crowned by a fur cap.

The face cradled in a fur collar of a long cloak was enchanting. The woman looked at him with mesmerizing eyes, heavy lidded and sleepy, eyelashes flickering darkly like the wings of a raven. The directness of her gaze sucked him in as if it were a powerful whirlpool.

"You following me, *ja?*" She smiled, and Ephraim nearly swooned.

"What? No…" But he hesitated. She had a thick accent, like sweet syrup. Ephraim was grabbed from behind in an iron grip by one of the Austrians. "Let me go! I'll call for the constable!" he cried.

Other Austrians appeared and laughed, a cold sharp sound filled with irony and disdain.

The men conversed in their native tongue with the woman, who seemed to be in charge.

"Villains! Unhand me!" demanded Ephraim.

The woman nodded, and the grasp loosened on Ephraim's arm. He twisted and freed himself.

It seemed a proper plan at the moment. He would topple the surprised Austrian, then run, hoping to encourage pursuit and therefore remove attention from Mr. Armstrong, wherever he might be. Ephraim was confident that his smaller, more agile body could elude them in the woods and undergrowth of the park. However, when he threw all his weight into a charge against the nearest Austrian, Ephraim merely bounced off the solid form and fell to the ground. With a grim smile, the man reached for Ephraim again and delivered a powerful punch that sent the boy reeling into darkness.

Emerging from unconsciousness was slow and torturous. Ephraim's jaw and neck ached. He thought he was perhaps still groggy, but the shadowed blurriness of his vision was due to the settling dusk. Ephraim figured that he had been out for less than thirty minutes. Rising unsteadily to his feet, he looked around. Of course, the Austrians were gone. He decided to go home before night fell, and from there he could make inquiries about Mr. Armstrong.

When he arrived home, he found his father in conversation with another man. They already had the information Ephraim sought.

"Ephraim!" said Mr. Noble, ash dropping from the cigar in his hand to the floor. "There you are. This is Mister, er..."

"Sobczak," the man introduced himself. He was thin and birdlike in appearance, standing with military erectness and dressed smartly in a valet suit of a long tailed coat and knee breeches that exposed spindly calves. "I am Mr. Armstrong's secretary. He instructed me to deliver this note to you."

"Mr. Armstrong? Is he all right?" asked Ephraim.

"My orders are to have you read the letter. It will explain everything."

Despite his anxiety, Ephraim received the note with a deliberate politeness and unfolded it.

My Dear Ephraim,

I write to you because I have developed a serious illness of a foreign nature. I am bedridden, and the doctor tells me I will be so for quite some time. I have a most important request to make of you. You must take my place in the fencing match. I trust you will acquit yourself with courage and raise the trophy in honor of the States.

Secondly, do not further pursue those lines of inquiry that brought you to the park. These are things better left to others older than you.

Your obliged and affectionate friend,

Julius Armstrong

"Illness, my foot! He was attacked by the Austrians!"

"What?" his father scoffed. "Ephraim, what are you babbling?"

Ephraim sighed, but he realized that no one was going to believe his story if Mr. Armstrong was not going to be forthcoming. Ephraim turned to the secretary.

"Tell me, Mr. Sobczak, is he badly off? Are his wounds—illness, I mean—severe?"

"I can only tell you that the doctor has ordered that he have no visitors until further notice. I am also supposed to return with a reply."

Ephraim did not hesitate. Honor dictated his answer.

"Tell him yes."

The day of the match arrived. Ephraim felt a chill in his toes and a dead weight in the pit of his stomach. He regretted agreeing to this. He wanted to be at home reading and being ignored by his father.

Ephraim knew that he was the best substitute from the club for Mr. Armstrong, but he was also aware of the disdain such a choice had ignited in all involved. There had been general disbelief at the announcement that a boy would replace Mr. Armstrong as the Champion of the United States.

Maitre Grincheaux joined him in the changing room.

"Come, Ephraim. We must get you suited up. This is all chicanery, dressing you like a harlequin. *Ma foi*, it is not proper fencing."

The steam pressure suit was bulky but light, flexing as Ephraim moved and providing no hindrance to action. He had expected it to look like some awkward diving bell uniform, but instead resembled a well-padded fencing jacket. A belt underneath the pressure jacket held the miniature pump and condenser. The water was charged by the motion of the fencer on the strip. A thin hose ran through his jacket, up his sleeve, and connected to a flexible tube of metal that was the fencing sword. When the tip of the sword was thrust at the opponent and made contact, the steam power was released and engaged a bell that signaled the scoring of a touch. His eyes were outfitted with goggles to protect them in case any steam was to spray at his face. This cut his peripheral vision sharply, so he would have to tilt his head, but the fencing strip was not wide, and according to the rules, his opponent must remain in front of him.

Ephraim hesitantly peered through the curtains to the stage of the theater. It was one thing to feel certain of his abilities in the familiarity of the fencing club. This was far beyond anything he had ever experienced.

The Park Theater was luxuriously decorated. Its stout gold columns were inlaid with silver workings. A gigantic glass chandelier hung from the domed roof. Blood-red curtains of velvet hung to either side of the stage. Before him stood Count Strattofenza, who was possibly the best fencer in the world and beside the count was the fencing automaton.

Ephraim could only wonder at its appearance. The head was cylindrical, with glowing electric eyes and a grating for a mouth. It sported a broad, curled moustache, also made of metal, giving it an unnatural sneer. The body was also a cylinder, with rivets forming a line to the left side of the torso, imitating the buttons of a fencing jacket. The arms and legs were long pipes with ball bearing elbows and knees. Claw-like fingers grasped a Pressure Foil. In response to the incredulous guffaws from the audience, Strattofenza pulled a lever on the automaton's back, and it began to do deep knee bends and precise lunges as steam puffed from a funnel in the back. The audience laughed, and the Italian scowled. He also had a foil and placed himself in front of the steam fencer. Immediately the automaton took a proper fencing guard, and when the Italian made a thrust at the machine, it parried and began a blurring display of blade movements that the Italian only barely followed. The laughter changed to applause from the audience, which was made up of a mass of bushy side whiskers, black formal evening wear, and self-important throat clearing.

The floor creaked, and Ephraim's footsteps echoed in the acoustics of the theater hall as the boy strode to his place on the stage. Ephraim felt very small, and his hands shook involuntarily. He heard a snicker from the audience. Strattofenza returned to his countrymen and began gesticulating temperamentally, obviously upset at the change of adversary. Ephraim hesitated and looked back to the maitre. The Frenchman nodded and shooed him forward. As the presiding judge of the bout stood ready, Ephraim took his spot and gave a confused salute towards the Italian fencing automaton. It silently returned the salute as the Italian champion grumbled. This finally piqued the boy, for he despised rudeness, and his nervousness was replaced by a determination to perform his obligation.

Prior to commencing the match, the opponents executed the formal tradition of the Grand Salute. Ephraim faced the automaton. They both began a series of complex preparatory maneuvers that served as a courteous salutation to the audience. The fencing automaton was meticulous in its movements, and Ephraim's trained body showed perfect balance and control as they alternated lunges, parries, and ripostes in a display of the action that would be employed once the true competition began.

The audience applauded while Ephraim and his opponent remained on guard, waiting for the signal to begin. At the word *Allez*, uttered by the presiding judge, the two combatants began their assault.

The first few moments of the bout Ephraim had to adjust to fencing in the pressure suit, and in that time the precise actions of the automaton scored its first point. Steam hissed and the bell clattered, signaling the touch. There was a smattering of polite applause, almost disappointment, at the seeming ease of the score.

The automaton scored twice more, then Ephraim finally parried an attack and hit with a disengage riposte that slithered beneath the machine's high guard. The automaton returned to its guard line, gears clicking as calculations echoed from the cylindrical head. The next time Ephraim attempted the same move, it expertly blocked the attack.

The automaton launched itself into the next several points, savagely overwhelming the young boy. At first, Ephraim wilted at the brutal onslaught, but Mr. Armstrong had instructed him to fight gallantly. He defended as best he could, blocking the attacks and opposing the blade, so that he slid another riposte on his metal opponent and then gained another point with a risky counter-attack. The audience slowly developed an admiration for Ephraim's fortitude, and soon there was enthusiastic applause when he scored. Still, by the intermission of the match, he was down ten hits to four.

Maitre Grincheaux brought a towel and a cup of water for Ephraim.

"Your tierce guard is sloppy," was his initial comment. This made Ephraim smile as he expected no compliments from the crusty Frenchman.

The hall lights were up during the break, and Ephraim chanced a quick gaze to the crowd. They were excited and entertained. He could see some gentlemen reenacting sword thrusts with pens as they discussed the bout.

"Do not be intimidated," advised Maitre Grincheaux, observing the weak smile on Ephraim's face. "It is nothing but a *retailleur*, heavy handed with its blade."

"Even when I score, it seems to analyse my attack and prevent me from using it again," complained Ephraim.

"It is only a machine, a calculator. I have given lessons to students who are much like that. They show great precision in the lesson, but lose in the assault because all their actions are programmed, without inspiration. You must be creative, devise attacks that it cannot anticipate. It is *l'art de l'escrime,* not simply a science."

Ephraim sighed; it was easier to say than to accomplish.

A flash of movement diverted his attention to a figure in the audience. In the back of the theater, he caught a glimpse of shiny black hair and drowsy eyes the color of twilight. It was the Austrian woman, and she was leaving with her cohorts. Ephraim deduced they were there to make sure Mr. Armstrong wasn't present, and now they were leaving to finish the job they had begun in the gardens.

The crowd quieted at the end of the intermission, eager to see the finale. After the salutes, the two combatants assumed their guard positions, and the order to commence was given. Ephraim, distracted, felt the automaton score again. Hiss and clang.

Ephraim decided, one way or another, he needed to end the match quickly so that he could help Mr. Armstrong. He *could* lose. The match was not as important as the well-being of his friend. The steam fencer had an aggressive style, and up till now Ephraim had relied on his defense and counter-attacks to make any points. He would not surrender, but he could get the match over with early by simply going all out in what would probably amount to fencing suicide.

This resignation loosened up the young man, his tightness replaced by a cool relaxation. He pressed his attack against the steam fencer with a ferocity that surpassed the automaton. This bewildered the machine, and it reacted wildly, opening holes in its defense that Ephraim could have sailed through in one of Cervello's steam boats. Ephraim no longer tried to analyze each engagement, but lost himself in the subconscious action of fencing. Each attack was new and unexpected, from unusual angles and at counter time. His blade whistled and darted like an arrow shot from a bow.

The automaton only managed two more touches, and Ephraim finished the match in a matter of minutes with a winning score of twenty to thirteen. None could argue the veracity of his hits, for the bell rang at each touch. Ephraim was as stunned at the display as the audience, who began cheering wildly after a hesitant moment of disbelief. Count Strattofenza shouted in

Italian and ripped the steam sword from the automaton's grip.

Ephraim did not wait. Though Mr. Armstrong had expressly told him to stay and raise the trophy, that order would be disobeyed. He stripped off his helmet, goggles, and fencing glove. Tubes flailed as he ran past Maitre Grincheaux.

"Ephraim! *Mon dieu*, where are you going? The awards ceremony!"

"I will explain later!" he cried as he disappeared down the aisle and out the door.

He stopped at the edge of the street. He had rushed out without thought, and only now realized he had no idea where to go. Luckily, there was a doorman, his blue uniform tight around a pudgy waist.

"Excuse me, did you see some men, foreigners, come out about twenty minutes ago?"

The doorman shrugged. "Lots o' people pass by. Don't ask 'em where they's from, you know?"

Ephraim was frustrated. "There was a woman with them. She had… hair… and eyes…" His powers of description failed him as his mind raced in muddy circles.

"Oif," responded the doorman, as if expelled from the depths of his round belly. "The lady. Yeah, I seens her. Hair… eyes…"

At first, Ephraim thought the man was ridiculing him, but then he realized he was serious. "You know who I mean?"

"Yeah, couldn't miss 'er, what a pretty piece! Got 'er a liv'ry coach to take 'er down the street to the City, wif some men."

"Thanks!" cried Ephraim, and he dashed south through traffic for six blocks to the City Hotel, New York City's finest accommodations. It stood five stories tall with over 100 rooms. Only the spires of Trinity Church stood taller.

Ephraim raced into the spacious hotel lobby, tiled with marble and magnificently frescoed. He had to wade through a sea of well-dressed men and women. An incessant buzz of conversation and tobacco smoke filled the room, making all the inhabitants appear like social versions of the steam fencer.

A few people glanced at him, but no one took much notice. Seeing no sign of the Austrians, he strode up to the polished counter of the visitor's register. A thin-faced clerk with a receding hairline that emphasized the deep glower of his eyebrows acknowledged him with an unfriendly stare.

"I'm looking for a group of foreigners."

The clerk's pen scratched dismissively in his ledger. He examined the boy from his flat-soled shoes to the unbuttoned collar of his shirt. Ephraim was embarrassed at the sloppiness of his dress, then he remembered he still had on the steam fencing uniform. He smiled sheepishly and began fussing with his loose collar.

"I… I was in the fencing match," he explained.

"Uh-huh. You must be looking for the Italians." He seemed to have even less regard for them than for Ephraim.

Ephraim realized that the Italian fencing contingent must have rooms at this hotel. Perhaps the Austrians were not after Mr. Armstrong, but instead were laying a trap for the Italians? Such a thing would be an embarrassment to the States, and Ephraim knew the Austrian Empire despised his liberal and anti-monarchical government.

"Yes. Yes, I am."

"Fourth floor." The clerk waved a hand at the staircase.

"Where on the fourth floor?"

"All of it."

"Thank you!" shouted Ephraim as he raced off for the massive staircase. He was sweating and out of breath when he finally reached the top floor. He looked around and saw an open door. Were they already gone? Or worse, kidnapped? Ephraim crept silently to the door and peered around the frame. At first he saw no one, just a luxurious suite with oak tables and satin curtains. Then, a shadow appeared, followed by a well-tailored figure of an Italian, displaying a colorful, wide cravat and silk vest. Ephraim sighed. He was not too late. He stepped into the room to give a warning. The man saw him and gestured frantically.

"I am here to rescue you. RESCUE…" Ephraim said loudly and slowly, as if that would be more comprehensible to someone who obviously did not speak English. Then another man appeared, and it was the slight form of Dr. Cervello.

"*Santo!* What are you doing here?" inquired the doctor.

"I have no time to explain, you are in danger. Why are you here? Aren't *you* supposed to be at the fencing match?"

The first Italian, a tall, thin man with long, gangly arms, pointed at Ephraim and said something with a commanding voice. Two more Italians came at him from either side, grabbing his arms.

"Wait, you don't understand." Ephraim struggled, but could not break their grip.

They dragged him out to the hall, and there stood Count Strattofenza. Ephraim was astonished. The count must have had a carriage waiting and left at the same time as Ephraim. When he recognized the boy, he gave him a baleful glare.

"Let me go!" cried Ephraim. "I am telling you, you have got to get away. I think someone might be trying to kidnap you."

Dr. Cervello looked surprised at Ephraim's statement. Then he laughed.

"*Va bene!* You are closer to the truth than you imagine, young man. Alfonso, bring him with us."

"Going somewhere, Doctor?"

It came from behind him, and Ephraim couldn't believe his ears. The bold voice belonged to Mr. Armstrong.

As a group, the Italians turned, pulling Ephraim with them, and produced caplock pistols aimed at the dapper American. He was dressed immaculately in a broad-shouldered jacket and a striped vest that hugged a perfectly healthy and uninjured physique. Mr. Armstrong was also armed, brandishing a compact, three-barreled percussion pistol specially manufactured by Deringer of Philadelphia, and a stout walking stick with a gilded silver knob. He stood unflustered that five men had guns trained on him.

"Mr. Armstrong. You seem to have amazing recuperative powers," noted Dr. Cervello.

"Proper living. I abstain from drinking and dancing, like a Quaker."

"I doubt that."

Mr. Armstrong shrugged. "Ephraim, are you okay?"

"What is going on?" begged the boy. "I thought you were bedridden."

"I may have exaggerated my condition. I will explain later. I thought I gave you explicit orders to finish the fencing match."

"I did! I beat the Italian Steam Fencer!" Mr. Armstrong nodded. "Congratulations."

"Bravo, bravo," interrupted Dr. Cervello. "I will send him a trophy. But we are leaving now, Mr. Armstrong, and you cannot prevent us."

"Perhaps I cannot, but they can."

They turned again as a group, like some carousel at an amusement fair. At the crest of the staircase were the Austrians, the beautiful woman standing lead, clad in a military jacket, trousers, and boots that still could not hide a shapely and imposing figure. A hand gloved in a long, leather gauntlet held a slim but lethal "Baby Viennese" muff pistol. Her comrades were armed with Linz flintlocks.

The Italians holding Ephraim loosened their grip, and the boy shook free as they recognized a more imminent threat in the Austrians. One of the Italians fired his pistol, and chaos ensued.

Men ran for the shelter of open doorways in the long hallway. Ephraim ducked behind a statue as bullets flew like swarming bees.

The boy crouched low until everyone had spent their shots, and as quickly as the altercation started, it fell quiet. There was a moment of hesitation, as if no one was quite sure how to proceed, then the Austrians rushed forward.

"*Avanti!*" shrieked Dr. Cervello.

The Italians met the charge in a flurry of blocks and tackles, like some rowdy football match. Ephraim was frozen with confusion as Mr. Armstrong deliver a punch to the midriff of an Italian. Not only were the Austrians not trying to kill Mr. Armstrong, they appeared to be working with him. Meanwhile, Dr. Cervello had returned to the suite room from which he had originally emerged. It looked as if the Italian henchmen were determined to delay their opponents, and so Ephraim decided to follow the Doctor.

In the room there was an open window, and when he investigated, Ephraim found a rope ladder hanging from the roof. The boy looked down, which he regretted; the four floors seemed even steeper above the dark abyss of the city streets. Girding himself, he swung out onto the ladder. The air was arctic as the wind blew bitterly. Swaying precariously, he managed to climb up and pull himself onto the roof.

It was too dark in the moonlit evening; something blotted out the glow of stars. Not the vaporous shadow of a cloud, but an object of solid mass. He heard a hissing sound above, followed by a shout from the rooftop. Suddenly, light flooded the roof. Ephraim gasped as he shielded his eyes, catching a glimpse of a Directable Balloon hovering just above the hotel. Wings protruded from a gondola that dangled below the balloon. Written on the side of the ship was the name *Nero Falcone*. The wings operated manually, enabling the ship to fly silently. Oil lamps shone down from the ship, illuminating Dr. Cervello, Strattofenza, and, unfortunately, Ephraim. The boy glanced around the rooftop, but there was no escape besides the way he had come. The roof was flat and empty except for a domed center sporting a flagpole, and the walled edge was crenellated like a castle.

Cervello saw him. With a sigh, he tapped Strattofenza on the back and motioned him towards the boy. For the first time, Ephraim witnessed the fencing champion smile, a ruthless glitter of white teeth illuminated in the spotlight. Strattofenza shouted to the balloon, and soon metal rattled on the rooftop. A slim shaft of silver glinted in the light, and as the Italian picked it up Ephraim recognized a real sword, no sporting steam foil. There was another on the ground, and Strattofenza hooked a booted toe underneath the blade and kicked it in the air towards Ephraim. Ephraim caught it by the grip and assumed his fencing guard.

Strattofenza chuckled and approached leisurely, his own dueling position more casual, not the strict form of the fencing strip. Ephraim kept his distance. Strattofenza, still laughing, took a stance that mocked the boy's fencing guard. He gave a couple of hops and waved his sword. Dr. Cervello yelled something at him, and the Italian champion gave a nod of his head as if to respond that he was through playing.

Without warning, he engaged Ephraim. The boy desperately retreated, finding the weight and balance of the sword difficult to maneuver. The Italian was comfortable with his sword, as if he had used it many times before. Ephraim parried two thrusts, but a third glided imperceptibly through the inside of his guard to deliver a cut on his forearm. It sliced through shirt and skin, a burning incision that forced Ephraim to drop his sword as he became trapped against the ledge of the building. The Italian's blade flashed, but no blow landed. Metal cracked against wood.

Mr. Armstrong clambered over the wall, finding leverage against Strattofenza's sword with his walking cane. "Ephraim, dear boy, if you'll excuse me." Ephraim scooted away, giving Mr. Armstrong room to move. "Now, I believe this was to be my fight after all."

Twisting the head of the cane, Mr. Armstrong drew forth a long, slim blade. The Italian growled, and there was no amusement in his efforts now. They circled, lunged, retreated, ducked, and dodged. Both men were skilled with real blades, cautious in their attacks, and efficient in defense, leaving no openings.

Without pausing, Mr. Armstrong addressed the youth. "Ephraim, be a good boy and please stop Dr. Cervello from leaving the rooftop. I would appreciate it."

Ephraim had been so captivated by the duel, he forgot about the doctor and the balloon. The boy dashed to where Dr. Cervello was struggling to gain purchase on a ladder that draped down from the airship. Winds buffeted the balloon, and it was far from stable even with the wings correcting its course. The doctor may have been a genius, but he was frail, and it looked as if he couldn't make it up the ladder. Then a man climbed down from the cabin to assist the doctor as he dangled helplessly, arms knotted around the rope rungs.

The balloon began drifting, and shortly it would stray away from the roof. Unsure how to prevent the doctor from escaping, Ephraim took a deep breath and bounded forward, leaping as he reached with both hands towards the ladder. The balloon lurched, and Ephraim barely reached the bottom rung of the ladder, his inertia swinging him out precariously from the roof. He hung, legs kicking, as blackness loomed beneath him, fear grating his every nerve.

"*Che cavolo fai?*" screeched the doctor. "What are you doing?"

Cervello tried a few halfhearted kicks at Ephraim, but was too frightened to put much effort into them. Ephraim soon gained a good hold, but other problems were edging his way. A knife glinted in the hand of the man crawling down the ladder. The boy shuddered, knowing that a couple of slashes to his arms and hands, and Ephraim would careen from the ladder into the pit of blackness far below.

If only he had some weapon! Then he remembered the steam hose wrapped around his waist. If the small vacuum pump and condenser still operated, he might be able to use it. He checked the end of the hose while holding on with one hand, making sure the valve was in the off position, then plucked the sword connection from its hook. It was made to operate as a pump from the motion in fencing, and Ephraim hoped both that there was water left and that the swaying of the ladder was movement enough to build pressure and activate the steam component.

The man climbing down was now even with Dr. Cervello, but the doctor actually hindered his progress by latching onto one of his arms. This gave Ephraim time to unhook the plug rod, and as the man tried to shake loose, Ephraim aimed the hose at him and pushed the valve with his thumb. Steam burned the boy's fingers, but he held on long enough to spray scalding water at the man's face. The Italian screamed and gurgled, losing his knife, then his grip. The doctor had regained his hold on the man, perhaps thinking he was going to be able to keep him on the ladder, but instead they both lost their balance. As the pair toppled off, the balloonist got his hand bound in the tubing around Ephraim's waist, and a strong tug pulled the boy from his perch so that all three fell.

To Ephraim's relieved surprise, they did not fall far. The balloon sailed back towards the top of the building where they plunged to the roof, landing with a smack of flesh and bone. By benefit of being last, Ephraim was cushioned by the others' bodies, though it still jarred him so hard that he thought his head would crack.

He looked up and saw Mr. Armstrong still engaged with Strattofenza.

The Italian observed the prostrate forms of the doctor and redoubled his efforts. He launched himself with incredible power, and his attack was unstoppable. Mr. Armstrong, however, did not attempt to stop it. Instead, he stepped towards Strattofenza with his back foot and twisted to the side. The distance closed faster than the Italian anticipated, and his blade shot past without injuring the other man. Mr. Armstrong had pulled his blade back, but kept the point on the count. Strattofenza hurtled onto the tip of the sword, forcing it through his stomach. The American let go of the blade as the Italian dashed several steps past him, like a wounded bull passing a matador. Strattofenza collapsed to the roof with the cane sword imbedded in his body.

At the defeat of the count, the roof suddenly fell dark, and Ephraim could hear the thunk of ballast bags landing on the rooftop and the hiss of the steam engine cruising away.

"Ephraim, son, are you all right?"

Ephraim's eyes began adjusting to the darkness, and he could see the outline of Mr. Armstrong. The boy's shoulder and neck ached from the fall, and the scratch on his arm bled, but he did not feel seriously injured. "I think so, sir."

More forms appeared on the roof, making Ephraim apprehensive until lamps were lit and it proved to be the Austrians. They immediately attended to the doctor, who was alive and moaning.

Noting that everything was secure, Mr. Armstrong returned to Ephraim. "Now, my boy. What are you doing here?"

Ephraim's questions spluttered out like an exploding boiler. "I thought… Well, I thought the Austrians had been the ones who attacked you. Were you attacked? And then I followed them after the match. I thought they were trying to kidnap the Italians. Were they?"

Mr. Armstrong stopped him with a raised hand. "Hold on, maybe it would be best if I just explained. Several months ago, the United States government received word from the Austrian Intelligence Service that Dr. Cervello was going to make an attempt to defect back to the Italian Kingdom of Naples and join a secret revolutionary society against the Austrian Government. He has been developing a new weapon for the United States, but as it turns out, he was in league with his compatriots all this time, using our resources, and then planning to escape with a little help from the *Nero Falcone*. The fencing match was a cover so that the Italian agents could extricate the doctor. The Austrians decided the doctor was less dangerous remaining in the United States than returning to Naples, and were willing to share their information if they were directly involved in foiling the liberation. I had to fake my injury so that I would be available to coordinate the intervention."

Ephraim searched Mr. Armstrong's face, and he replied with a grin.

"Yes, why am I involved, you ask yourself? Let us just say I occasionally pick up this sort of work, and I happen to have close…connections…with fräulein Misztikus of Austria's Office of the Imperial Police."

"That is not a very good answer—"

"It is the best you'll get from me. Now, I had two reasons for asking you to take my place in the Grand Assault. The first, which you proved, is that you are the finest fencer in the Club, though we may have to get you some practical dueling lessons in the future. The second was that you seemed to be snooping around and uncovering things you weren't supposed to. You misjudged both the Austrians and the Italians. Do not let your prejudices replace facts. So I thought this would get you out of the way during the actual confrontation. Obviously, I was wrong. Perhaps next time I should resign myself to simply asking for your assistance."

"Really?"

"Hmmm… Perhaps."

Ephraim sat at home trying to study, but his mind wandered to the events surrounding Mr. Armstrong and the Italians. It made him starry-eyed to think of Mr. Armstrong as some international agent for the States. He wondered if he would truly ask him for assistance next time.

His father appeared, drink in hand. "Say, how did that fencing match go?"

"Good. I won."

"Well done, Ephraim. Showed those Italians a thing or two, eh?"

"Yes, I think I did."

After a sip of brandy, his father said, "I suppose fencing is the thing for you, then. No boxing lessons. This fencing, all about honor and doing the proper thing. That suits you, doesn't it?"

Ephraim thought about it for a moment. He had disobeyed the instructions of Mr. Armstrong by involving himself in the case of the Italians. In truth, he had not acted in a completely honorable manner, though he had done it for pure reasons.

He looked to his father with a newfound grudging respect. He would not abandon his ideals, but he recognized that things were not always black and white.

"I think that rules are important guides, but a person should examine their conscience to decide if they apply."

Ephraim Noble, Sr. smiled. "It is an important distinction. I am proud that you finally recognize it."

It was Ephraim's turn to smile.

About J. Woolston Carr

J. Woolston Carr currently lives in Dallas, Texas. He works for the Dallas Public Libraries in the Youth Discovery Center for children and teens, and is an avid reader of 19th century history. Mr. Carr is also employed as a fencing instructor for the Fencing Institute of Texas teaching modern Olympic style fencing, and is president of the Victorian Fencing Society for the study of the martial art of fencing as it was practiced in the nineteenth century. Mr. Carr has a blog for the Victorian Fencing Society with articles on nineteenth century fencing at http://victorianfencingsociety.blogspot.com/.

The Steam Horses of Stem Park by Robert B. Read, Jr.

Emerging from the forest, a squirrel and a rabbit crept slowly and quietly toward the ancient ruins of an ancient civilization, which had halfway crumbled to dust, leaving the other half to mark its existence.

"Why are we creeping along like this?" the rabbit asked the squirrel.

The squirrel stopped creeping on all four legs and walked upright on two, replying to the rabbit, "It seems like we should."

Walking along normally, the rabbit observed, "There has obviously been nobody here for millions and millions of years."

Together, the two friends carefully looked in through the doorways where doors had fallen away and windows where glass panes had broken away, looking for anything interesting inside.

The sun was in the east, early morning now, so they could see in many places. In the afternoon, when the sun had moved to the west, they would be able to see in from the other side. They had been warned many times to keep out of old ruins, which were unstable and could collapse.

Making their way around the two dozen buildings and seeing nothing much, they came to a building which had already completely collapsed, revealing a large rectangular plastic case, apparently intact and undamaged.

The squirrel waved excitedly. "One of those storage things!"

The rabbit tried to shake the container, then knocked on the container and listened. The rabbit tugged on the squirrel's tail. "It's too big and heavy for us to move. We need to go get help."

The squirrel jumped up and pulled on the opening mechanism, and the end of the container swung open, exposing the perfectly preserved contents.

Boxes and boxes made of plastic containing books.

The two of them opened a few, flipping through the pages. They noticed the same word on many of the books.

A few boxes contained a few items which were unfamiliar to them.

The squirrel wanted to try to open more, but then figured it would be best to bring the container back to their village first and open them there.

"Skyler!" someone called.

"Over here!" answered the squirrel as he emerged from the forest into the village of mostly wooden huts and a few stone buildings.

"Gilda!" someone called.

"Over here!" answered the rabbit as she emerged behind the squirrel.

They walked by many other squirrels, rabbits, monkeys, beavers, gophers, raccoons, and other assorted animals, to the two who had called out to them.

The raccoon known as Pluton informed them, "You two missed lunch again."

This was of no concern to the two young animals.

"We found a container!" Skyler explained.

"In some old ruins." Gilda pointed.

The gopher known as Erisen joined them, standing tall next to Pluton, and looking down at the two youngsters. "You should not be poking around in old human places by yourselves." Before either of them could reply, he added, "I know you were with each other."

Pluton waited patiently, and then as he expected, the two young animals began to tell what they had already found inside the container.

"Books filled with pictures, all about some place called Stem Park," Skyler told them.

Gilda nodded. "Oh yes, we must have been in what was left of that place."

"Stem… Park…" Pluton repeated. He turned and waved to two horses nearby. "Hubert, Harold, we need your help retrieving a new discovery."

The two horses hitched themselves to a wagon, securing the hitches with their stubby finger-like toes, then slipping on their metal walking shoes for travelling, and followed the other four animals as they led the way back to the mysterious ancient ruins.

Although the smaller animals could move through the trees and bushes easily, the horses had a difficult time pulling the wagon along, but managed to navigate through the forest until they emerged into the clearing where the ruins stood.

Pluton and Erisen gazed at the old buildings for a moment. Neither of them had ventured this far into the forest, so they had never seen these, but had seen other similar places in their travels.

Skyler and Gilda led the way to the container.

Skyler pulled it open again and drew out a few of the books, handing one to Pluton and one to Erisen. They paged through the books, regarding the pictures.

"See," said Skyler. "All of them are about this place called Stem Park. It must have been fantastic when it was here!"

Pluton looked at the cover of the book he held, then at the cover of the book Erisen held, then at some of the other books in the collection. "Uh, Skyler, Gilda, I think you two need to practice your reading a bit more," he told them. "These books say 'Steam Punk,' not 'Stem Park.'"

"Steam… Punk…" Gilda repeated. "What does that mean?"

Pluton shook his head and shrugged. Erisen did the same.

Skyler speculated, "It's obviously the name of this old village. But I think Stem Park sounds better. We should fix up the place and call it Stem Park."

While Pluton busied himself in a box of various items, Erisen showed the title of a book to Skyler and Gilda, sounding out the letters.

Skyler grunted. "We speak the human words and use the human letters, but how do we know we are saying them correctly?"

Gilda nodded. "Yes, since they are all gone, we would never know if the sounds are correct. If they heard us speaking now, they would probably laugh at us for saying everything wrong."

"Like Stem Park," said the two horses together, laughing.

Ignoring them, Skyler and Gilda entered the container to see what Pluton was doing. He seemed fascinated by a small wind-up model, which resembled a horse whose legs and head moved.

Setting the object back into a box, Pluton looked through another box of books. "Annual Steam Punk Anthology… issues 5975 through 6048…" he muttered as he examined the first and last book in the stack. "Somebody's lifetime collection," he figured.

Erisen examined the contents of the boxes of items, then turned his attention to the books. "Why do you suppose somebody preserved all these documents and artifacts?" he asked Pluton.

Pluton had no idea. He asked Erisen, "Whom do you suppose these documents and artifacts were preserved for?" Erisen had no idea either.

Something drew Pluton's attention. A metal horse on the cover of one book. The metal wind-up horse in the box was almost identical. Paging through the book, he found additional pictures of the horse and showed the others. "Hey, look at this. A steam-powered, mechanical horse!"

Outside, Hubert and Harold asked, "A what what what ?!"

Repeating what he had said, Pluton brought the book into view for the horses.

Studying the pictures for a moment, Erisen began to have an idea. "These humans figured out how to make mechanical horses to pull their wagons. If we follow this example, we could make mechanical horses to pull wagons around."

Hubert and Harold stared blankly for a moment, then laughed.

Erisen snapped the book shut for attention. "I am an engineer. Pluton is a scientist. I am certain we could figure out how to construct something like this—" He drew the wind-up horse out of the box. "—as big as you two."

Hubert snorted. "Pulling wagons is our job. No wind-up, metal horse can replace a real horse."

Erisen told them, "We could build mechanical horses to pull animals in wagons to ride around the future Stem Park."

Pluton, Erisen, Skyler, and Gilda removed all the boxes from the container, then Hubert and Harold lifted the container into the wagon.The others filled the container again with the boxes.

As they all walked along back the way they had come through the forest, Pluton and Erisen discussed how they could possibly construct a horse-sized mechanical horse that could move by itself and also pull along a wagon. Hubert and Harold listened without making any comments or contributing any suggestions apart from an occasional laugh or sigh.

Arriving at the village, Pluton indicated a storage hut. Repeating the process in reverse, they transferred the container into the hut, setting it among a few other similar large plastic containers that had previously been found by other expeditious animals. Several other animals had now gathered around, and Pluton assured them that they could all see the contents after it had been first examined and cataloged by the scientists and archaeologists.

After unhitching from the wagon, Hubert stomped over to Erisen. "Hey mister smarty engineer," he called to get Erisen's attention. "Just how could a mechanical horse possibly pull a wagon the way Harold and I just did?" He indicated, pointing with his tail, the path they had taken. "Stepping over all those rocks and roots, winding through bushes and trees and branches, pulling wagon wheels over stuff on the ground like those metal lines."

Harold noticed that Erisen now had the small wind-up horse in his paw. He plucked the horse away, wound it up, then set it on the ground, kicking a small pebble into its path.

The mechanical horse walked along, but when it encountered the pebble, it stumbled and fell on its side, continuing to move its legs until it wound down and stopped.

Harold then picked up the horse and set it back in Erisen's paw. "You can make a horse-sized toy horse, but that is all it would be, a big toy."

Hubert nodded in agreement, then the two horses stomped noisily away.

"What are these things anyways?" Harold asked Hubert as they stepped over two long lines of rusted metal running along the ground.

"Some old human things," Hubert guessed. "They're all over the place, making a nuisance for anyone hauling things along on wheels."

Days passed, and each day Skyler and Gilda tried to borrow books from the container, but Pluton said not yet, as they were still being reviewed by the scientists and archaeologists.

Also each day they tried to see what Pluton, Erisen, and several others were doing in secret in a hut at the edge of the village, but Erisen said no, as they were too busy designing and building and testing whatever they were constructing.

Skyler counted on his fingers. "Eight days. We found the books eight days ago, and we have not seen them since then."

Gilda told him, "Next time we find something, we should keep it a secret for a while."

Hubert, Harold, and two other horses were walking by when the hissing sound of a steam engine inside the hut drew everyone's attention. The horses, being tall enough to see in through the windows, galloped up to the hut and peered inside.

Inside, Erisen was enclosing a small steam engine inside a large metal cylinder, which was about the size of a horse body, and was supported by four metal shafts each about the size of horse legs. Erisen then attached something on top of one end. It vaguely resembled a horse head.

Slowly, the shafts moved, bending in the middle. Then the entire construction began to move.

"I think it's finally working," said Erisen hopefully.

As the construction neared the door, Pluton opened the door, and the construction walked out into the sunlight.

There, walking along a step at a time, was the finished preliminary version of the steam- powered mechanical horse.

As the horse walked through the doorway, emerging from the hut, the clanking and hissing sound drew the attention of other nearby animals who came scampering over for a closer look.

Erisen shut the door behind the horse, obscuring the view of the remains of several other failed attempts, which he and Pluton had made constructing what was now walking out in the village.

When the horse had walked far enough to prove that it could walk with a regular horse-like pace along the ground, Erisen reached up and flipped a small switch on the horse's back, stopping it. Then he moved the switch further, and the horse walked in reverse. As it neared the now closed door, Erisen stopped it again.

"What do you all think?" Erisen asked.

"Amazing!" answered Skyler.

"Wonderful!" answered Gilda,

Other animals had similarly favorable comments.

Then Hubert, Harold, and several other horses came closer to inspect their work.

Harold made his appraisal. "That looks nothing like a horse."

Pluton explained, "This is only the inner workings, the steam engine to propel it, and the skeleton of the necessary gears and rods. We can leave the task of making it look like a real horse to the artists and crafters of the village, to give it everything from two pointed ears to a fluffy tail."

Hubert gathered together the other horses a short distance away, where they whispered some plan with each other.

Animals were already volunteering to work on the mechanical horse.

"I'll make the ears," Gilda offered.

"I'll make the tail," Skyler offered.

Pluton explained, "We plan to make three more of these, to have two pairs, to pull two wagons around a circular track. So we would need four pairs of ears, four tails, four of everything."

At this point, the horses returned, hauling along with them a wagon containing another steam engine, to which was attached a myriad of musical instruments.

Hubert selected one of a collection of metal cylinders, and inserted it into a circular hole in the engine. The horses stood ready in a line.

"Okay then, let's see if you two smarties can make your horses do this."

The musical instruments played, controlled by the cylinder and driven by the engine. The horses danced in a line, an identical dance, moving their feet and turning around. Then one started a pattern which was repeated down the line to the final horse. They finished in a circle as the musical piece ended.

The gathered animals applauded, and the horses bowed in acknowledgment.

Harold called over to Erisen and Pluton, "Can a mechanical horse do that?"

Erisen strolled forward slowly and said rather confidently, "I am quite sure that given the required time, a mechanical horse can be constructed to do exactly what you have just done."

"Required time…." repeated Hubert.

Erisen turned away and patted his construction. "But these mechanical horses are not intended to perform musical line dances on stage. They are intended to pull wagons filled with animals on rides around on a circular road. For that purpose, they are already quite adequate."

Harold grunted. "Pulling wagons is a job for a real horse. Your horse cannot see where they are going. Someone will need to start and stop them, and turn them left and right, and—"

Hubert nudged Harold, telling him, "Let the 'smart' animals figure that out themselves."

As the horses wandered away, Skyler asked, "Can we read the stone pork books now?"

"Steam Punk," Pluton corrected. "Yes, yes, children. We shall put all the books into the library for everyone to share now."

As Pluton and Erisen were about to reverse the mechanical horse back into the hut, Hubert trotted by, setting a shiny stone behind it. "See you at the park!" he called as he galloped away.

The next morning, Skyler and Gilda, along with several other young animals, met at the library, a large stone structure in the village, where all sorts of books had been stored. Many of these had been brought to the village from elsewhere when the original animals had settled in this place. Many others had been manufactured and written by animals residing in the village since then. But quite a number had been discovered by explorers and archaeologists, those which had been manufactured and written by humans. These were kept in a separate room.

The large plastic container filled with steam punk books had been hauled into the room. Two kangaroos were unpacking the books, leaving each in its clear plastic protective cover and placing them on empty shelves.

When the kangaroos had finished sorting and stacking the collection, the young animals searched through the books.

Skyler soon found the book which had first drawn his attention. The cover showed tall silver towers of a city unlike anything he had ever seen before.

Gilda searched from one end of the shelf to the other. Finally, she found what she had been seeking, the book which showed what appeared to be a candy-making machine producing brightly colored candies.

Skyler and Gilda sat in two of the reading chairs in the corner of the room where overhead prisms directing external sunlight provided sufficient reading light.

Skyler showed Gilda a two-page picture in the book. "I wonder if this city still exists someplace."

Gilda studied the picture for a moment. "Even if we could find it, the towers have probably all fallen down by now."

Gilda showed some pictures in the other book to Skyler. "I wish we could find some of these machines to make all the candy we can eat."

At this point, a horse head poked in through a nearby window. "You kids know those are all stories, right?" Hubert asked. "All those books are just made up stories about stuff that never really happened."

Skyler waved the book at the horse. "Hubert … Pluton and the scientists, and Erisen and the archaeologists, all of them say these are hysterical dogmints."

"Historical documents," Hubert corrected. "But I say they are stories."

"Stories can be real," Gilda insisted. "Real places, real events."

Hubert snorted. "You find any place in those books out here in reality, then I'll believe those are historical documents. Otherwise, they are mythological musings." Hubert withdrew his head and scampered away.

In the afternoon, Skyler and Gilda brought the two books with them as they went to consult Pluton and Erisen. They were found at the edge of the village with their mechanical horse.

"How can we know if these stores and real or not?" Skyler asked them.

Erisen answered, "They must be real. Why would anybody write about something which never happened or never existed?"

Pluton suggested, "Perhaps somebody could write about what could be rather than what was."

Unseen among nearby bushes, several sets of horse ears perked up to listen to their conversation, and eyes peered through the leaves.

Erisen and Pluton were attaching a small box to the mechanical horse with a wire. Erisen operated switches on the box, and the horse moved, stopped, moved again, turned left, turned right, stopped, reversed, and stopped again.

"Perfect!" Pluton commented. "Now whoever is riding in the wagon can operate the horse."

Hubert gathered the other horses together and whispered to them, "I have a new plan…"

Over the next few days, Pluton and Erisen constructed a second mechanical horse identical to the first horse. Various animals brought coverings and other items to attach to the horses to make them look more like a real horse. Gilda brought eight painted wooden ears, attaching two to the head of each completed horse, and Skyler brought four fluffy cloth tails, attaching two of them.

The horses were hitched to two identical wagons, into which planks had been nailed to create seats for the animals who would ride in them.

"Next, we need to test the pulling power of the horses with a load of animals in the wagons," Erisen announced.

Pluton agreed. "I am sure we could find some volunteers for the test." Immediately, a number of the nearby animals volunteered. "We should bring the wagons out to a clear flat area."

Pluton and Erisen each maneuvered one horse and wagon out to a clearing at the edge of the village, a location where many of the village children played games. Then they went to gather up a few more animals to fill the wagons, to determine if the horses could pull the wagons with a full load.

When they returned to the clearing a short while later, they found Hubert and Harold, one sitting in each wagon with the controllers for the mechanical horses.

"What are you two up to now?" Erisen asked.

Hubert explained "You need somebody to drive the wagons. Who better to operate a horse than a horse?"

Neither Erisen nor Pluton had a good answer to that.

Harold added, "You will also need somebody to bring all the paving materials to make a road around the park, and operate that big cylinder gizmo to flatten out the road. Who you intend for that?"

They knew the obvious answer was horses.

Hubert offered, "You let horses drive the wagons, and we help build your park rides. Deal?" Pluton and Erisen quickly discussed this with each other, then agreed to their proposal.

Animals piled into the wagons, then the mechanical horses were set into motion, pulling them along easily. Hubert and Harold clapped each other's hooves as they passed by each other.

Weeks later, the park opened, only containing the horse rides around the perimeter, but that was only the start of what would become of the place, when many of the wonders seen in the newly found books would someday be constructed there, once the animals figured out how.

Skyler and Gilda first rode the wagon pulled by Hubert in one direction, then rode the wagon pulled by Harold in the other direction. It became an on-going tradition that as the wagons passed each other, the horses would clap hooves, and the passengers of each wagon would clap paws with the passengers of the opposing wagon.

At the end of the day, while the horses gathered in their barn, Harold wondered, "Why did they put the steam engines in the horses anyways? It would have made more sense to put the steam engines under the wagons to turn the wheels directly."

Hubert and two other horses quickly covered Harold's mouth. "Shhhh!" Hubert shushed him. "We have a good thing going now, so don't give them smart animals any new ideas."

Harold whispered, "They will certainly figure it out eventually."

Hubert nodded. "True, but until then, we real horses will still have our places."

Weeks passed, and one day Skyler and Gilda were sneaking out of the village again.

"Where are we going now?" Gilda asked.

Skyler asked, "Have we been in that direction yet?" He indicated the metal strips leading away from the village. Gilda waved him onward.

The two animals crept along the ground, following the mysterious metal strips.

About Robert B. Read, Jr.

Robert Read was born in 1965 and lives in Rhode Island. He is currently a computer programmer for the state. He writes a mixture of science fiction and children's stories, such as the self-published *Country Club Cats* series, and the forthcoming *SteamyTown PunkyPops* series.

Jewels from the Deep by Nils Nisse Visser

A Sussex Steampunk Tale

I'll give thee fairies to attend on thee
And they shall fetch thee jewels from the deep
(Titania, *A Midsummer Night's Dream*)

Rottingdean, 1872

Bartholomew Stapleton suppressed the urge to gag. The curled ends of his immaculate moustache threatened to wilt and droop, disheartened by the pungent, briny air. The stench was vile. Stapleton reached for his handkerchief and pressed it to his nose. As a Londoner, he was frequently exposed to the corruption of the Thames at low tide, but that familiar odour of decomposition faded into insignificance on Rottingdean's small shingle beach.

Fishing boats were pulled up on the shingles and parked in a neat row near to where nets had been hung out to dry on large wooden racks. Weathered fishermen mended nets, scrubbed down beached fishing craft, or tended the rusty steam-powered winches used to haul their boats up and down the shingle beach. Grim-faced women scaled and gutted the last of a fresh catch. Glistening scales covered their coarse dresses, the crude tables they were working on, and the shingle around them. Fish guts festered in the feeble spring sunshine, attracting swarms of buzzing flies.

Though he had blended in perfectly in Brighton earlier that day in his brocade long coat and top hat generously adorned with finely wrought silver cog and gear brooches, the same made Stapleton completely out of place on the beach. Just like him, many in the seaside town had been wearing the latest FlightFunk fashion in celebration of modern engineering. The marvellous technology which had allowed humanity to not only master land and sea, but even extended human dominion into the skies above! Stapleton was a pragmatic man, not easily swayed by popular fancies, but he shared the collective optimism that there had never been a more exciting time to be alive than the second half of the nineteenth century, the Age of Steam.

Rottingdean was but a few miles away from Brighton, but what a difference those handful of miles made. The grim and grimy fishermen and women were dressed simply: The men in sailcloth smock frocks, and the women in drab dresses and aprons. Stapleton couldn't see a single brass cog or gear pinned on their clothes, or even one of plain iron. The only bright colours were worn by a pair of Queen's Men in their scarlet coats, ambling along the row of fishing boats with muskets slung over their shoulders. They threw Stapleton frequent curious looks, as if to emphasise he stuck out like a sore thumb. Even the screeching seagulls whirling overhead mocked him.

Beating a retreat from the beach, Stapleton wandered into the village. Small cottages lined the main street. A horse-drawn carriage rumbled by on the cobblestones. More Queen's Men were patrolling. Barefoot children played catch or chased hoops. An elderly woman, her face lined with years of woe, was furiously scrubbing her door step. Nobody in Rottingdean seemed to be aware of any human advancement since the invention of the wheel. It was inconceivable to Stapleton that Brighton was merely a few miles away, and London just a couple of hours by train. They might as well have sent him halfway across the world to some far-flung, primitive outpost of the Empire.

He recalled what his supervisor had told him back in London.

"They are a quaint lot down on the Sussex coast, Stapleton, very peculiar indeed. Backward as savages and stubborn as pigs. They're so proud of being obnoxious that they sing songs about it. Best smugglers in England though; it runs in their blood."

Belgrave Quality Purveyors Limited was a London firm specialising in the unquenchable appetite for luxury goods. The business was sometimes sadly inconvenienced by unreasonably high tariffs imposed by Her Majesty's Customs & Excise, but there were ways to get around that. BQP shop assistants were adept at conducting deferential chit-chat with genteel customers, interspersed with discreet whispers about wares *not* on display. Stapleton facilitated the logistics of getting that under-the-counter stock into the various BQP West End shops.

"The Rottingdean lot are reputed to be top dog," his supervisor had told him. "Led by a chap they call 'The Poet.' You'll find him at the Black Horse Inn. We've sent word you're coming. Go assess the operation, and if you think they're up to scratch, secure their services. If things go awry for any particular reason..."

"...leave no witnesses," Stapleton had finished, citing unwritten BQP company policy.

Before long, Stapleton arrived at an old timbered building. A faded sign suspended from its wrought iron bracket pronounced it to be the Black Horse Inn. Stapleton glanced at his pocket watch and entered the pub. The interior was a murky maze of alcoves and discreet corners with no decoration other than a few fishermen's tools hung on the walls and corked netting suspended from the low ceiling. There were only a few customers scattered about the interior. There was no bar, just a corner with neat stacks of casks, and little diversity on offer. Stapleton ordered a pint of Sea Cider, praised by the innkeeper as a local brew, but drew a blank look when he asked for a glass.

Stapleton made his way to an empty corner with a pewter tankard in his hand, shaking his head at the backwardness of a place that didn't offer glassware. He didn't like pewter because of the tangy taste it added to a drink, but his estimation improved on his first sip. The Black Horse's innkeeper had coated the inside of the tankard with beeswax, adding a hint of honey rather than pewter, which complemented the clouded, tart cider well.

Nonetheless, Stapleton glowered at everything in sight. He was pleased that he had secured his lodgings at the Old Ship Hotel in Brighton and not here. Although he wasn't as refined as BQP's customers, whose decorative cogs and gears were fashioned from gold rather than Stapleton's silver ones, he considered himself to be a modern man of civilised tastes.

"I hope Rottingdean is to your liking." A man slid out of a nearby alcove. "Not too quaint for your tastes."

The man was slender and keen eyed. An untidy entanglement of long black hair half concealed his gaunt face. Dressed as a clerk, his dark clothes were old and frayed, his hands stained with ink. He reminded Stapleton of a hungry magpie about to gorge on a songbird's nestlings. Stapleton wasn't in the mood for idle chit-chat with the locals. He had come to talk to the kingpin of Rottingdean's collective smuggling efforts, reputed to be a criminal mastermind, not some lowly clerk.

"You've had a busy morning," the clerk continued, not put off by Stapleton's stony silence. "Been up at the Beacon Mill, prowling about The Green, inspecting the beach…."

Stapleton's eyes widened as the clerk began to recite.

You came, and looked, and loved the view

Long known and loved by me.

Green Sussex fading into view

With one gray glimpse of sea.[1]

"You are the one they call The Poet?" Stapleton asked.

"No need to look so surprised, Mr. Stapleton of Belgrave Quality Purveyors in London. Or am I not what you expected?" The Poet asked, his thin lips quivering in a brief, knowing smile.

"I had expected a man of standards on a par with his reputation," Stapleton replied curtly.

"You're honest in your bluntness," The Poet said. "But think of this, Mr. Stapleton. Of the two of us, who was more likely to get noticed this morning in a village crawling with scarlet-clad Rozzers? For my part, I had expected

---

[1] *'Green Sussex' by Alfred Tennyson.*

a man displaying some professional discretion."

Stapleton accepted the rebuke, for it was painfully obvious that he hadn't exercised due caution in his choice of dress. He had dealt with smugglers from Ramsgate in Kent to Penzance in Cornwall, and should have known better. He was used to having the upper hand in these encounters and now found himself off balance. Elsewhere, there had been gratitude in recognition of the honour of being associated with BQP. Here, Stapleton was starting on the defensive, startled by the gnawing suspicion that he wasn't in charge of the situation.

"Enough scorsing of pleasantries, Mr. Stapleton. Let's retire to my office and talk shop." The Poet waved a hand towards the alcove from which he had appeared. Stapleton noticed the simultaneous nod at a stout, bearded fisherman, who moved forward to stand outside the alcove after the prospective business associates took a seat around a sturdy oak table.

"We collect off the coast: either on sea or in the sky," the Poet said. "Bring it in, store it, and transport it to pubs around the Wyrde Woods in the Sussex Weald. Further transport to London is for you to arrange."

"I have Spitalfields night-fliers at my disposal," Stapleton said, pleased to be discussing business after the awkward introduction. "And am acquainted with the Carfax Inn, Raven's Roost, and Earl's Barrel in the Wyrde Woods. The Carfax has my preference. But this village of yours is crawling with Queens' Men."

A flash of hatred crossed the Poet's face. "The Rozzers in the village are the least of my worries. The coast is lined with Coast Guard cottages. There are searchlights and anti-aerocraft guns at Brighton, Seaford, and Eastbourne. Fire-trains operate between Lewes and Polegate, as well as Pevensey and Hastings. Worst of all, we get more than our fair share of Royal Aero Fleet attention."

"I was under the impression that the pressure was eased somewhat after that diplomatic mission last year."

"Yarr, but then that Viscount of Some-Place-or-Other got himself killed on a patrol."

"Viscount Seymour of Upton Snodsbury," Stapleton supplied. "He plummeted off the cliffs, didn't he? Was there foul play?"

The Poet grinned. "The Viscount's night patrol atop the cliffs followed a trail of whitewashed rocks laid out to mark a safe route. Mayhap some of our youngsters accidentally shifted some of those rocks about in their play."

"Sounds like foul play to me," Stapleton said. "It's done you no favours."

"Yarr. London is once again intent on grinding rebellious Sussex under its heel. But we scratch by, Mr. Stapleton, we scratch by. Sussex wunt be druv."

Stapleton nodded. The government was trying to crack down on smuggling, or Free Trading as locals preferred to call it in Sussex, a region engaged in illicit trade since Medieval times. The natives took pride in outwitting the authorities time and time again, something Stapleton could appreciate well enough. Of late though, there had been an infusion of political perversion—French notions of equality. For all of its charms, Brighton was a revolutionary hotbed of sedition, and that wasn't much to Stapleton's liking. Apart from an occasional difference of opinion with Customs & Excise, he was a fierce loyalist. The British Empire, he reckoned, could only function if everyone knew their place in it and didn't aspire to best their betters.

It was best to avoid politics though. That wasn't why he was here. "Her Majesty's Government isn't much amused by Free Trading antics, nor by Brighton politics. But I wasn't aware there were so many obstacles. Rottingdean might not be the best place for BQP's activity after all. The stakes are high."

"Mayhap that is so," the Poet conceded. "But if it is a trial run that brings you here, my guess is that you've got a Channel-Runner waiting out at sea somewhen this week. Meaning there is a crop to harvest, isn't there?"

Stapleton pursed his lips, caught out again. The Poet was amused by him, not the least bit impressed, nor apparently aware of Stapleton's reputation. That might have been mere rural ignorance, but this Poet was proving himself to be an adept thinker. Surely, he knew Bartholomew Stapleton wasn't known to suffer fools gladly? Even the most vicious scumbags in London treated Stapleton with deference. Those who didn't tended to find themselves making intimate acquaintance with the bottom of the Thames, or else visiting a certain pig farm just outside the city.

"I have come to ascertain if your lot measure up to BQP standards," Stapleton said, allowing a hint of disdain in his voice. "As there are some questions whether or not you've recovered from that Rozzer raid a few years ago."

"The Massacre on the Green was a costly business," the Poet said. "But we're back in business. And Rottingdean's Free Traders desire to see if your lot measures up to *our* standards, Mr. Stapleton. As I see it, you can take a gamble and try to get in touch with Free Traders in Worthing, Seaford, or Hastings, but that will take you time…and you might not find the response you want."

The confident sparkle in the Poet's eyes told Stapleton what reception he was likely to receive along the east Sussex coast if he spurned Rottingdean. Even so, he couldn't resist saying, "There's always the Mudlarks of Romney Marsh." It was unlikely the Poet had any sway in that corner of Sussex.

The Poet shrugged. "In Rye they say the world is divided into five parts—Europe, Asia, Africa, America, and Romney Marsh. They're foreright folk in the Marsh Country, prefer to be left alone. But consider this, if fellow Sussex Free Traders are viewed with suspicion there, how would they look upon you? By my reckoning, Mr. Stapleton, we're your bettermost option."

Stapleton took a sip of cider, dislike and admiration competing within him. He set his personal feelings aside. "*The Kestrel* captained by Fitzsimons Noakes. Eight miles south of Beachy Head. I've got the coordinates and altitude." Stapleton patted his pocket. "Noakes will be there for the next three nights, at the hour of the witch."

"I know *The Centennial Kestrel* and its captain; he's a fine aeronaut, despite his blustering boasts. Cargo?"

"Twelve crates. Sumatran clove cigars and Javanese kretek cigarettes out of Ostend."

The Poet let out a low whistle. East Indies tobacco was all the rage in London. A dozen crates of it represented a small fortune.

Encouraged by the Poet's appreciation, Stapleton added, "The Belgian seller claims the crates 'accidentally' fell off the deck of an inbound Dutch schooner returning from the East Indies."

"A fortuitous event. But indeed, a one-off then."

"No, the seller assured us such a miraculous coincidence could occur with predictable regularity. A quarterly affair."

The Poet laughed. They haggled over the price, half of it to be paid upfront, the other half upon handover in the Wyrde Woods. If the goods were intercepted, the first half wouldn't be reimbursed and the second half wouldn't be paid, as was standard.

"It'll have to be tonight," the Poet said after they agreed on the fee. "The Rozzers go back to their barracks in about an hour and won't be back until morning. But they'll report your presence. It would be better if you were gone when they return on the morrow. Aside of that, tomorrow is Thursday, and it's bad luck to sail or skirr on Thor's day. And Friday is an even unluckier day to set out, surely."

Stapleton nodded his agreement. He didn't care much for local super-stitions, but wasn't inclined to spend any more time in Rottingdean than absolutely necessary.

"You'll fly out in *The Liddle Mew*, Mr. Stapleton. Our fastest sky-skiff, captained by my bettermost skipper."

"How far will we have to travel to get to this sky-skiff?"

"*The Liddle Mew* is anigh, no further than it takes to walk from The Black Horse to the beach, which is precisely where we'll be going in a few hours. In the meantime, would you care to join me for a bowl of fish stew? Today's catch and speciality of the house."

The notion of fish stew repelled Stapleton, who suspected that the nauseating smells from the beach still lingered in his clothes, so he decided to opt for a bowl of vegetable soup and some bread instead.

Shortly before sunset, Stapleton and the Poet made their way to the beach, followed at a discreet distance by the stocky fisherman, now armed with an axe, who was joined by a companion sporting a brace of pistols and a cutlass.

Stapleton was expecting the sky-skiff to skirr in from the sea to pick him up, but was astonished when they reached the beach. There were three gaps in the row of fishing boats. The missing vessels had been dragged farther up the beach, their lee-boards replaced with propeller outriggers and darkened, inflated envelopes secured atop of their masts. Crews were busily making the last preparations for take-off.

"Almost indistinguishable from the hog-boats," the Poet said proudly. "Unless you know your hoggies real well."

Stapleton was unable to keep the admiration out of his voice. "Right under their noses."

"And the Rozzers none the wiser, addle-headed puckstools that they be. Allow me to present you with *The Flittermouse, The Humbledore,* and *The Liddle Mew.* We've also got a cutter, *The John Hawkeye,* but she's too large for this particular game of hide and seek, so parked elsewhere."

"Busy night, I see."

"Them that ask no questions, isn't told a lie, Mr. Stapleton. Your only concern is *The Liddle Mew.* Come, let's meet the *Mew's* crew."

Stapleton wasn't much impressed by the sky-skiff as they approached. The hull and envelope were unevenly patched with lengths of wood and leather hides, giving the impression of a slovenly craft feebly skirring through its dying years. Stapleton was increasingly of a mind that tonight's rendezvous with the *Kestrel* would be the first and last time that BQP worked with the Rottingdean smugglers.

All three were dressed in plain fisherman's smocks. A grey-beard introduced himself as Barry, but it was the other two who raised Stapleton's ire. The Poet's "bettermost" crew seemed nothing less than a calculated insult. They were just children, twelve years old at most. At first, Stapleton assumed they were boys, but when they introduced themselves, he realised they were girls. The dark-haired one named herself as Liss, the fair-haired one as Lot.

Ignoring the girls, Stapleton turned to the Poet, fury on his face and in his voice. "Your best crew?"

"Yarr, the bettermost aeronauts between Black Rock and Beachy Head," the Poet answered calmly. "And I'll remind you, Mr. Stapleton that you are here to observe. You may write whatever you want in your assessment, but you won't intervene with our operations. Savvy?"

Stapleton stared at the Poet, trying to control his rage. In any other circumstance he would have stormed away in a huff, but he was acutely aware that the Channel-Runner wouldn't wait forever. Free Traders didn't like to be stationary as it was, especially not with the Royal Aero Fleet patrolling the skies. Stapleton swallowed his bile, subjecting himself to the humiliation of the Poet's misguided joke. He boarded *The Liddle Mew* in stony silence.

To add insult to injury, it turned out that the girl called Liss captained the sky-skiff, directing the other two as the *Mew* took to the sky. Watching the crew, Stapleton had to grudgingly admit that Liss handled the craft well. Upon closer observation, he also noted that there was more to the *Mew* than first met the eye. The pectoral and dorsal sails were neatly furled and securely tied to their booms. The lines stretching to the twin masts holding the inflated envelope aloft were taut, and there was no unnecessary clutter littering the deck. The small, sturdy steam engine in the low engine house at the stern chugged smoothly. Its almost gentle rhythm concealed the considerable power which drove the propellers, one fixed to the outrigger on each side of the hull.

Regardless of the evident and cleverly concealed qualities of the *Mew*, Stapleton's mood didn't improve. Girls in men's clothing. Doing men's work. It just wasn't right. Nor was their behaviour. The girls bantered incessantly, in between bouts of laughter and spontaneous songs—bawdy blackguard verses like "Lily White Thighs."

By the light of a candle I happened to spy
A pretty young couple together did lie
Said Nelly to John if you'll pull up my smock
You'll find a young hen full as good as your—

The girls dissolved into gales of mirth.

Barry tolerated it all with a foolish grin on his face, although Stapleton noted that he hovered over the girls with an air of fierce grandfatherly protection and kept a wary eye out on Stapleton.

Stapleton had little time for females. Their main useful purpose could easily be bought for a bob a go, far cheaper than courtship or marriage. As far as he was concerned, women should be subservient, suitably grateful for a man's prowess, money, and perhaps the occasional charitable interest shown in their petty worries and otherwise empty thoughts. Liss and Lot displayed far too much cockiness as they swaggered about the *Mew,* making it appear as if skirring an aerocraft was mere child's play.

Grinding his teeth, Stapleton savoured the thought of intricately planned retribution. He had been in this business for longer than he cared to remember, but had never before encountered anything like the *Mew's* crew. Now that he had, he'd sooner sell his own mortal frame to the body snatchers than offer this lot a contract. Moreover, Stapleton vowed that the Poet would pay for humiliating him in this manner. Stapleton's fingers stroked the folded ivory-handled knife in his pocket. The blade was razor sharp, and Stapleton could strike fast as a snake. Although vexed by their behaviour, he wouldn't harm children. The Poet however, was fair game after making a mockery of a serious BQP request.

They found the *Kestrel* without problems. Liss seemed to know the captain because the two exchanged cheerful insults as the crew transferred the cargo from the *Kestrel's* hold to the *Mew's* deck. This was never an easy task at high altitude, but proceeded smoothly. Before long, the *Mew* was headed back for the coast, carrying Stapleton's precious cargo, while the *Kestrel* discreetly slipped away into the darkness.

"No longer skirring into the wind," Liss pronounced from the open steer house at the *Mew's* stern, just in front of the low engine house. "And a fair breeze. Let's have the 'toral and dorsal sails out."

She set the helm, then helped Lot and Barry unfurl the sails and swing the booms out. The crew sang while they worked.

Here's to the grog, boys, the jolly, jolly grog,
Here's to the rum and tobacco.
I've a-spent all my tin with the lassies drinking gin,
And across the briny ocean I must wander.

Stapleton shook his head. There was no reason to caution silence as the rumble of the engine would betray their position long before the crew's noisy malarkey, but children should be seen, not heard. No good could possibly come of letting girls run wild and feral like this.

Tired after a long day, Stapleton sat down, resting his back against the tarpaulin covering the stack of crates amidships. He dozed off for a while, abruptly awoken when a seagull took position behind the *Mew's* stern, issuing plaintive cries loud enough to compete with the engine's steady chugging.

Scrambling to his feet, Stapleton took stock. A thick fog was rolling in, lending the darkness of the moonless night an unnatural shimmer. Normally, any aeronaut worth his salt would avoid skirring into dense mist, but the young captain of *The Liddle Mew* plunged the sleek sky-skiff right into it.

Stapleton shivered as the ghostly shroud enveloped the *Mew*. The fog was so dense that the oblong helium-filled envelope suspended over the deck was reduced to a vague shadow. A chill crept across Stapleton's skin, and he shook his head as if to clear it from superstitious fear.

"Steady now," he growled to himself. "A proper London pea-souper hides far more trouble than an empty sky over an empty sea."

The gull shrieked. Stapleton frowned. Something had changed. The fog below the *Mew* had become darker, a vast pane of gloom which seemed to be gulfing upwards towards the sky-skiff. He realised the expanse of darker shadow was stable, and it was the *Mew* which was moving down to meet the surface of the sea. Liss adjusted the propellers to level out. The sky-skiff shuddered briefly as it came out of its descent. The hull broke through the lowest level of the fog, allowing sudden visibility, although the envelope above remained shrouded. The sea's choppy surface churned all around them, the *Mew* skirring a bare ten feet over the water.

Stapleton's previous estimation of Liss's skirring skills tumbled rapidly.

This, he thought, *this is why The Poet is a fool. Why you don't let children do an adult's job, let alone a girl do a man's job.*

"What's going on?" Stapleton hollered as he made his way to the steer house. "You've come far too low, girl. You'll get us all killed."

"Royal Aero Fleet patrol, Mus Stapleton," Liss answered calmly.

Lot pointed upwards.

Stapleton gazed at the blanket of thick fog. In vain, of course, nothing could be seen at all. "How do you know?"

"The mew reckoned so, Mus Stapleton," Liss said.

"And mews can hear the wind whisper," Lot added.

"Mew?" Stapleton asked.

"Sussex word for seagull," Barry explained. "We speak proper English, not that furrin gibberish Lunnoners speak."

"Blast and hellfire!" Stapleton barked. "I'm not a gullible land-lubber. Speak plain, cut the nonsense. Seagulls don't talk."

Liss shrugged and peered at her instrument panel, pointedly ignoring Stapleton.

"Some folk can hear the mews," Lot insisted. "Liss has the gift, like her father."

"Her father?"

"Yarr," Barry said. "None other than Cap'n John Hawkeye."

It was Stapleton's turn to shrug, though he was actually impressed. John Hawkeye was a legendary smuggler, his name still toasted in taverns all along the south coast where his deeds were retold with unceasing relish.

"I reckon the 'how' bain't as important," Liss said, "as the fact that there be a Royal Aero Fleet chaser overhead, Mus Stapleton."

"And the Seven Sisters dead ahead," Barry said. "We'll be kissing 'em drackly."

Stapleton turned. Ahead of them waves crashed against the base of pale cliffs rising high into the fog. The *Mew* was headed straight for them at considerable speed.

"Starboard vert-prop full power," Liss said, adjusting levers on the steer house instrument panel. "Port vert-prop in neutral spin. Lot, Barry, bring in the booms, furl the sails."

The skiff turned larboard until the cliffs were off the beam, after which the *Mew* followed a course parallel to the cliffs. More seagulls joined the *Mew's* plaintive escort, circling the aerocraft and screeching manic laughter. Stapleton gripped the railing, watching the waves roll ashore to dash themselves against the cliffs in explosive sprays. He could even hear the roars of impact, despite the Mew's chugging engine. Tiny drops of water moistened his face, the taste of salt on his lips.

"You are putting us in danger," Stapleton complained. "No sky captain ventures this close. It's insane."

"Liss knows what she's doing, Mus Stapleton," Lot said reprovingly. "She's the daughter of—"

"Captain Hawkeye," Stapleton completed. "And my mother is the Queen of Timbuktu, none of which makes this any less insane."

"Zackly." Liss threw her head back and laughed. This close to the cliffs they caught the updrafts of air, and her long dark hair billowed around her head, lifted by the momentary breeze. "Insanity is zackly the point, Mus Stapleton."

Lot and Barry laughed. Stapleton shook his head even though he understood the point; they were safe from Royal Aero Fleet pursuit here. Not even the boldest Fleet pilot would venture this near to the deadly cliffs.

"Barry, take the helm," Liss ordered.

"Yarr, Cap'n." Barry stepped up to the steer house to take the helm.

"What we're doing, Mus Stapleton," Barry said conversationally, pointing at the cliffs, "is called 'kissing the Seven Sisters.'"

"Kissing…? Hey, you two, what are—?"

Liss and Lot had moved towards the cargo stored amidships. They fumbled with the tarpaulin, lifted an edge of it, opened the lid of the crate thus revealed, and then started rummaging about in the crate.

"Stop that!" Stapleton was about to step forward to drag the girls away from his precious goods, when Barry laid a grizzled hand on his arm.

"Captain's prerogative," the old aero-dog said amiably enough, but there was an ominous warning in his voice. Stapleton ground his teeth and stayed where he was. A sky captain's word was law on board of an aerocraft during flight. Tempted as he was to take his belt off and give the girls a damn good thrashing, he knew it would be interpreted as mutiny. Despite Stapleton's skills with his knife, instinct told him Barry was a formidable foe, even in his elderly years. The old man's outward joviality didn't match his eyes, which were ever wary and alert.

The girls turned around. Lot held up a cigar box, Liss clutched a carton of cigarettes.

"That doesn't belong to you," Stapleton hissed. "Put it back."

Liss shook her head. "It bain't for us, Mus Stapleton. It be for the Pharisees."

"Farawhat?"

Liss gazed at the cliffs. A breeze was slowly dismantling the fog's integrity, dividing and subdividing it into interwoven strands. The newly formed gaps of clear air revealed that the forbidding cliff walls rose ever higher, with no end in sight.

"Well," Lot said, liberating a bundle of Sumatran cigars from her box. "There is the crew's share."

"And the captain's share," Liss added, deftly freeing a packet of Javanese kretek cigarettes from the carton in her hands. "Other than that, the Pharisees demand their due, and they bain't like it when it's withheld, surely."

"What in the blazes are Pharisees?"

"Faeries," Lot said helpfully.

"Hush, that name bain't to their liking," Barry admonished her.

"FAERIES?" Stapleton fumed.

"So the Lunnon man shouts it at the top of his voice, of all chuckle-headed things to do," Liss said, shaking her head in disbelief. "The Pharisees will have their due so we can skirr home safely, Mus Stapleton. Under their protection. Tis how we do things in Sussex."

"You people are beyond belief." The box and carton were just a small portion of the cargo, but still worth more than anybody in Rottingdean was likely to earn in a whole year. Stapleton wasn't about to sacrifice them to please some backward natives babbling on about faeries.

The *Mew* skirred into a pocket of turbulence. Barry rapidly trimmed the propellers to steady the skiff. With Barry thus preoccupied, Stapleton seized the chance and dashed forward, snatching box and carton from the girls' hands. He let his momentum carry him forward to the stern where he whirled around, a snarl on his face.

"That bain't a wise move, Mus Stapleton," Liss said.

"You'd risk this run's entire crop?" Lot asked.

"Now listen here, girl," Stapleton snapped at Liss. "I don't know what century you think you live in, but in the civilised world there are advances you cannot even begin to comprehend. Modern thinking is what we do these days. 'Out with the old, in with the new,' I say, and good riddance. If you think that I'm going to part with my goods to appease these…these…"

"Pharisees," Lot supplied helpfully.

"Bloody hell. Faeries are an invention from children's story books. They don't exist! They don't dance around in circles at full moon, just how ignorant can you—"

"By Pize, but they middling do," Liss countered. "Dance on the hilltops in the moonlight. There's those what has seen them on the Downs. But there bain't just Pharisees on land, Mus Stapleton, there be plenty that live in the sea, in the clouds…"

Stapleton launched into an angry tirade, roundly condemning the ignorance of irrational superstitions, trying to convey to these simplistic nincompoops just what was happening in the country, the marvellous inventions that were changing human life forever, the rationale of science, the power of mechanical might.

The girls and Barry seemed entirely unperturbed by his outburst. Barry continued to trim the propellers and steer the *Mew,* while the girls just let Stapleton's torrents of words wash over them. The stubborn look on Liss's face told Stapleton he ranted in vain. That only vexed him further.

"—and if you think that I'll destroy precious cargo because of some imbecile notion of—"

Stapleton caught a flicker of movement up by the envelope. He looked up only to see it was gone again.

"—mere faery tales—"

New movement. On the water. Movement that didn't equate with the choppy waves. He turned his head and focused, but he was a fraction of a second too late. There was nothing to be seen other than the waves rolling steadily towards the cliffs.

"...women's hysteria...."

Stapleton's words dried up and his mouth dropped open. He stared at a long, scaly tentacle emerging from the sea, joined by another, both briefly exploring the air with their tips before sliding below the surface again.

"That...that was..."

"Pharisees," Liss said calmly. "Pooks."

Stapleton opened and closed his mouth, but no words came out. There was renewed movement by the envelope, and he looked up to see smaller shadows circling the envelope's vague outline, bulbous things trailing a slew of writhing tentacles.

"Sky-squids," Lot explained. "Their venom can melt through the envelope."

"Or your skin," Liss added.

Stapleton's eyes were drawn back to the sea. The surface teemed with movement as a plethora of shapes emerged, some vaguely humanoid, others monstrous, large and small.

"Sea Pooks," Barry said. "None too pleased."

Stapleton blinked, speechless. He took in the grotesque scaly forms. Many were draped in seaweed, exposing wide mouths to reveal rows of vicious teeth. The creatures stretched out arms, fins, claws, and tentacles, the slit pupils of their eyes conveying an ancient malevolence which left Stapleton trembling. He hung on to the railing for dear life, his mind frantic as he tried to understand what he was seeing.

The creatures shrieked and bellowed with such a volume that the sounds of the *Mew's* engine were drowned out altogether. Their serpent-like eyes blazed with fury. Stapleton was convinced that he could feel the exquisite pain of being torn apart and then shredded by all those teeth and claws, his soul afterwards dragged down into the depths for more torments. The absolute surety of this, the uncompromising totality, was so petrifying that he could feel the warm trickle of urine running down his leg.

John Hawkeye's daughter was calm, showing no fear. She caught his eye and directed a pointed look at the box and carton in his hands. "Bettermost give 'em what they want."

"They'll drag us down into the sea otherwise," Lot warned.

It took all of Stapleton's usually indomitable willpower to raise his arms, then feebly throw box and carton overboard.

The monstrous cacophony reached a high pitch as grotesque appendages reached for the offerings. Then, with startling abruptness, it ceased altogether as the creatures disappeared beneath the waves at once.

Stapleton stood quivering by the railing, gasping for breath, and clawing for comprehension.

"They bain't like your picture book Pharisees." Liss stepped up to the railing next to him. "Sussex Pooks can be a mite irate."

"A *mite?*"

"Bettermost to give them what they want, Mus Stapleton." Lot came to his other side. "It bain't much, surely."

Stapleton nodded dumbly. He felt lost, bereft of all his certainties.

"Think of it as a toll," Barry suggested.

Stapleton nodded again. A toll was something his mind could work with. He stared down at his wet trousers with disbelief and shame.

"Most folk are frit, the first time," Liss said. "For bettermost reasons. It bain't something to feel shameful about, surely."

"Most?" Stapleton asked, narrowing his eyes.

"Yarr, most. Not all. There be a handful of exceptions." She smiled confidently, and he could see steel resolve in her eyes. "We'll be away from the Seven Sisters drackly, Mus Stapleton, Cuckmere Haven is anigh. We'll slip over the estuary and land the *Mew* behind the crest of Hindover Hill. There bain't no Royal Aero Fleet or Queen's Men about the Cuckmere Valley tonight."

"The seagu…mews told you?" Stapleton forced himself to ask. He needed something resembling normality to clutch on to, no matter how absurd…. Or was it? He simply didn't know anymore. Talking seagulls made more sense than the forms writhing in the water, hungering for his flesh and soul.

"Yarr, that they did." Liss shrugged. "Tis how things are done 'round here, Mus Stapleton. Tis different than what you be used to in Lunnon, mayhap?"

Stapleton took a deep breath, regaining his composure somewhat. "Yes, indeed. All considering, Miss Hawkeye, you have yourself a contract."

"Good." Liss smiled brightly, all child for a moment, before she revoked that impression by lighting one of the Javanese kretek cigarettes. She inhaled deeply. The distinctive, exotic aroma of the clove spices filled Stapleton's nose.

"Bettermost news," Lot said with a smile. She held out her bundle of Sumatran smokes to Stapleton. "Care for a cigar?"

About Nils Nisse Visser

Nils Nisse Visser writes contemporary fantasy, contemporary and historical fiction, historical fantasy and Steampunk stories. As well as non-fiction magazine work, he has published ten novels and novellas, and contributed stories to four anthologies, including two award-winning WriterPunk Press anthologies. His short steampunk story "Limbs" (which can be read on his website), was awarded second place in the Steampunk Readers & Writers 2018 writing competition. His first Steampunk book, *Amster Damned*, has been positively received by critics, who have encouraged him to continue exploring the genre. Find out more at www.nilsnissevisser.co.uk

The Bronze Bomber by Briant Laslo

The war had gone on longer than anybody expected. From that very first battle at Manassas Junction, everybody knew it was going to be bloody. And, given the outcome of that fight, it looked like the Confederacy was going to have a swift victory. But, as is the case in many wars, the Earth itself seemed to demand a higher price in blood to make up for the idiocy of the human beings inhabiting her lands, and the war dragged on.

It wasn't until Antietam, when opportunities were both missed and seized by one side or the other, that the tide began to turn. While most people viewed it as a tactical draw, the fact was that Antietam was the first turning point when the North began to shift things in their favor.

And then the siege of Vicksburg, locking in control of the Mississippi for the Union, seemed to almost guarantee that the war would be over soon.

But, on July 1, 1863, a new sun rose over Gettysburg, Pennsylvania.

No one from the North knew what they were seeing. The object appeared as large in the sky as the sun itself, reflecting the daylight off its polished surface. It moved through the air more than one hundred feet above the ground, somehow flying as easily and as quietly as a bird.

The shadow that it cast confounded the mind when trying to comprehend the size of the thing. Three hundred feet long and cylindrical, the entire surface was a highly shined, brassy material. There was a platform, no more than twenty or thirty feet across and perhaps 75 feet long, positioned directly at the underbelly. It was upon this platform that people could be seen moving about. As it closed in on the northern soldiers, shouting voices and the sounds of cranks and gears echoed down.

Death rained down upon the fields of Gettysburg.

Six-pounder guns, 24-pounder howitzers, and some sort of repeating flintlock that fired up to thirty rounds per minute, decimating anyone in the proximity of the behemoth that now seemed to soar above the chaos. It was called the Nepomuk Repeater, named after its inventor, Johann Nepomuk, an immigrant from Weitra in the Austrian Empire. The Confederate President had become acquainted with Nepomuk somewhere around 1837. Following the death of his wife in 1835, Jefferson Finis Davis disappeared for seven years, traveling across the sea toward Europe. When he returned in 1842, he brought the farmer who had an innate talent for building mechanical wonders with him.

At the time, Nepomuk's creations consisted of things like a self-driven plow that could be set loose upon a field and would till in a straight line all on its own. However, as the years passed and events unfolded, Jefferson turned to Nepomuk more frequently, seeking assistance with ideas and concepts that could help change the flow of the war in which Jefferson now found himself a principal participant.

Thus, the Bronze Bomber was born.

Propaganda spread about the "Technological Terror of the Heavens" and its capabilities. Depending upon wind conditions, it was able to travel up to thirty miles per hour, or roughly twice the speed of the fastest trip down the Mississippi. Its armament was easily interchangeable, allowing it to house up to three dozen howitzers if attacking fortifications, nearly seventy of the repeaters if attacking open field, or any number of weapon combinations. There was also a twenty by thirty foot section of the platform that detached from the main vehicle, suspended by multiple chains and cranks allowing supplies, foot soldiers, or even cavalry to be lowered onto a battlefield up to 75 feet below the Bomber itself.

A week later, the South announced that the Bronze Bomber was just the first in a line of airborne weaponry for the newest branch of the Southern Army, the Nepomuk Airship Armada of the Confederate People.

Now, nearly five years after the Gettysburg Massacre, the North finds itself on the brink of defeat. And while battles still actively rage in different parts of the country, it wasn't these battlefields that would decide the fate of the country. It would be decided by an undercover union agent sitting in the corner of a bar in Richmond, Virginia and passing for a Confederate citizen.

Albeit, a drunk Confederate citizen.

"Barkeep! Another Pernod Fils if you would." The clarity of the agent's words belies her level of inebriation.

Tiny beads of water twinkle their way down the glass container at the top of the silver absinthe fountain upon the table. The design of the metal base, a woman with fairy wings holding the glass container filled with icy cold water above her head.

"I think that perhaps you have had enough."

This early in the afternoon there are only three other people besides the agent and the barkeep in the establishment, and his words easily find their way without him having to step out from behind the bar.

"There's only one person who can tell Jacqueline Whitney Holmes when she has had enough, and you, kind sir, are not that person. However... If you no longer wish to engage in the beauty of free enterprise, then I will bid you adieu."

A deep voice joins the conversation from the entrance. "I shall purchase the libation requested and make sure the lady makes it back to her abode safely."

"Who the hell are you calling a lady? Ya hornswoggler," Jacqueline intends for the insult to sound surly, but her smile instantly demolishes her façade.

The man holds up two fingers, extracts a small purse from one of his many pockets via a gold chain, and pulls out a coin for the barkeep. "Now, now my dear, you and your marvelously red hair know that my acquisitions are always on the up and up," with a quick flip of the tails of his frock coat the man joins Jacqueline at her table, sliding one glass of Pernod Fils to her.

It fits into her hand as if it is a natural extension of her body. It belongs there. It has always belonged there.

She nods at the man now sitting across the table. "That never has been a problem for you, has it? Being up… and up."

They both guffaw, bending over the table to embrace the other.

"What can I say Jacqueline, I've never cared whether it's notch or trinkets. As long as I get mine, everybody can be happy."

"Happy you say. Is there such a thing nowadays, Roman?"

"Always… Fleeting and fragile though it may be at times."

A silence envelops the table, broken only by the trickling sound of water. They both place a single cube of sugar on the intricately designed spoons resting atop their glasses. The ice-cold water drips over the sugar, dissolving into the emerald liquid beneath and forming the magical clouds that have captured the fascination of so many.

"How are things with your brother?" Roman asks, taking a drink and then using an overly opulent handkerchief to wipe away some residual moisture from the Franz Josef hugging his upper lip.

"John?" She laughs. "The bastard is off playing Richard III, I think in Chicago."

"Chicago? I thought he was a diehard supporter of the Confederacy?"

"Oh, he is! That doesn't stop the wagtails from paying to see him up on the stage and hope they can catch his eye, and Johnny will go wherever the money is."

"Well, we all have our vices."

Jacqueline lifts her glass at that, drinking down nearly half her absinthe. She inhales the aroma, tasting the delightful combination of anise, fennel, and the frequently overlooked melissa. It runs down her throat and into her chest, and she imagines tiny green fairies floating upon the vapors up toward her mind. She wonders if they will be terrified at what they find there.

"So, why are you here?" She leans both elbows on the table, looking at him curiously. Also, it helps her focus getting a bit closer to him. "Did you come to say goodbye? Or do you have something useful for me?"

His voice drops nearly to a whisper as he also leans forward. However, his arms notably stay under the table. Roman would never be caught with his elbows on a surface other than a mattress. "I came to make sure you actually volunteered for this mission. Just because you and I are the longest serving members of the B2S Regiment, other than Hiram himself, doesn't mean we always have to step forward for the missions nobody else wants."

"Of course I volunteered for this mission. You know I've been waiting for this mission ever since that bitch of an airship attacked Philadelphia. Ever since Edwin."

"I know he was your favored brother, and what happened at Philadelphia was a travesty, all those innocents dying. But that was over four years ago, and the Bronze Bomber is practically retired now. This 'Greatest Show Above the Earth' they are planning is just a publicity stunt for Davis and Nepomuk. Both sides are starting to accept the fact that they can't do this much longer. The North has the numbers, but the South has the technology, and England is watching as their former colonies destroy each other. If things stay as they are, it's only a matter of time before we are all hailing Queen and Country again."

"What are you suggesting?" Jacqueline takes a moment to concentrate on not squeezing the glass in her hand too tightly. "Retreat into the shadows? Just let the cards fall as they may and then pick up the pieces when everything is a little less bloody?"

"Pshaw! You know I've lost as much as anybody in this war, Jacqueline. I'm just pointing out that even Lincoln has said this war is inevitably becoming as much of a popularity contest as a militaristic one, and that, perhaps, this particular mission is not a necessity."

"So we just let them have their Greatest Show, then?"

"If we were talking about simply sabotaging the show, making a mockery of it, that would be a different story. But we both know that isn't the mission."

Jacqueline puts on her most polished nonchalant face and times the finishing of her drink to coincide with the shrugging of her shoulders. Roman shakes his head in resignation and drinks down the rest of his cloudy, green liquor as well.

"Fine," he says as he stands, running his hands over his coat to smooth it down into place. "I said I came here to make sure you had truly volunteered for this mission, and I see that you have. I know better than to try to talk you out of something you have set your mind to."

"Are you headed back north immediately then?"

"I think it is probably best that I do. There will be questions regardless of whether you succeed, and a known member of the B2S will be among the first asked. Why?"

"If you find yourself in Chicago, tell Johnny that if I get out of Richmond, I am coming for him next."

"You're drunk."

"Well, you know how I get when I am drunk." She stands slowly, intending to strike an enticing pose leaning against the table. Unfortunately, her hand slips as the world tilts, and she stumbles off to the side, knocking over the chair she had sat guzzling spirits in for far too long.

Roman proves as agile as ever, catching her about her shoulders and preventing a full-on sprawl. For a moment, she feels like she is witnessing the entire sequence of events from above and she finds it hilarious. She can hear and see herself laughing as Roman lifts her back into a balanced position and she drifts back to her body.

As her perspective returns to the first person, Jacqueline sees Roman with his hands still upon her shoulders, holding her steady as he laughs. He has seen her like this more times than she can remember.

"You did say you would get the lady, that's me, safely back to my bode… my ab-ode… That's a funny word…ab-ooowed. Why do you always use such funny words?"

Roman shakes his head and laughs softly as the bar darkens.

"That's an intriguingly astute question. Let me get you home and we can try to figure it out."

"Ass toot." Laughter. Darkness.

Darkness gave way to light as the sun rose in the East, as it always does. The Austrian is in the final stages of work on a music box.

When the music begins, The Blue Danube by Johann Strauss II, the ballet slipper will shatter, 64 tiny, platinum slivers shifting in unison to form the ballerina herself. Then, as the dancer would begin to rotate in the classic arabesque position, moving in time with the music to a full one hundred eighty degree penché, she would proceed through the entire routine, ending an impossible grand jeté where the ballerina gives the appearance of completely separating herself from the base before landing in a bow.

Or rather, that is what is going to happen if he could ever finish it.

"I really don't think all of this is necessary," Johann says to his friend of over thirty years.

"Of course it isn't *necessary*," President Davis replies. "But, it may very well be required. Your astonishing apparatuses have given us the opportunity to keep our cause alive these past five years. Without you, things very well may have ended back at Gettysburg in '63, and the right for states to create their own laws would've been lost forever!"

"We both know that is not what is at the heart of this war, my friend."

"Oh, but it is, Johann. It is! Regardless of where you stand on the practice of slavery, this conflict is about the true nature of our country at its core. Are our states free to form their own governments, independent but united as was intended? Or, does our unification, the federal government, have the right to control how the individual states choose to live?"

"I have no desire to debate this topic with you again. Regardless, what is the point of this Greatest Show Above the Earth? Do we really need to have acrobats on the Bronze Bomber?" Johann tinkers with one of the minuscule gears responsible for the position of the ballerina's support leg

"Not just acrobats," Jefferson laughs as he slaps his hands together. "Acrobats, camels, strongmen, snake charmers, a belly dancer, and an elephant! And the point of this event is exactly what I was just saying, to celebrate your unparalleled mechanisms."

"I'm just a farmer, Jefferson. I have no desire to be celebrated."

"Nonsense! Once upon a time, you may have been just a farmer. Had our paths never crossed you may have spent your entire life doing nothing more than rotating crops, tilling the soil, and making offspring to help you do more of the same. But our paths *did* cross, and you have nearly single-handedly reshaped the course of our entire world."

"So too can a meteor strike transform the planet, but it is not necessarily a cause for festivities."

"Ah yes, but the ability to harness that kind of power and direct it… That is certainly a reason for praise. And that is precisely what you have done. Even that dullard Lincoln realizes what is happening. He knows his numbers are negated by your technology, and he is finally starting to understand that England is watching everything. That's why old Honest Abe is focused more and more on popularity. It just so happens that, in this instance, he is right."

Johann puts down his magnifying glass and pulls out a piece of paper from one of the inner pockets of his vest. He unfolds it and spreads it on the table in front of him, then picks up his mechanical pen.

"What are you doing?" Jefferson asks.

"Oh, just scratching that off my List of Things I Will Never Hear Jefferson Say… Abraham… Lincoln… is… right. There we go."

Jefferson snorts, slapping him on his back. "That's one of the things I like most about you, your sense of humor. And that's what we need to show the people! Show them that you are not some mad scientist enraptured by creating weapons of mass destruction. I know that's not who you are, and I know that you don't want to be remembered that way. So, please, embrace this celebration. It's still a couple of weeks away, why don't you reach out to the man running the show? Maybe you can create some of your mechanical marvels to thrill and delight the crowd."

Jefferson always did know how to get the inventor interested in an assignment.

"Very well, very well! I know better than to try to talk you out of something you have set your mind to," Johann smiles, standing up from his workbench to hug his friend.

"Excellent!" The embrace from Jefferson is strong and filled with joy. Hope. "I'm sure that with some of your creative contraptions as part of the show, we will enchant the public and help everyone understand what the South is truly fighting for."

"What is the name of the individual running the show?"

"His name is Phineas Barnum."

"Phineas!"

Phineas knew that tone in Charity's voice. His wife was not happy with him about something. "Yes Dear?"

"Phineas Taylor, what are you thinking?" She comes out into the yard where Charles and he are enjoying some wine and cigars. She is carrying some papers, and instantly recognize them as his notes.

Evidently, Charles knew that tone in Charity's voice as well. "I think it best I start getting ready for the show!" he says, hopping down from his chair. Charles is thirty years old, barely three feet tall, and can easily drink most people under the table and still be ready for a performance the same night.

Phineas extinguishes his cigar. "What is it, Love?" he asks, though he already knows the answer.

She holds up one of the papers and reads, "A human soul, 'that God has created and Christ died for,' is not to be trifled with. It may tenant the body of a Chinaman, a Turk, an Arab, or a Hottentot—it is still an immortal spirit."

"Yes, yes, it's quite good I think, don't you?" Phineas smiles, standing to turn toward his wife of nearly forty years. "It is how I plan to introduce the new belly dancer. I am billing her as 'The Ghost of Ireland'!"

Without commenting, she shuffles to another paper and reads, "For although the elephant may be taught to plow, or the dog to carry your market-basket by his teeth, you cannot teach them to shave notes, to speculate in gold, or even to vote."

"This part is intended to get a bit of a laugh. See, Victoria has trained Jacko the dog to climb into a voting booth designed by Mr. Nepomuk, which will then somehow transmogrify into a desk…" He chuckles nervously as Charity's expression remains unchanged. "And then… And then Jumbo, our elephant…"

"I know our elephant's name, Phineas!"

"Of course you do, of course you do! Well, then he comes out wearing a stock market hat and an oversized pencil…"

"Oh Phineas." He smiles hopefully as he detects the definite addition of pity to his wife's tone. "I know you mean well, honey, but you have to remember where we are. You've been very public with your beliefs that the Negro should be free and permitted to acquire an education, own land, and even vote, and you know I completely agree with you! But, despite what Jefferson Davis is trying to sell to the public, we all know what this war has been about."

Phineas can only nod, she is of course right on in her assessment.

"I was against you doing this show for that very reason," she continues. "But, I know better than to think I could ask you to pass up the opportunity to be the first show of its kind to be performed a hundred feet above the surface of the Earth! But please… please, think about your audience. They have read newspapers. Newspapers that have almost certainly printed interviews with you in the past and made your stance clear. These people are able to read between the lines."

"I don't know what I would do without you, Charity," he says with complete earnestness. "You are right, of course. Sometimes I just let the showman in me take a bit too much of the lead."

"Of course you do, dear," she says taking his hand in hers. "That showman was one of the reasons I fell in love with you all those years ago. Because he's not just about putting on a great show, but he wants to affect people. I would never ask him to stop thinking that way, to stop wanting to make a change for the good. But I also want to make sure he's around for many years to come."

"Absolutely," Phineas says, embracing his wife. "Absolutely."

"So, what do you say? Shall we focus on making this show the most memorable one of all time and leave the social commentary to the newspapers?"

"Newspapers here!" The young boy's voice calls out from the corner of East Grace and Sixth Streets. "Each and every issue comes with a program to the one event everybody is going to!"

It was April 14, 1868, and a huge crowd gathers throughout the day at Richmond's Monroe Park to experience "The Greatest Show Above the Earth," a sprawling circus-like environment designed by the one and only PT Barnum. The event itself is a spectacle the likes of which has never been seen before.

Admission is free to the public, and anyone on the ground is able to partake in everything one would expect to see at a carnival such as this—games of chance, clowns, lion tamers, tightrope walkers, cotton candy, and foods of all sorts.

In addition, there are rides so spectacular that they befuddle the attendees. Even those who themselves ride The Centrifuge, which rotates so rapidly that it allows people to defy gravity itself as the floor drops out from underneath their feet, struggle to explain the sensations.

And then there is the Nepo-Wheel—an immense, wireframe wheel, 75 feet in diameter. It allows people to easily and smoothly rise into the heavens, overlooking the entire fairgrounds from the comfort of one of three dozen canopy-covered benches attached to the perimeter of the wheel.

All of this is dwarfed by the Bronze Bomber itself, circling one hundred feet above the fairgrounds throughout the day. To the screams and delight of the crowd below, Jules Leotard performs several death-defying shows on his flying trapeze suspended beneath the primary platform.

However, the real show is on the deck of the airship. Admission is restricted to the wealthiest citizens and a few select journalists, and the scene before them is nearly beyond words.

Statues that first appear to be solid granite suddenly dissolve into hundreds, thousands, of tiny metal flakes, only to re-form as a completely different sculpture. The Nike of Samothrace somehow transforms into the Aphrodite of Milos in only a few seconds.

Strongmen lift platforms with camels upon them as snake charmers glide across the floor of the airship on carpets that are supported by dozens of tiny, millipede-like legs.

There isn't any kind of story holding together the display. One isn't needed as everyone finds themselves overwhelmed by the visual ostentatiousness.

And so, it extends throughout the day and into the evening, one unfathomable sequence of events leading into the next on the airship while the crowd below continues enjoying themselves.

The snake charmers come out for a second act and form a ring around a large, coiled basket at the center of the Bronze Bomber's control deck. Playing their murli instruments in unison, they begin to revolve around the basket as if captured by its gravity.

Just as the lid of the basket falls off to the side, the voice of PT Barnum rings out, "I give you, the Ghost of Ireland!"

Moving in time with the music, a woman clad in sheer, green silk scarves gyrates her way out of the snake basket. Her ivory, unblemished skin stands in stark contrast to the shockingly red hair that falls about her shoulders. A veil of more opaque material covers her face. The only other accoutrements to her form are elegant, emerald-colored gauntlets encasing each of her forearms.

At the behest of the ringmaster, the president of the Confederacy, Jefferson Davis, and his Chief Scientist, Johann Nepomuk, step forward. The ring of snake charmers separate before them, providing an unobstructed view of the steamy spirit.

The Ghost extends her arms, encouraging both men to move closer; the sensual motion of her body promises unimaginable delights.

And then, a puff of smoke escapes from the gauntlets, diminishing straight upward as quickly as it appeared. Hardly anyone notices the vapor; they are too distracted as the red-haired beauty steps from the basket and both Davis and Nepomuk fall to their knees.

The spectators begin to laugh. They believe this is all part of the show, the men theatrically overwhelmed by the mysterious beauty before them.

Until she points at the pair and shouts, "Bloody thou art, bloody will be thy end!"

Both men crumple, and the woman sprints across the deck. Several officers are on her heels, nearly close enough to tackle her.

Without hesitation, Jacqueline leaps over the railing of the Bronze Bomber, still easily one hundred feet above the surface of the Earth.

People are screaming, "They're dead!" as the officers look over the banister. The Ghost maintains an unfaltering swan dive position, the scarves covering her body flapping wildly as she falls.

Then, the material becomes nearly rigid, forming wings connecting each of her wrists to her ankles. The scarves immediately catch the air beneath them, and Jacqueline's plummet changes from fall to flight. By the time the officers on the deck of the Bronze Bomber pull their weapons, the assassin is nearly out of view.

Shortly after the airship lands, her victims are pronounced dead. Tiny darts laced with poison are found buried in each of the men's throats. P.T. Barnum is immediately arrested and questioned, but ultimately released. No one employed by the carnival is able to give any significant details about what the Ghost of Ireland actually looks like, other than "beautiful." A massive hunt for the assassin is ordered, but other than the vague trajectory in which she traveled, there is very little to go on.

Witnesses reported she traveled, "in the general direction of Chicago."

About Briant Laslo

Briant Laslo has been defying the odds for a long time. Born with a form of Muscular Dystrophy, his parents were told he would be dead before he was five years old. He will turn 48 later this year. Despite the wheelchair and extremely limited use of his arms, he has driven across the country four separate times with his friend and believes in experiencing as much of this life as possible. Having spent the last 15 years working in the world of Social Media, building relationships between Fortune 1000 companies and their members, Briant has seen the impact a good story can make. An avid reader, he now is beginning his journey in the world of writing, seeking to bring his creations and stories to a larger audience.

La Muerda by Mercury

The dark metal of the branding iron was now orange-red. It sat on top of a rack, hanging over a barrel of fire till it glowed. The only noise inside the shop was the snap and crackle of the fire. Andy rolled up her sleeve to expose her forearm. The smith eyed her. He was a burly and greasy man, with a thick mustache that hid his upper lip and dark, small eyes that she didn't trust.

"It needs to be higher. More skin," he said. "Take your shirt off."

Andy gave him a flat look.

"Unless you changed your mind. That's understandable; La Muerda ain't no place for girls."

Cackling came from another man sitting on top of an oil drum. His gaunt face and skinny figure were a gangly silhouette against the cloudy, glass-pane windows.

"Andy ain't no girl. She a hard-cooked Wrangler from West Tracey," Buck said.

"Wrangler? So, that's why you want the mark." The smith grunted. "Cowgirl or not, La Muerda will eat you up, spit you out, fuck you, then eat you again."

Andy stood. She wore a brown under bust vest, which she unbuttoned. After she slipped the vest off, she did the same with her shirt.

"I didn't pay you to talk. I paid you for the mark," she said. "And Buck, this better work, or you're next on my list."

Buck whistled as she stripped down to her bra, but she knew that he wouldn't take her threats lightly. Her upper torso was decorated with old scars she had gotten on the job. She didn't joke when it came to hunting.

"I hear ya," Buck said. "It'll work. Right, Max?"

The smith, Max, grunted again and picked up the branding iron. Its metal was in the shape of a six-pointed star with a hollow space in the middle that would form a tiny skull.

"You'll get what you're looking for with this. Don't no tourist sport this brand, missy. Only the real dirt and slim of La Muerda."

"Don't call me 'missy,'" Andy said, frowning. "Do you have a name for me?"

"No one big," Max said. "But he works for one of the reina's lieutenants, I hear. Junked-out dealer. They call him Pinocchio."

Andy raised a brow, but didn't question it. She sat back down and rested her arms on the armrests of the wooden chair, fingers gripping the ends. She took in a deep breath and looked at the filtered light of the moon coming through the windows.

"Let's get this over with," she said.

At night, the desert was cold. Andy stepped out of the smith's shop, the breeze raising small bumps along her arms. She buttoned her shirt back up before shrugging on her vest, wincing from her fresh brand. Buck joined her out back. The old lamps outside the shop buzzed as insects flew around them. It was quiet. Not many people went out into the desert at night—not if they wanted to see the morning light. The deserts of La Muerda were vast. The sand dunes stood tall and dark against the horizon; she knew they went on for miles each direction. The only haven on such an inhospitable planet was Necropolis, the City of the Dead.

"From here, you could almost call this place beautiful," Buck said.

Andy looked up at the night sky untainted by the glow of the city, overflowing with the pinpricks of light that were the rest of the galaxy. She rarely missed Earth, but for once, she longed for her home in West Tracey.

"All this over one guy? Why?" Buck asked.

"He's not just one guy. Morgan was—is my partner," Andy said. "He's family, Buck."

"That's right, you two were in the same orphanage back on the homeland." Buck showed his snaggle in a toothy grin. "Was there a time you two weren't glued to each other?"

They had been friends since they met in St. Mary's Orphanage. He had been her first kiss, her best friend, her partner in crime, and her partner in justice.

"I'm going to find him."

"Anne—"

She narrowed brown eyes at him.

"Andy. How long has it been?"

"Six months," she answered.

"Six months? Someone goes missin' for six months, it's more likely they get found dead," Buck said. "Max had a point. La Muerda isn't like other places. It's a planet outside law. You go into Necropolis, you may not come out in one piece. No badge protects you in there."

Andy checked the holster at her waist and pulled the straps tight. She checked her pistols and made sure each was loaded.

"I wasn't planning on it."

Whether Morgan was dead or alive didn't matter. She was going to make the queen of La Muerda pay.

"You runnin' a suicide mission?" Buck asked.

"Not planning on that either. I just want to know where he is."

"And if he's six feet under sand?"

Andy pulled out a switch knife and flipped the blade. "Then I collect a bounty."

Buck cackled and pulled out a carton of Piston cigarettes. He stuck one between his lips, then a small flicker of flame lit up his taut face.

"Well, I can't come with you on this one, cowgirl," he said.

"I wouldn't ask you to, Buck."

He offered her the cigarette, and she took a drag before handing it back.

"If I get stolen off by some evil seductress, promise you'll come save me?" Buck asked.

Andy rolled her eyes. "Wouldn't you rather stay with your seductress?"

"I like my women hard-cooked, Wrangler style."

Andy chortled. "That ain't ever happening."

"A man's gotta try."

It was nearly time. Andy walked around the shop to where the horses waited out front. Hers was a black and white mare with dark hair and a spot on her left rear. A hat was hooked on the horn of the saddle. In the distance was Necropolis, a glowing pollution of red and white lights with tall buildings surrounded by a gate of crooked metal.

Andy grabbed her hat and untied her horse, then took hold of the saddle horn. The brand on her arm pinched and stung with the movement. She paused, then turned to Buck.

"Hey, thanks for getting me in and arranging the mark," she said.

"Don't thank me. All I got you was a death sentence."

She hoisted herself up onto the horse and took the reins.

"I don't die that easily," Andy said.

She turned her mare, then tipped her hat at Buck before starting towards the red glow of the city.

Buck cackled behind her. "Ain't that the damn truth."

Necropolis never slept. Behind its walls was a city of dusty streets walked by prostitutes, drunks, gamblers, criminals, and ex-Wranglers looking for a fight. No one cared if you slept on the streets, beat your lover, or stabbed someone for drugs. It was a city ruled by the dead—by those who had lost everything.

Andy walked the dirt streets, surrounded by the laughter and swearing of patrons exiting from saloons and whore houses. The beat of clubs could be felt through the soles of her boots, and the smell of booze and bodies made the haze that hung in the air seem toxic.

"To hell with you, Rio," a woman screamed as she was tossed from a bar in her garters and corset. Make-up ran down her face. "You don't tell me when I've had enough!"

A big man, who Andy assumed was Rio, poured the contents of the bottle of beer in his hand all over the woman before smashing it on the ground next to her. Andy looked at the woman and saw her eyes were glossy with a look as though she wasn't all there. Most people that Andy passed had that look.

Andy turned away, fists clenched. The only law in Necropolis was the reina's. Her word was absolute. There was nothing Andy could do to help anyone here.

Plus, she had a job to do—find the reina herself and where Morgan had been sold off to. Andy looked over her shoulder before turning down an alley between two tall, brick buildings. The small walkway smelled of piss and whiskey. Trash lined the walls and overflowed from the giant garbage bin that sat at the far end of the alley. Halfway down, two men stood smoking beside a pair of wooden shutters, under a flickering neon sign that read "The Hogwash."

Andy changed her demeanor, pretending the smells didn't disgust her, that she didn't want to cuff them all and beat the hell out of them. She let her face droop slightly and eyes get lost. She pretended she was part of La Muerda.

"Hey, boys," she drawled.

The men looked at her. The one to her right wore a denim vest that looked like his arms had punched its sleeves into a cut-off fringe. A cigarette sat between his lips and a tan Stockman hat perched on his head. A shorter, skinnier man to her left gave her a yellow-toothed grin.

"Hey, girl, lookin' for a little fun?" the skinny man said.

"I'm looking for Pinocchio."

"What's a tight, young thing like yourself want with that piece of junk? I got all you need right here."

Andy gave a smile, rubbing a thumb across her leather holster. "You can tell me what I want to know. Or I can pistol whip it out of you. I'd find the latter more entertaining."

The skinny man stopped smiling and sneered. The man in the cowboy hat held a hand up. He eyed her, then nodded his head to the back of the alley.

The men stared at her as she passed. At the end of the alley was the garbage bin and nothing more. Andy glanced back to make sure the men weren't coming after her, but they'd gone back to their cigarettes and cat-calling, so she kept walking. Trash was piled up high at the sides of the garbage bin, and its top wouldn't close completely. Andy went around the bin and stopped.

When Max said Pinocchio was a junked-out dealer, she didn't think he meant literally. Pinocchio sat on the ground, leaned up against the garbage bin and dressed in rags, his rusty limbs creaking. His flesh peeled away in places, revealing the metal underneath. He would have had a pleasant face if not for his deterioration.

One of Pinocchio's eyes looked a normal blue, sitting in a perfect piece of his face, while the other eye was bare in its socket. Where tissue should have been, their were wires and metal peeking out. Andy recognized his series; the first in a line of robot deputies meant to help keep the peace. They were called Triple Stars. They tried deploying them in West Tracey. It worked until the sheriffs realized the bots couldn't tell a harmless drunk from a licensed Wrangler or actual criminals. Even with their defects, they managed to put fear into petty outlaws, promoting peace and justice. Pinocchio should have been cleaning up Necropolis, not festering in old oil and dealing drugs to its denizens.

Andy kicked the bot's foot. He looked drunk—if that was even possible.

"You Pinocchio?" she asked.

The bot looked up.

"Who's askin'?" He sounded as normal as any man.

"A customer."

Pinocchio looked her up and down, then got to his feet, joints squealing. Andy wondered how he was still together.

"Thirty deno," he said, holding out a dirty, but human-like hand.

"I'm not here looking for drugs," Andy said. "I need information."

"That'll still cost ya thirty."

Andy reached into her back pocket. She flipped through a few bills and tossed them at the bot. "Now talk," she said. "I'm looking for a lieutenant."

Pinocchio shoved the money somewhere out of sight and glanced around nervously. "A lieutenant? You tryin' to be one of the reina's girls?"

Andy shrugged. "Maybe."

"Well, you're bitch enough for it."

She snorted. "I'll take that as a compliment."

"Well, I do happen to have a lead," he said.

"And?"

"And, you didn't hear it from me."

She gave him a hard look and exhaled slowly. "I know the deal. Spill it before I run out of patience."

The bot's eyes shifted again. "Her name's Neera. She's a lieu to the reina. Around this time, she can usually be found at the Queen's Corral. It's east of here. Not too far."

"She?"

"Reina's become bent on making Necropolis a true matriarchy."

"Funny for a woman who's tricked out women across the galaxy," Andy said.

Pinocchio grunted. "Well, that's been changin' too."

Andy considered the bot. She thought the Triple Stars were pretty cool as a kid. They had brought justice—for everyone, even orphans like her and Morgan. Something in her gut tightened seeing the bot as nothing but a discarded piece of junk.

"What's a Triple Star like you doing in Necropolis?" she finally asked.

Pinocchio sat back down in his pile of trash, looking out at the street. "Look around. This is a city of failed dreams."

She didn't even know bots could have dreams. "And what was yours?"

Pinocchio looked up and gave a crooked, oil-stained smile.

"I wanted to become a real boy," he cooed.

The way he said it made her believe that wasn't all there was to it. Andy resisted the urge to shudder. She left him there and stepped out of the alley. She was getting closer. Andy crossed the dirt road, weaving through pedestrian traffic and horseback riders. She had left her mare outside the city, at the ready, should she need it.

Most of Necropolis was a stronghold of bars, clubs, and casinos—a city of endless indulgences. Andy read every neon sign and placard she passed, glancing down alleys for hidden hangouts. She didn't bother asking for directions. She didn't want anyone to remember her face or her destination; she would be a ghost in the city of the dead.

"Step right up, honey," called a feminine voice.

Up ahead, two women wearing bustles, mini shorts, and corsets whistled and called out to prospective patrons. One woman was more rounded and curvy, filling out her corset. The mole drawn on one breast jiggled with every movement. The other woman was more broad of shoulder, taller, and leggy, with a squarer jaw and firm thighs. They both stood under a giant wooden sign that read "Queen's Corral."

"Welcome, sweet thing, come take a gander at our girls," the taller woman said with a deep voice. A couple of men entered, howling and cackling in excitement.

Andy took in a breath and walked towards the two showgirls. The tall one spotted her first as she walked up. Up close, Andy could see she had a mole drawn on her powered face.

"Hey there, darling. Looking for a show?" she asked.

The shorter girl laughed, making her breasts bounce. "Queen's Corral offers top of the line entertainment. Don't be shy, honey. Come right in," she said.

"My pleasure," Andy murmured, stepping past them.

The lobby was dark, lit only by black lights, which gave it an eerie purple-blue pall. Andy paused, but was then ushered by two men wearing nothing but tight shorts and bowties. They led her to a set of double doors. They opened them for her, and Andy stepped inside. The soft pulse of music and dark lobby suddenly became a sensory storm of beats, smells, and lights.

Cages were set up around the stages. Inside, half-naked women twirled and spun around neon poles. Andy spotted one dancer who used a light-up Lyra hoop, spinning and flipping around with ease and grace. Some dancers had flashy pasties on their nipples, and others had discarded them to shake their bare, glittered breasts at the men and women who watched them. Tassels spun and shimmering skirts came off to the beat of the club music. Patrons sat around the stages, drinking and desperately shoving their money through the wire of the cages, trying to earn the attention of the dancers. The floors of the stages were green with deno.

There was only one woman who sat at a stage alone, her "fuck off" aura keeping the other patrons away. Her eyes were fixed on the aerial dancer in the cage, whose naked body twisted and spun with the help of pink aerial silks. The woman watching her had a mohawk of blue and black braids that fell down one side of her head. Her dark skin glowed with the shifting colors and lights of the club.

Even as Andy pulled up a seat and sat next to her, the woman stayed fixated on the dancer. Andy caught curious eyes peeking over at her, but no one had stopped her from sitting. Andy swallowed and stared at her. The woman picked up a glass of dark liquor and took a drink.

"Lieutenant Neera?" Andy shouted over the music.

Neera set her glass back down. One side of her nose had two silver hoops. She had barbells in her eyebrows, and a stud in her lip. Neera still paid no attention. She reached for her glass again, but Andy took it instead. She brought it to her mouth, nose burning with the smell of hard bourbon. She drank every last bit and set the glass back down. Neera was staring at her now, and not with a friendly look.

"Who the hell are you?" Neera asked. Her eyes were hazel, with hints of green and murderous intent.

"Someone looking for the reina," Andy said, body tense.

Neera laughed. "We don't need any more hoes," she said. "Now get out of my sight."

Andy looked at the bar and raised her hand to signal the bartender for another round. "I'm not here to turn the corner," Andy said.

Neera looked at her for a long moment. A man in tight shorts and a bowtie brought over two glasses of bourbon. Neera took hers. Andy set a few denos on the stage while Neera took a drink.

"What, you another ex-con trying to make your way up the ladder?"

Andy pushed her sleeve up to show the brand on her left arm. She tried not to wince as the fabric rubbed against the burn.

"Still looks fresh," Neera said.

"Well, I got to start somewhere."

The lieutenant grunted. "You got thirty seconds."

Andy dropped her sleeve, heart racing. "I need to see the reina."

"Why?" When Andy didn't answer, Neera laughed. "You think we just let any piece of tail show up and demand the presence of our queen? I can take one look at you and tell you ain't looking for no position in this trash hole planet." She took a long, dismissive pull from her bourbon.

But Andy was so close to finding Morgan, she couldn't leave now.

"Hey," the lieutenant said. "That was your cue to fuck off."

"I have information the reina would like to hear," she said.

"Don't we all?" Neera went back to drinking her bourbon.

"It's about the attack on her trade post six months ago."

The slave trading post she and Morgan staked out was a popular spot for trading people illegally. She had planned to put a dent in the trafficking business, but nothing went as planned. She'd been shot, and Morgan was taken. Neera raised a brow. "You know something about that?"

Andy swallowed and nodded. It was all she had to offer.

"I heard it was some balls-out cowgirl trying to take down the whole operation," Neera said. "You telling me you know who's behind it?"

Andy nodded again.

Neera looked her over before setting her drink down. Andy didn't blink.

"Well," Neera said. "The reina did give orders to send anyone who knew something about it to her. For your own sake, you better not be lying."

The lieutenant reached into the pocket of her jeans, then slid a business card over.

Andy took the grimy card with its weathered lettering. "Sweet Water Saloon?"

"The one and only. Go to the bar and ask for water, extra sweet," Neera said, turning back to the dancer.

Andy pocketed the card and tipped her hat before picking up her glass of bourbon and drinking it in one shot. It burned on the way down. She wiped her mouth, gave some more deno, and left the club to go see the reina of La

Muerda and avenge the only friend she'd had.

"What'll it be, missy?" the bartender asked. His bushy mustache curled up on the ends.

"I'll take a water. Extra sweet," Andy said.

Sweet Water Saloon looked like it had come straight out of the back end of West Tracey with its hardwood floors, earth tone wallpaper, and round tables. The bar took up one side of the room, and above it was the second floor. Only one set of stairs led up. It had white banisters that matched the stools she sat on. A piano sat in one corner of the room where a man played an upbeat tune. The people at the tables played poker with fat cigars hanging out of their mouths. They didn't need to say it. Andy felt it. They were the reina's men.

"Coming right up," the bartender said, giving her a sideways glance.

He walked down the bar and disappeared around a corner.

Everyone in the bar went about their business, but they weren't drunks or hookers. Their eyes were clear, and their ears just as sharp. Though no one looked at her, she could feel their attention. There was no backing out now.

The bartender came back, a mug and rag in his hand. "Your water is ready," He cleaned the mug and set it down on the countertop. "Upstairs," he murmured, nodding towards the right.

"Thanks." Andy stood.

"Hey," he said. "No guns."

Andy licked her lips, then drew her pistols and placed them on the bar. She still had a knife in her boot. The bartender gave her a once over and took the pistols, storing them below the bar top. Andy didn't feel safe going to meet the reina unarmed, but it was the only way she'd get her audience.

She walked past the bars and tables, the chuckles and taunts of men playing poker accompanying the music. Andy could feel their gazes as she turned to walk up the stairs. She didn't look back.

Upstairs were several rooms. All the doors were closed, so she took the hall down the middle. More doors, all closed except for one. As Andy walked the hall, the music grew fainter. She got to the door and pushed it completely open, slowly revealing a lavish room. The floors were carpeted in crimson that matched the drapes and loveseats. The walls were a light, lacquered wood, and a small chandelier hung from above. The only other color was the matching ivory vanity, desk, and chairs. In the middle of the room were three loveseats that sat at the sides and head of a small, square coffee table. Behind the sofas was a queen-sized bed, draped with crimson curtains on an ivory canopy.

Andy swallowed and took a seat on the sofa facing the door. The reina was powerful in the worst ways, and no one could stop her since she operated on La Muerda, a planet outside regular law. The reina was queen, and if she didn't want to give up information, she didn't have to. But this wasn't going to be a negotiation. Andy would get her answers.

Heels clicked on the wooden floorboards outside. Andy felt her stomach tighten. She clenched her fist and watched as a woman filled up the doorway. She was tall and all leg. Black, lace stockings stopped at ruffled garters around her thighs. A sheer, ruffled trim petticoat brushed the tops of her thighs and gave way to a dangerously short skirt. Its sides puffed out into more sheer layers that topped the petticoat and the bustle that trailed behind her. Her black and violet skirt matched her corset. Black silk gloves, a lace hat, and a matching choker and broach completed her outfit.

The reina shut the door behind her, then walked to the loveseats and stopped. She was taller than expected, beautiful, and certainly not the vile hag Andy thought she would be.

With a deep voice, the reina asked, "Andy?"

Andy stood. The woman's plush lips were painted red, her eyeliner and shadow applied perfectly. Her unblemished face was outlined by auburn curls that fell to her shoulders. Andy squinted. She recognized her honey-colored eyes and thick lashes.

"Morgan?"

The reina smiled. "Anne-Denise Rummel, don't you recognize me?"

Andy stared at her childhood friend, the man she hunted with for years. She let her jaw drop.

"I know. I look amazing, right?" Morgan chuckled, a sound she thought she'd never hear again.

"I see you've changed your hair…." Andy felt almost breathless. Was she dreaming?

"This thing?" he said.

Morgan reached up and took off the lace hat. His nails were painted red. He tossed the hat to the side and took off his curls to reveal the long, jet black hair Andy had known him for. He set the wig on the table and took his hair out of its bun, mussing it a bit. It had grown since she'd last seen him, falling around his shoulders like dark silk.

"How are you still alive?" Andy asked.

She stepped around the table to get a better look at him, afraid to blink and have him disappear. Behind all the make-up, she could finally see her friend.

"I thought you were sold off to some mid-galactic trash-coon or… Dead."

"I *was* sold," he said. "After the mission went wrong, they took me and the girls still alive up to another post. There, they traded most of them out. They tried to do the same to me but… Let's just say my new 'masters' could never keep me long. You know I don't go down without a bit of a fight."

In the past, Andy had nicknamed him the Gentle Firecracker; easy to handle, right up until it blew your hand off.

"So, you got away?" she asked.

"Sort of. After a while, the former reina had heard of me and my antics. She thought it was bad for business for her clients to go through such hassle. She sent for me, and I was sold into her service."

"'Former'? You killed the reina?"

He shook his head. "It's almost impossible to get close enough to kill the reina."

"I got to you easily enough."

Morgan smiled. "That's because I told my lieutenants to send anybody with information about the attack to me. I knew you'd come eventually."

Andy took a deep breath. "So, how did you become…"

"Queen of 'Capital Crime'?" he asked.

Morgan walked to the loveseat at the side of the table and sat down. He was tall, heels or not. Andy took a seat at his side.

"After I was sold into the reina's service, I was made to work for her," he said.

"What kind of work?"

He looked at her, brown eyes distant for a moment. "The kind of work you wouldn't approve of." Morgan tucked an arm around her in a hug. "You have no idea how much I've missed you, Andy," he said, kissing the side of her head.

She hugged him back and pulled away, eyes stinging slightly. She didn't know if she wanted to hit him or cry. "It's been six months, Morgan. And you've been alive this whole time."

His smile faded. "I know... I just—"

"Had a criminal empire to run?"

He opened his mouth, then closed, then tried again. "La Muerda isn't a good place. I know that. But the last reina saw something in me. I fought my way up, gained respect. I survived here on my own. No Andy to save me this time."

She blinked. "What is that supposed to mean?"

"Andy, we both know you were the tougher kid. It was your dream to be a Wrangler; to stop what happened to our parents from happening to any other child," he said. "It was noble. But I was just a sidekick."

"You aren't a sidekick, Morgan. You're family."

He smiled. "Thank you, but Necropolis changed me," he said. "And I'm changing Necropolis."

She frowned. "I was out there. Doesn't look too changed to me."

"It's not easy, but slave trade is down, and I keep prostitution on a tight leash."

"What about gambling and drugs?"

Morgan shrugged. "You can find that on any other planet. Necropolis is a city of vice. But it can be maintained and controlled."

Andy thought about Pinocchio, living in filth and dealing drugs. She shook her head. "This place cannot be controlled," she said.

"Not everything is black and white. Good and evil."

What could she say to that? In the six months they were apart, he built himself a throne on a city of sin that would break most people upon entering it.

"Anne." Morgan swept a hand under her chin and lifted gently. "I'm sorry I didn't contact you. I didn't... know how."

"A phone call, a letter?"

"No, I mean I didn't know how to tell you," he said. "I didn't know how to face you."

A warm tear slid down her cheek, and he swept it away with his thumb.

"I missed you, Andy. Not a day went by that I didn't think about you and what happened," he said. "Last I saw you, you were shot and bleeding out. But I know you don't go down that easily. I believed you would come for me, and I was right."

He cradled her face in his hand, then leaned in and pressed his mouth to hers in a soft kiss. Andy closed her eyes and set a hand on top of his smooth, shaved thigh.

"You taste like cherries," Andy whispered, licking her lips.

Morgan chuckled, a noise that rumbled through his chest. His slender fingers found the small of Andy's back as he turned her body to face his. He hiked one of her legs against the side of his hip and wedged himself between her legs, moving in to kiss her again. A tongue slid from his mouth and into hers. His black hair fell around their faces and tickled her neck.

"Wait," she said, placing a hand on his lace trimmed top. His lipstick was smeared over his mouth, and Andy was sure her lips matched.

"We said we wouldn't," she said.

"Yeah, when we were working together," Morgan said. "I got it. Bad for business."

"We're still partners," she said.

Andy watched as Morgan's eyes fell down the line of her neck and vest.

"We haven't worked together in six months," he said. "I think we can make an exception."

She rolled her eyes. Andy looked at the lace brushing the tops of his thighs, then slid a hand up his soft skin and under his skirt. She found the bulge hidden by the puffiness of the petticoat and rubbed her fingers over him.

Morgan tilted his head back and moaned.

"You do look cute in a skirt," she said.

"I can keep it on if you want."

Andy smiled.

"But only if you keep on your hat," he said.

Andy gazed into his dark eyes, caressed the familiar line of his jaw. Without him, his gentleness, and his voice of reason, she felt her self control slipping. Being a Wrangler had made Andy rougher, more ruthless, and quick to anger. She was changing, too. She wanted for just a moment to pretend everything was as it used to be. Andy gave him a small smile, tracing her fingertips over his collarbone, a look in her eyes he was familiar with.

"You've got a deal," she said.

From the silk sheets of the Reina's bed, Andy watched Morgan at the ivory vanity desk, pouring hot water into teacups. He was dressed in only a silver satin robe. He reached into a drawer and produced two bags of tea, opened them, and steeped them in the two cups. Andy watched, sheets pulled up to cover her bare chest. The sweat beaded on her forehead was drying. Morgan lifted up a ceramic jar of sugar, looking at her. Andy nodded and he smiled, grabbing a teaspoon.

"So," Morgan said. "I never asked you how you found your way to me. It couldn't have been easy."

Andy turned to flash the healing, six-pointed star brand on her upper arm. Morgan winced. Andy had discovered he had a similar burn on his lower back.

"It was the mark, a cross between bravery and stupidity, and not taking no for an answer," Andy said, shrugging.

Morgan took out the tea bags, threw them in a dust bin, and carried the two cups of tea to the small coffee table between the couches.

"You make it sound easy, but getting that mark is near impossible without the right connections and cash," Morgan said.

Andy moved to the edge of the bed and crawled out, picking up her pants and shirt. She shrugged them both back on as Morgan sat down. Her short hair was a mess. She ran her fingers through it a few times and went to the couch to sit down beside her friend.

"You remember Buck?" Andy said. "He had a guy. And yes, it cost a fucking fortune."

Morgan chuckled. "Would it help if I said I'd reimburse you?"

Andy huffed and chuckled, picking up a cup of warm tea and taking a drink.

Morgan's smile faded and he gave her worried eyes.

"You shouldn't have taken the mark, Andy. It's semi-permanent and the sort of thing that follows you. No law abiding citizen is going to hire someone branded as an outlaw of La Muerda. And what if the sheriff finds out? You'll have a bounty on your own head."

"Let me worry about that," she said.

"You're lucky you even got the correct branding. Some of the junkies out here will try to sell you anything for a bit of deno."

"Buck took me to a smith friend of his. He knew what he was doing."

"I remember Buck was always a bit crazy," Morgan said.

"Still is," Andy said, chuckling. The warmth of the tea felt good in the pit of her stomach. They drank in silence. When Andy had finished half of her tea, she set the cup down.

"So… What now?" she asked.

Morgan lifted a well-groomed eyebrow.

"Don't look at me like that. I waited almost a year. Ran around half the galaxy chasing leads and trying to find you, Morgan."

Her former partner sighed and drank from his teacup.

"I know, and I'm grateful, but—"

"I thought you were dead," she said. "Tortured and murdered, laying out in some godforsaken desert."

Morgan frowned and set his cup down. He looked at her.

"I don't want to leave La Muerda," he said.

Andy looked at him as if he had lost all reason.

"Andy, I'm the reina."

"And what the fuck does that even mean? You're Morgan Terrifield, not some damn outlaw." Andy shook her head. "Is this about being a Wrangler? At one time, it wasn't just *my* dream, it was yours, too."

"This isn't about some dream I had of shooting guns and playing cowboy as a kid. After the reina took me in, I changed—no, I became something more," Morgan said. "I used to be weak. I was lost, and I know that you could feel it, too. I didn't belong out there chasing bandits and criminals. I was just following you, the woman that could never love me back in the way I wanted."

Andy opened her mouth, then closed it again.

"You don't have to come back as my partner, Morgan, just... Come back at least."

Morgan looked down at his manicured hands.

"Within the last six months, I've come to know the girls here as family." He smiled slightly. "It's like how we were back at the orphanage. Living the only way we could, in the only place we could call home."

"Necropolis isn't your home."

Morgan pursed his lips. "I'm building something here. A new family, a new home. An empire."

"And how many corpses will you step over to get there? How many women must be beaten, how many men killed, and how many androids must be trashed for you to be satisfied?"

Andy clenched her fists, tight enough to feel her nails dig into her palms. Morgan looked at her, his honey eyes unreadable.

"As many as it takes," he said.

Andy felt light headed. She stood up, jaw tight.

"I'm a Wrangler, Morgan, employed under the Alliance to follow galactic imperial law, chosen to uphold the rights of all living creatures and bring under justice those who have stepped outside lawful boundaries." Andy swayed, her body heavy. "If I leave this planet without you... If you stay here as reina then... Then...." Her voice sounded more distant.

"Then that makes us enemies," Morgan finished. He shook his head. "I figured you'd say as much."

Andy stumbled and caught herself on the arm of the couch, vision dark around the edges. She glanced at her cup of tea.

"Son… of a *bitch*."

"Relax. It'll just make you sleep. You've earned it," Morgan said.

His voice was accompanied by ringing. Andy slumped into the couch, and Morgan went to kneel in front of her, taking her hand in his.

"Come back with me… Come back to West Tracey… Earth," Andy mumbled, eyelids as heavy as rocks.

"I'm sorry, Anne, but I can't leave just yet. I've still got things I need to figure out. Please, when you wake, don't try looking for me again."

Darkness swept over her.

"Don't come back, Andy."

Water splashed her face, the cold liquid jolting her out of her sleep. Andy gasped, eyes blinking open and heart racing. The sun was almost blinding, and the heat made her clothes stick to her skin. She looked up, making out the figure of a man.

"Morgan…?"

"Name's Javier, darlin'," the man said in a thick accent.

Andy gave him a confused look, then felt the wet tongue of a dog on her face. She scrunched her nose and turned her face away from the collie that had decided to greet her. She sat up, head pulsing slightly as she took in the house, a chicken coop, and a small patch of field with a corral filled with a few pigs and horses.

"How did I…?"

"Some horsebacks dropped ya off here. Said give'er a horse and handed me some deno," the man said. He reached up and took the hat off his head, handing it to her. "This be yers."

Andy glowered and dusted her hat off before slowly getting to her feet.

The man grunted and shrugged, then handed her a small canteen of water.

"Horse is right over there. I want no trouble, just be on yer way."

Andy brushed her pants off and spotted the tan horse waiting off to the side. In the distance, over the wavering horizon of heat, tall metallic buildings of Necropolis loomed.

"Did you see who dropped me off here?"

The man nodded. "Some big feller. Scaly lizard. One of dem crocodile men," he said. "Oh, and left ya this."

The man handed her a folded note. Andy took it and opened it up. The paper had an imprint of red lipstick in the form of lips she recognized. There was one thing written on it. *"It's your choice."*

Andy folded the note back up and put it in her pocket. She checked her hip for her holster and guns. Her clothes were in place, and her badge and deno untouched. She went to the horse waiting by the poorly built fence and mounted it. She sweated under the heat of the sun. The shimmering city in the distance looked like a faraway dream—or nightmare. She had a choice and a job to do. Andy grimaced and coughed, throat dry and aching. She fixed the hat on her head, securing it, then turned to look down at the rancher.

"How far..." She glanced at the city, then back to the man. "How far to the nearest airship corral?"

The man scratched his brow, then pointed east. Andy tipped her hat and clicked her heels against the flank of the horse. The man nodded and watched as she set off. She followed his directions. East and into the desert, with the city of sin shimmering behind her.

About Mercury

Mercury (Zoë Woodard) is a recent graduate from California State University Long Beach and an aspiring writer with a minor in Creative Writing. They write anything from Horror, Fantasy, and Science Fiction and they run a Youtube Channel (Mercurythescribe), producing audio stories.

Divine by E. A. Catania

A cool kiss of steel pressed lightly against Captain Jonathan Shaffer's neck. Dropping his pistol, he raised his hands while his mouth thinned into a grim line. Of course the first time he went out to sea, they would be boarded by sky pirates. The man behind him kicked the gun away before prodding him with a hard metal elbow and growling, "Easy does it." Keeping his arms up, Jonathan followed the rest of his crew as they, too, were herded from different parts of the ship and onto the main deck.

Catching the eye of his right-hand lady, he offered Dianna a humorless smile. "I should've gone for the Navy. I could be piloting an airship right now instead of bobbing around in the open on the waves."

From somewhere down the line, a disgustingly cheerful voice sang out, "Look lively! Captain Warren on deck!"

Jonathan glanced around and saw no one; it wasn't until a shadow fell over him that he looked up to the airship hovering above them. A tall man with jet-black hair strolled casually to the ropes, hopping up on the rail of his ship before swinging himself down in a display of flair and pomp. He landed squarely in front of Jonathan, released the rope, and grinned. Much to Jonathan's annoyance, Captain Warren was in perfect condition, from his worn yet well cared for boots, his billowing white shirt (half open, of course), colorful scarves around his hips, and a gaudy assortment of earrings and necklaces which shone and jingled on various parts of his person.

"Hello, chap!" Warren said. His voice was carefree and low, the sort of deep voice one would imagine from a fictional villain. "I like what you did at the end." He leaned in and slapped a hand down on Jonathan's shoulder, next speaking in a stage whisper. "But it probably would've been best to just *keep running.*" The pirate released him and leaned back with a shrug. "We would've caught you anyway, but at least you wouldn't have lost all your cannon power. I could've used that."

Squaring his shoulders, Jonathan replied crisply, "When the Queen hears about *pirates* looting her ships—"

The tall man rolled his eyes, twisting away with a dramatized sigh of annoyance before he swung back around and punched Jonathan square in the face. Pain exploded across his left cheek and he stumbled back into Dianna, knocking into Rebecca, who barely budged. Rebecca set them both upright and crossed her arms, glaring a warning to Captain Warren.

"While I wouldn't ordinarily stop you from calling us *pirates*—" Captain Warren dragged the words out slowly, as though he were speaking to a child, and reached into his shirt for a rolled piece of paper. "—*this* time we're here on authority. So, I believe that makes us *privateers.*" He held the paper out and smiled pleasantly. "Cheers, mate."

Jonathan ignored the paper Warren was holding and wiped his face with the back of his hand, wincing. He didn't need a mirror to know one of Captain Warren's rings had left a long gash slashed across his cheek. "Is that so?"

"What? You don't want to see?" The other captain asked, waving the paper in front of him like a treat before a dog.

Dianna reached across Jonathan and snatched the scroll. *"I'll* read it."

"Ah. Women." Warren sneered in her direction as she broke the royal seal. "Do you even have the *education* to read?" A few of his crew snickered.

Dianna glared daggers at the man before dropping her gaze back to the parchment. She frowned. "This isn't sanctioned by the Queen."

"No, darling," a voice drawled. "It was sanctioned by *me.*"

Dianna paled and whipped her head around. A tall man was strolling toward them, adjusting his shiny, golden cuffs. His light brown hair was tied low with a silk ribbon, and his clothes were beautifully tailored to his form; the entire ensemble was probably worth more than Jonathan's yearly salary. The man had disembarked from the pirate ship unnoticed, and he approached with a lazy smile.

"I looked *everywhere* for you the night you ran away." The man placed a well-manicured hand on his chest as if wounded. "You can't *imagine* how betrayed I felt when I found out you'd run off with that Baron fellow. To think, he actually gave a legitimate recommendation—and so quickly, too!" He stopped directly in front of Dianna. "I'd nearly figured out the best way to poison you before you deserted me. Shame. I was quite interested in learning herbology." He paused. "But, 'death at sea' has a rather nice ring to it, don't you think?"

Jonathan stiffened the more the man spoke, realizing about halfway through his commentary that he was Dianna's soon-to-be ex-husband. From what Dianna had told him, Richard Maddox deserved to be shot on the spot. Dianna, keeping her temper much better than Jonathan, simply lifted up the letter of marque and ripped it in two.

Richard chuckled, unperturbed. To Warren, he remarked, "I *did* tell you she'd do that, didn't I, Raph?" Looking back at his wife and smiling smugly, he divulged, "*That* was a copy, my dear. You really should learn to control your temper."

Jonathan did his best to hide his smirk when Dianna placed one half of the document on top of the other and, shrugging, ripped it once again. "If it's a copy, then you won't be needing this one."

The smirk fell slightly from Richard's face. "Now you're just being contrary."

Dianna smiled, tearing the scroll into smaller and smaller pieces before letting them fall from her fingers and flutter away in the breeze. "There's nothing of value on this ship to take. We haven't picked anything up yet." She fixed her gaze on the pirate captain. "So what are you here for?"

Sniffing in disdain, Richard said, "If you'd bothered to *read* the letter—"

"Why bother? I'm sure it's all a bunch of drivel written in a grandiose and convoluted manner, affecting a sort of false bravado and an insufferable ability to be both ignorant *and* pompous."

Jonathan snorted and promptly covered his mouth.

"That's enough," Captain Warren cut in, annoyed. Making his way down the line of Jonathan's crew, he spoke so all could hear. "We *were* going to kill all of you. All except *you,* anyway." He looked Dianna over in disdain. His eyes shone unnaturally in the bright sunlight. *"But!"* He cheerfully continued, turning and resuming his stroll. "If you decide to become part of my crew, I can promise your safety and livelihood. I'll even pay you, if we find something worth splitting, and while it won't be *easy* being the newest of my crew, it'll certainly be better than sinking into Davey Jones' Locker." He stopped once again before Jonathan, and the two stared each other down for a brief moment. "Except you. We don't need you."

Before anyone could react, Warren pulled out his pistol and shot Jonathan at point-blank range. Jonathan's eyes widened in shock. He looked down, barely registering pain as blood blossomed across his chest, before his body crumpled next to a horrified Dianna.

"So!" The tall man put his gun back into its holster as two of his men threw Jonathan's lifeless body overboard. "Who would prefer to stay alive?"

Dianna sat on a crate across from Richard, her face set to a stony mask. "I do apologize for that." Her husband lounged with a foot crossed over his knee in a small, windowless room. "It wasn't my plan to kill him, but, you know, *pirates.*"

Dianna sat on a crate across from the man she once thought loved her, her face in a stony mask. "I thought they were privateers."

"Same difference, really." He leaned back, looking very much like a contented cat. His eyes, dark brown and hooded, gazed at her with what less observant people might mistake for affection. Dianna knew it to be something else entirely. *"I thought it'd be best to throw them all over."*

After Jonathan had been shot, Dianna quickly ordered the rest of her crew to accept Captain Warren's offer. She didn't want to be the reason for any more deaths. They were shoved, jostled, and yanked onto the airship and immediately dispersed to do the most menial tasks. All except Dianna, who was escorted roughly into this room. Richard watched her in the dim lantern light for a few long moments, his face unreadable, before he leaned forward and rested his elbows on his knees.

"Where is your ring?"

Dianna's eyes narrowed into a withering glower. "I left it with you." She'd dropped both the engagement ring and wedding band on their shared bureau, along with a note clearly stating her intentions to divorce him as soon as possible.

His smile was faint and unamused. "Don't be coy. The one your mother gave you."

She stared at him warily. "Why?"

"Because I found *this*." He answered, pulling a gold chain from his pocket. A pendant of brilliant emerald wrapped in golden leaves swung at the end. Dianna reached for it, but Richard pulled it away. "Ah-ah," he chuckled, shaking his head. "I didn't bring it to give to you. I came to get your ring." He held the pendant to the lantern light, turning it this way and that so the stone sent shattered shards of green light all over the room. "The two are a pair. They belong together."

"A pair?" Dianna asked, incredulous. "You came all the way out here so you could have matching jewelry?"

He smiled. "Yes."

"How did you even get that?" she snapped. It had been buried deep in a chest her mother had left her. A locked chest. A locked chest that didn't have a visible way to unlock it.

"It's *amazing* what new wonders are being created." His voice intoned idle dismissal.

Captain Warren slammed the door open, letting in bright light as he entered. When the latch clicked shut behind him, the room was once again in doused in dim, flickering light. Eyes shifting between the seated pair, the captain's gaze finally fell on the pendant in Richard's hands. "Well?"

"She has it, like I said she would."

Captain Warren crouched down in front of Dianna. "Give me the ring and *maybe* I won't kill you."

Dianna snorted. If they had needed only the ring, they could've killed her, and her crew, upon catching them. "Not likely. I bet you need me alive."

"Clever." He smirked, though the expression was cool and calculating. Glancing over his shoulder to Richard, he said, "No wonder you couldn't do anything with her. A popinjay such as yourself could never call a woman like this to heel."

Bristling, she snapped, "I think your definition of marriage is a little outdated, *Raph*. Being called to heel is for a dog like you."

His eyes slid back to her, the dual colors bright even in the dark room, and he chuckled. Returning to his full height, the pirate captain put his hands on his hips and mused, "What shall we do with you?" He rubbed his chin thoughtfully. "I could threaten to throw a member of your crew overboard for every hour you deny us."

"For a ring." Dianna replied, her eyes flat hazel. "For a matching set of jewelry. You're both mad."

"Oh *no*." A slow grin spread across Captain Warren's face. "You don't know the value of your ring. Shall we show her, Richard?"

Richard straightened and held up the pendant. He fiddled for a second before a blaze of greenish light projected a broken map onto the wall. Dianna slowly stood, her eyes wide. That was technology more advanced than anything she'd ever seen. She felt as though she could touch each of the islands despite knowing they were nothing but light. Richard wasn't smart enough to figure it out on his own. *She* hadn't even realized the pendant held a secret like that.

"How did you know to do that?"

He shrugged. "I was tinkering with it. It's not important." He tapped to the bottom of the pendant. "The ring goes here."

Dianna narrowed her eyes before hesitantly pulling out her ring, which hung on a simple leather thong around her neck. The ring was made up of delicate golden strands wrapping together like vines around an identical green stone. Slipping the thin band off, she held out her hand for the necklace.

"I don't think so—" Richard started, only to be interrupted by the captain.

"Just give it to her. What is she going to do? Run away with it?" Warren raised one eyebrow at Dianna's husband. With a reluctant shrug, he turned off the map made of eerie green light and handed the pendant over.

The stones were two halves of a whole, although the cut wasn't clean. It was as if someone had hastily chopped the original gem in half before creating the pendant and ring around them. Carefully placing the two gems together, broken end to broken end, she heard a soft click.

Richard leaned forward eagerly. "Turn it on!"

Dianna turned the pendant over in her hands and found an impossibly tiny clockwork mechanism, which she gently turned. The map beamed back on, showcasing a complete map. Islands and borders of larger continents sprang into being in the airless room. In the middle of the ocean there was a small, glowing star.

Richard leaped to his feet, his eyes narrowed. "But there's nothing *there*, we checked!" He growled in aggravation and ran a hand through his hair, disheveling the brown locks in a way Dianna *used* to think was handsome. Now he just looked like a spoiled child.

Captain Warren leaned forward, not nearly as frustrated as the other, and studied the map intently. "We're missing something, then." His eyes flicked up to Dianna, "Well? What do you see? It *is* supposed to be from your mother."

"I thought you didn't like women," she sniped. She hadn't actually been studying the map. Something else had happened when the hologram kicked on, singing in her mind like a whale song heard across great distances. She didn't look at the map now, meeting the pirate captain's stare with her own unflinching one.

His smile was thin. "I fully expect you to lie, though I wouldn't suggest it." He tapped his finger just under his bright green eye. "I'll know."

The luminous color immediately made sense. "That's not your natural eye," she almost accused, both annoyed and impressed in spite of herself. Not many people could wield an implant like that. Not many people could *afford* it.

Captain Warren grinned. "Good girl."

Reluctantly turning to the map, Dianna let her eyes travel over all the islands and continents represented there. Nothing seemed particularly interesting or stood out aside from the fact it was holographic.

After a few long moments of silence, Richard sighed loudly. "Would you just get *on* with it?"

Dianna rolled her eyes. "If you're *bored* you can always go strut about on deck and show off your new jacket."

He looked down at the tailcoat he was wearing and pleasantly remarked, "You noticed? I had to have something *new* to find treasure."

She snorted in disdain. When her gaze returned to the map, she caught sight of something she'd been missing. Standing a bit taller, Dianna squinted at the upper-left corner. It was a date. Her eyes widened and she re-checked a few of the islands before letting out a short laugh. "No wonder you couldn't find it. This map was made in 1276."

"Was it?" Richard was fixing his cuffs again.

Ignoring his lackluster reply, Dianna turned to Captain Warren and pointed at an island. "What island is this?"

He squinted at it, muttering under his breath before coming back with, "Those are the Caraway Isles."

Dianna smirked. "No, they aren't. Look again."

Warren narrowed his eyes at her before staring hard at the islands again. Shaking his head, he straightened. "Those *are* the Caraway Isles. This one is Parrot Bay and *that* one is Nyra." He was visibly annoyed. "Get to the point."

Shaking her head, she helpfully provided, "It's 1808. 1276 was *years* before the first Big Shift." Warren's eyes widened in sudden understanding. "You're going in the wrong direction." Dianna turned the projecting gems upside down and the map corrected itself. "*This* is the correct bearing. True North, prior to 1354. That makes this coastline Bulvaria and *this* large island New Greenland. Whatever you're looking for is between Cicera, Roma, and Ethermane."

She didn't get time to gloat. The map shimmered, breaking up into hundreds of lines and numbers before the pendant unexpectedly shattered in Dianna's hand and threw them into darkness.

Alone in a small room, Dianna chewed on her thumb and thought about the map. Why would her mother put a map into a pendant, and how had she done it? With a frustrated sigh, she sat heavily on a line of crates masquerading as a place to sleep and slouched back against the wall. It didn't make sense. None of it did. Her mother had been a simple woman. Any money or status had come from Dianna's father, hadn't it?

She touched the little pouch hanging around her neck. It held the ring and what was left of the pendant. Now that they had a heading, both items were useless to the captain and her husband. They weren't useless to Dianna, though. The vaguely familiar singing in her head had put itself on repeat, but she couldn't place it with any known memory. She ran a hand through her thick, black hair before ruffling it in frustration, and let her head fall back against the wall.

There was a swift rap on her door.

"Come in."

The door was pushed open to admit Benjamin and Rebecca. The steel-barreled chest attached to the former swallowed up a significant amount of room, which left Rebecca to duck under his arm and plop herself down on the crates. With a cheery smile, Ben offered Dianna a bowl of soup.

"Thanks." She smiled, taking the dish and setting it on her lap. "I'm guessing you didn't just come to feed me, though."

"Well, that was part of it." The large man spoke quietly, which was quite a feat for someone who had a metal voice box. Leaning against the wall with his arms crossed, one bulging with muscle and the other with an alarming mix of metals and weapons, he continued. "But Sebastian wanted to know if you had a plan."

Dianna picked up a piece of hardtack and knocked it against the edge of the bowl. It was rock solid. "Not as of yet." She'd spent most of her time trying to figure out the singing in her head and the rest of it coming up with ways to shove Richard off the airship.

"There's been word that we're going toward a treasure," Rebecca offered. She crossed her ankles and stretched her legs out, leaning back on her palms. "It's apparently supposed to be quite a heist."

Dianna snorted. "Is that right?" She dipped the hard biscuit into the bowl of watery soup, stirring it absently. When she finally took a bite, she was impressed with what Ben had placed before her. "Remind me to get you a spice belt you can wear all the time."

"No need." Ben's smile turned mischievous as he rapped on his metal chest. "I can carry whatever I need in here." Unbuttoning the shirt he kept modestly high, he revealed the iron barrel and a shoulder cleverly built into the fleshy parts of himself. Pressing on a panel Dianna had forgotten was there, the man next opened up his chest itself to reveal not just wires, tubes, and his beating human heart, but an arsenal loaded with pistols, daggers, and other small weapons. "Thought I ought to stock up." He winked, closing the hatch. "For whenever the captain needs us."

Realizing they were both looking at her, Dianna blanched. She hadn't wanted to be a captain, but apparently the universe had other plans. She sighed, wrinkled her nose, and took another bite of food.

"Well, what do you think?" Rebecca demanded. "Sebastian is chomping at the bit wanting to take these guys down for killing Jonathan."

Dianna shook her head. "Not here, not on their turf. They'd toss us all over before we could blink." She filled them in on what Captain Warren and her husband were planning. Brushing aside any questions about the treasure being rightfully hers, she plunged onward to say bluntly, "Richard isn't smart. He'll stroll just about anywhere without a second thought. Warren is craftier. We'll have to convince him we're no threat to keep him from getting suspicious." She looked between the two when they didn't respond and clarified. "You need to make him think you want to remain his crewmen. For good."

"What?" Rebecca spat in disdain as she narrowed her eyes. "Do you realize he's been having Maisy and me doing all their *laundry*? They may not be on sea, but these fleabags are still somehow crusted over with—" She stopped, shuddered, and rubbed her arms in a rare moment of uncertainty. "I won't pretend I want to be here, I refuse."

There was a brief moment of silence before Dianna quietly said, "That's an order, Miss Louis." She met Rebecca's stubborn gaze with her own and held it until the other looked away. "It won't be for long. It'll only take a few days as a crow flies to get to where we're going, and," she waved her arm in an encompassing gesture with a grim smile, "as it so happens, we're flying with the crows."

Over the next few days, Dianna's crew reluctantly took their turns loudly swearing allegiance to Captain Warren while she quietly went about his ship and admired how well it was built. It still looked like a traditional ship, but was made to cut through the air rather than water. That lent to a leaner, more streamlined hull with wings extending on either side to catch any updraft. It didn't operate with a simple open flame, either. Instead, the ship had a giant wood stove channeling all the hot air upward and into the envelope carrying them. There was even a backup of coal buried deep in the bottom of the ship, should they run out of wood.

Captain Warren's crew was made up of lean, muscular, half-metal men whose mechanical parts ran on steam. The ship was never silent. There were puffs and squeals and metal grating on metal constantly around them. If the wind hadn't been loudly buffeting the ship, Dianna might've gone mad from the sound. She silently thanked whoever had constructed Ben's body; without their expertise, he might've been as loud and cumbersome as these poor sods. He also didn't need to worry about running out of steam. *Sun-powered,* that was Ben, and his cheerful, loud singing and ever-smiling mouth seemed to be a testament to it.

Although she had originally intended to try and make friends with the opposing crew, it quickly became obvious that they both revered and feared their captain. They also seemed to carry the same disdain for women, which meant whenever she tried to speak with them, they sneered and kicked her away. She shrugged it off. Being pointedly ignored enabled her to wander about the ship unhindered, and it meant she could easily avoid speaking with or seeing Richard. Ever.

Sitting with the other two women on her crew for dinner late one evening, Dianna leaned over a scrap of paper she'd nicked and finished her sketch of the airship.

"It's well made and easy to handle. If we can get control of it, the rest would be easy."

Maisy nibbled on a piece of hardtack, frowning. "How did you even get past the stores?"

"They're not watching us. We can go wherever we want," Rebecca scoffed. She'd had the task of figuring out the steering.

Dianna grinned at her companions. "I'm actually rather glad Captain Warren has such a low opinion of us. He doesn't think we're smart enough to do anything dangerous, which gives us poor, wee, delicate females an incredible advantage."

Maisy brightened, leaning forward and nearly spilling her half-eaten soup. "We can sabotage the ship!"

"No, we want the ship. It'd be a sore disadvantage to get rid of it."

"Then what?"

Dianna smiled. "Ladies, we're going to stage a *mutiny*."

"A mutiny?" Sebastian, a tall and broad fellow with long blond hair, looked up from cleaning his gun with a dubious stare. Somehow, he'd charmed his way out of doing any mopping, which one of the steamed-powered crew was doing nearby instead. Keeping his voice low, he murmured, "Will any of these men even *go* for that?"

Maisy sat close to her husband, leaning her shoulder against his and pretending to mend something. "Probably not," she admitted. "But we want the ship." She put the shirt down and stretched her arms, using the chance to check if anyone was close enough to hear, before she added, "Captain said to wait until we get to wherever we're going. We can take it while they're distracted."

Sebastian scratched the side of his nose, looked up into the oblong balloon hovering over them, and shrugged. "I suppose that's fine, dearheart."

"It has to be," she stubbornly replied, elbowing him in the ribs. "So, until then, don't do anything reckless."

It was at this point Captain Warren's crew member stomped up to them and shoved the mop handle into Sebastian's face. *"That's* how ye swab a deck, ye miserable lump!"

Maisy's husband took the mop, leaned it against his shoulder, and then peered around the other crew member. "Ah. Yes. I see now. Masterfully done, sir." Standing and stretching to his full height, he lazily offered, "Is there anything else I can do?"

"Obviously not! Yer useless!"

Shrugging and leaning in to give Maisy a parting kiss, Sebastian strolled off to put the broom away and, presumably, go back to cleaning his pistol.

The other crewman swiveled to take his frustration out on Maisy, but she squeaked, scooped up the shirt, and scurried out of sight.

In various other areas of the ship, Dianna's crew were in casual conversation with each other, speaking poorly about Dianna's captaining abilities to any who would listen. It had been her idea. She wanted them to have full autonomy when the time came to take over. While they did their best to smear her name to Captain Warren's men, the plan made its rounds among *her* crew in conspiratorial whispers.

Later that evening, Dianna was waiting for Rebecca and Maisy in a hidden corner of the ship. Idly swinging the little pouch that held her ring, she heard the sound of boots and quickly straightened, tucking the pouch away under her vest. Unfortunately, the person to round the corner was the last person she wanted to see.

"There you are, darling!" Richard swept forward as if to hug her.

Dianna dodged his advance, slithering around his open arms and backing up a few steps. "What do you want?"

He dropped his arms. "Do I need a reason to want to see my wife?"

She recoiled. "As far as I'm concerned, I'm *not*."

Tsking, the well-dressed man placed a hand on his hip and inspected his nails. "You know that doesn't mean anything, my love. We *both* need to agree to divorce, and I simply cannot do without you."

"Which is why you tried to kill me."

"Don't be like that, darling," he crooned, stepping closer once again. "I'll be absolutely *devastated* without you. Would you prefer if I said you were *lost* at sea? I could walk the sandy shores every day, waiting for your return."

"I'd prefer if you didn't say anything at all," Dianna retorted, backing away from him. "It always ends up being a stinking pile of—"

"Temper, Dianna." The way he said her name sent her skin crawling. Captain Warren was blatant with his threats. Richard preferred a more subtle approach. Stepping forward again, he continued. "Honestly, we wouldn't be in this situation at all if you'd just done what you were supposed to."

"You mean if I had let you poison me," she said flatly, stepping back.

He looked wounded. "No, darling, of course not! I mean if you'd simply borne my *children*."

Dianna bristled. "You mean the maid, the cook, the laundry girl down the lane, our next door neighbor, and her *mother* weren't enough for you?"

Richard sighed. "Darling, if they had a child, it wouldn't be *mine*. Not legally." He stepped forward again and leaned in close. "Besides, I chose to marry *you*."

"Well, that just makes it *all okay*." She took another step back and hit the wall. Bracing her feet stubbornly, she crossed her arms and warned, "You need to back up. Now."

Richard braced one hand casually above her shoulder and chuckled. "Come back to my room. I'm sure my bed is more comfortable than yours. You could stay there with me, where you belong, and we could discuss this whole 'lost at sea' business and maybe…" He glanced up, thinking for a moment before saying with grand allowance, "…come to a compromise?"

"I think not." Dianna retorted, shaking with fury. "Do I look like an idiot,

Richard?"

"No," he drawled, smiling. "You look like my wife."

She slapped him. The look of surprise on his face was almost worth the hell she'd pay for it if she stayed. Shoving him roughly away from her, and grateful to be much stronger now than she had been a few months ago, Dianna hissed, "I've *never* been your wife." Spotting Maisy coming down the hall, she strode off to meet her.

"Are you okay? You're trembling." Maisy glanced behind her even as Dianna led them away.

Forcing a smile, she took a breath and shook her head. "I'm fine. Let's find Rebecca."

Take your bow, go into the woods
To catch the golden stag
He wears a crown
Of golden down
And guards the copiague.

Dianna woke with a start, sitting straight up from where she had fallen asleep on the floor. Her dark hair fell around her face, and she pushed it back in confused frustration until she remembered where she was. Letting her hands drop, her shoulders fell, and she leaned forward to rest her forehead on her knees. The pouch fell from inside her shirt to knock softly against her legs.

She gasped, jolting upright again. She remembered.

The song was a nursery rhyme, a child's song her mother used to sing to her before bed. Dianna sat up straighter, crossing her legs, and opened the pouch to fish the ring out. She turned it in her fingers several times, and then, on a whim, she put it on. The ring slid comfortably on her second finger. Holding her hand up, she admired how the stone glinted in the muted rays of moonlight. She wasn't prepared when a memory as clear and vibrant as the moon itself leaped to the forefront of her mind.

Take your bow, go into the woods
To catch the golden stag
He wears a crown
Of golden down
And guards the copiague.

"What's a copiague?" Dianna interrupted the gently singing voice. She was wrapped in a blanket and her mother's arms.

"It's our protected place, now hush. This is important, my little fawn." When she started singing again, Dianna's voice followed, obediently reciting along.

With your arrow, strike his heart true
And ring him round with twine
Then pull it tight
With all your might
And gaze at his bright shine.

Then call on Virbius loud and clear
And charm him with your wiles
When the moon shines
In silver lines
He'll lead you through your trials.

You are Divine, you're proud and strong
But keep your footsteps straight
Do not go near
The shallows here
And don't forsake your fate.

Dianna rested her chin on her arm, staring out the window. She'd stopped reciting it when her mother died, only a few months after she turned five.

As a child, she had thought the words were a magic spell to keep them safe, and when that belief was shattered, she had wanted no remembrance of it.

Thinking back to the singing in her head, she once again recited the words. The tune was a perfect match. She had remembered something, but she had no idea how to use it.

"She's *magnificent.*" Captain Warren leaned on the rail next to Dianna. A beautiful island with a natural, circular harbor of sandy beaches and high cliffs stretched out before them. "And right where you said she'd be." He turned his body toward her, one elbow still resting on the smooth and shiny rail, and laced his fingers together. "I suppose you're not *completely* useless."

Dianna grimaced. "Careful, Captain Warren, someone might accuse you of trying to compliment me."

He paused, looking thoughtful. "I think a compliment is warranted, don't you? After all, you've just led us to what should be the treasure of a lifetime."

"My inheritance, you mean." He only smiled, and she turned her attention forward again. "Forgive me if I don't leap from joy. Bad back, you know. All that *knitting.*" At that, Warren laughed and reached over to ruffle her hair. Dianna skillfully avoided the touch and faced him. "What do you want?"

Pushing himself off the rail, the man leaned over Dianna and chucked her under the chin. "You're the key. Show us the way in."

If he'd asked her a few days ago, she could've honestly said she didn't know. Swiveling on her heel, Dianna pointed to a rock formation that looked like a crudely carved stag head rearing up into the sky. A ring of golden brown trees crowned its head. Just like the song. "Look under there. You should find a protected cave or something similar." The rhyme rolled around in her head and she paused, wondering if she should tell him the rest.

"Go on." Captain Warren raised his eyebrows.

"Watch for traps."

"What kind of traps?"

Dianna shrugged. "Ones with arrows?"

About halfway down the cliff, between the stag head and the crashing waves of the ocean, they found an entrance. A large cave sat back among a cluster of trees, yawning wide on a flat outcropping. As Captain Warren's men scrambled to secure the ship to the rock face, Rebecca looked to Dianna expectantly. Dianna shook her head with the barest of movements. Even with the pirates distracted, they would still be outnumbered and outgunned. She wanted as few casualties as possible.

As soon as the gangplank was firmly set, Captain Warren clasped Dianna's elbow in a bruising grip and pulled her off the ship. About half the crewmen followed, weapons in hand and gleaming eyes peering into the dark as though they could see what someone else might not.

Richard strolled down the plank, fixing his cuffs and hair. Despite the long trip, he looked as though he'd just spent the last few days in a *spa* rather than on a ship with a hardened crew and nothing more than thin soup to fill his stomach. Linking his hands behind himself, he stopped next to Dianna and Captain Warren.

"Are we going to go in?" he asked, peering around with feigned curiosity. "Or are we going to stand out here all day?"

The pirate captain pushed Dianna forward and released her. "After you." He bowed extravagantly to the two of them.

Richard straightened his jacket with nonchalance and held his arm out to Dianna. He had no idea he was trap bait. "Well, darling? Shall we?"

Ignoring him, Dianna walked to the edge of the cave. She had noticed long lines carved deeply into the stone wall when she had been disembarking. She stepped closer, peering through the hardy trees, and found crossbows hitched up and ready to fire. Dianna gently touched the strings before rubbing her fingers together. The oil felt fresh, as if the bows were looked after on a daily basis, but the weatherworn backs suggested otherwise. Whatever their secrets, they were still armed and dangerous.

Turning around to warn the others, she saw Richard striding into the cave without her. Dianna hesitated, but as much as she'd *love* to let him get skewered by arrows, she didn't think she wanted to see another person die right in front of her.

"Stop!" she snapped. Taking a few long steps, she grabbed the back of her husband's coat, dragging him out of the entrance just as high-pitched twangs sounded from several directions. Thanks to her quick movement, the arrows flew harmlessly by and clattered against the stone. "Idiot." She let go of him and glared. "Didn't you read as a kid? Never walk straight into places like this. There are *always* traps."

"I see I was correct in having you go first," Captain Warren said. A few of his men were swiftly dismantling the traps left unsprung. "What else is there?"

Dianna looked into the cave. "I'm not sure. So, try not to get killed."

Once all the bows had been completely taken apart, Dianna took a lantern and entered the cave. The singing in her head was louder and more complex now. It was a whole symphony on repeat, drilling the words into her head until they nearly drowned out everything else.

The cave narrowed until they were walking single file. Richard's grip on her wrist tightened the farther they walked, keeping her close, and she found herself hating his cowardice. When the cave abruptly opened around them, Dianna stopped in surprise. They had gone from a tight passageway to a huge cavern with no floor. Her lamp barely threw out enough light to show the perilous, narrow path that spanned the length of the chasm. Something else glinted on the distant cave walls, too faint to make out.

"Keep going!" a man shouted from behind.

Dianna warily eyed at the stone under her feet. To either side, all she found was darkness and the faint sound of water. The path was wide enough for her to walk confidently as long as she put one foot in front of the other. Although it was an easy task for anyone who was even *moderately* paying attention, she seriously doubted the capabilities of those who followed behind her.

"There's an open fall out here." Her voice echoed in the vast cave all around them. "Watch your step."

She inched forward until everyone had entered the cavern. With all the lanterns illuminating the space around them, Dianna could make out the objects in the distance. The collective, reflected light of glass disks shone nearly as brightly as the sun; each lantern was reflected off the mirrored surfaces multiple times and crosswise, and Dianna realized too late what the reflections were for.

There was a sound like tearing fabric and a short whistle before a man yelped in pain. More tearing and shouts started to fill the air as one end of long, bamboo rods were released from the ceiling of the cavern. With their other end still bound to the cavern roof, the rods whipped out to strike everyone on the path like a lashing from above. At least one man fell, his cry cut short by a splash. She'd have to pick up her pace to get the rest safely across. Starting to trot, Dianna was nearly thrown off the path herself by Richard's vise-like grip.

"Don't go so fast!" he hissed.

She twisted her wrist until it slipped from his hand and ran to the other side of the cavern. He would have to fend for himself. The ground eventually widened, and the remaining crew scurried onto it, gasping for breath. While the men nursed bruises from the bamboo rods, Dianna walked to the edge and peered up at the cavern ceiling.

"They worked like magnifying glasses." She was impressed. Considering the level of technology needed to create the map, the simple traps designed here were a fascinating contrast. The bamboo had been held back, held *tight* like the poem had said, with thin twine. Under the bright shine and pointed fixation of the lantern light, the rope had burned until it snapped, thrashing anyone in the way like a switch wielded by an angry parent.

Captain Warren stood next to Dianna, his eyes fixed on the ceiling like hers. "For any man of my mine who dies from this point on," he calmly warned, "I will kill one of yours."

Dianna frowned at him. "It's not like I knew exactly what was going to happen." Captain Warren's gaze slid over to her, his implant shining brightly. "I'm not lying."

"We'll see." The pirate wheeled on his men. "Stop fussing about your bruises and get back in line." The men grumbled, but obeyed.

Richard stalked over to Dianna, rubbing a shoulder and glaring. "I swear, if you get me killed, I will kill you first."

Dianna rolled her eyes. Compared to Captain Warren, Richard was a mosquito. She shouldered past him and made a beeline for the ongoing path, the crewmen filing silently behind her. The narrowing passage grew dank and wet, and a cold draft lingered around them. A stream of water rushed by their feet with hasty whispers and roughly hewn walls pressed close on either side. Accompanied by the occasional drip from the ceiling, it was enough to make the largest of men shiver. Dianna rubbed her arms briskly and hoped they'd come across the next thing soon. If her inheritance was in there, it was buried deep.

After what seemed an eternity, Dianna stepped inside a narrow chamber and sidled over so the others could pool in after her. The lantern light cast a warm and friendly glow across a scene made of stone. A young man of smooth white marble held an empty bowl in his graceful arms. His face was serene and sweet, his eyes cast down to a young stag who frolicked beside him. Other wild animals sat or stood nearby, all of them looking toward the young man. Further back was an old tree with animals and symbols carved deep into it. Many of them were blackened from age and covered in moss to the point of being unrecognizable.

After admiring the scene, Dianna noticed a single dot of light on the cavern wall. A partially overgrown hole allowed bright daylight to stream in from far, far above. She gazed down at the woodland scene, silently reciting the next part of the poem, when she noticed one of Warren's men start to walk forward. She whirled toward him.

"Don't!"

The floor beneath him gave way and his leg plunged into the ground. One of his companions grabbed his arm and hauled him back up, but the damage was done. A long gash was cut across the metal of his leg, straight up to his knee. It wouldn't hurt, but it wouldn't be easy to walk on, either.

Dianna walked over and crouched to stare into the hole he'd opened. "That was stupid," she said. Beneath the crumbled stone waited large, sharp spears standing on end, their tips jabbing dangerously upwards. "Tiger traps." She glared at the man. He'd almost gotten one of her men killed. "Don't walk anywhere before I say how to. You're lucky that was your *metal* leg."

She carefully walked back to the statue and stared into his shy, sightless eyes. Following his gaze, she inspected the bowl, then looked back up at the ceiling. *When the moon shines in silver lines...* She snapped her fingers. "The moon! We need water and the moon."

"The moon." Warren's eyes narrowed curiously. "We're not staying here until night."

Dianna pointed to the statue. "This is Virbius. He's a woodland god. You can charm him by giving him something to drink." She tapped the bowl in his hands. "I'm guessing we should fill this with water and let the moon reflect on it. That should..." She trailed off before shrugging. "Well, it should do something."

Captain Warren fixed her with a calculating stare, his eyes flashing in warning, before he leaned back on his heels and suggested, "Why don't we *make* moonlight?"

"Don't be stupid," Richard scoffed. "You can't make moonlight, that's preposterous."

"Shut up." The pirate captain barely spared the other man half a glance. Speaking to Dianna instead, he raised his eyebrows. "Well?"

She met his gaze straight on. "I'm not an engineer."

"No?" Captain Warren strolled over to one of Dianna's crew and looked him over, before promptly shooting him in the knee. Sebastian leaped to the fallen man's side, ready to fight, but was held back by Maisy. Reloading his pistol, Warren didn't look at Dianna. "Here's some inspiration, since you seem to need it. You're a clever girl." He cocked the gun and aimed it at the young man's head. "Make some moonlight."

Every line of her trembled with anger, but acting against Warren now would be foolhardy. She had to be patient. Taking parts and pieces of metal from both her crew and Warren's, Dianna set to work. When she was finished, she had a wide, metal box with sloped sides and a hole on either end. After turning the sloped sides so they faced downward, she scanned the crew available. The tallest was, unfortunately, Captain Warren.

"If you want me to make moonlight," she said, standing up and dusting off her pants, "you'll need to help me. Richard, make yourself useful and put water in the bowl. You, Captain." She pointed to the space just in front of her and continued, "are going to give me a boost." She would've preferred to ask Ben for help, but he had stayed behind on the ship to encourage the remaining pirates to keep their mouths shut.

Handing the gun off to another one of his crew, Warren strolled over and looked down at her with an amused half smile. "How, exactly?"

"If you want the light beam to be as close to correct as it's going to get, I'll need to sit on your shoulders." Dianna fiddled with the box she'd made, carefully placing her lantern inside and locking it in. The little adjustments she'd made had the bright flame burning hot and nearly blue. If she touched anything but the handle, she'd be severely burned, but she hopefully wouldn't need to hold it for long.

"Do try not to burn me." Captain Warren drawled before he bent and scooped Dianna up around her knees, nearly causing her to drop the entire contraption on his face, burning lantern and all.

"Be careful!" she snapped, catching the lantern before it collided with him. She immediately regretted stopping it. He deserved to be smacked.

"I'm not *kneeling* in front of you," Warren replied calmly, adjusting her weight more comfortably and hoisting her higher. "This is about the same as sitting on my shoulders, isn't it?"

Dianna didn't respond. She was too busy carefully aligning the lantern exactly as she needed it. The second it was fitted, she held it out and looked around for Richard. Surprisingly, he was filling the bowl as she'd ordered. When the water was nearly overflowing, he stopped and looked up at her in question.

"Is this enough, darling?"

Any and all gratitude she'd felt toward him for doing as she'd said evaporated in an instant. "Yes. Now back up." He did as she ordered once again, and she lifted the light. "Douse your lanterns, everyone."

There was a brief moment of hesitation, which was immediately broken by Captain Warren backing up her command. The room was pitched into darkness. The only light in the cramped cave came from the hole in the ceiling and Dianna's experiment. The puncture in the bottom of the box sent a pinpointed ray of light directly onto the bowl, illuminating Virbius' face and arms with a silvery glow. The ripples in the water played tricks with darkness and light, making the statue seem come to life and breathe in the soft, reflective shine. For a moment, everyone was enraptured by the effect, until Maisy gasped.

"Look at the ceiling!"

Careful not to move the lantern, Dianna focused her attention upward and was once again awed by what she saw. Silver lines illuminated by the reflected light traced out constellation patterns. Each shining point marking the stars twinkled like a diamond, the lines between them flickering dimly.

"Orion and the Crow," Warren murmured.

From her vantage point on his shoulders, Dianna noticed the ground had very similar patterns chiseled into the stone. There was a gaping hole in another constellation where the unsuspecting pirate had stepped. "We need to follow the lines." She glanced up at the ceiling before trying to locate Maisy in the dim light. "Maisy, do you trust me?" She thought she saw a faint nod. "Follow my instructions carefully."

One of the pirates stopped Maisy from moving. "Captain?"

"Let her get on with it," Warren growled.

Instructing the young woman to gather up stones, Dianna carefully guided her across the floor. Placing a stone on every slab representing part of the two constellations, Maisy created a clear path to safety. Once she was on the other side, Warren released Dianna and ordered the other lanterns to be lit. The room burst into warm color again, and the haunting scene vanished.

As they filed along the path, Richard leaned over to Dianna and asked, "Darling, why couldn't those be seen in *regular* light? Why make us go through the trouble?"

"Moonlight is silver," she replied and glanced back at the statue. "Virbius was a god who hunted and wandered with Artemis, the goddess of the moon. If any regular light worked, the statue would've been Apollo." There was a long silence behind her, and she mentally sighed. "Riddles aren't riddles unless there's a way to solve them. Using a regular lantern or sunlight would be too easy."

Her husband made a discontented noise in his throat. "What kind of mother leaves *traps* for her child?"

Dianna chuckled quietly and dropped the subject, letting Richard grumble in confusion.

The last trap was eerily similar to the second. A thin stretch of stone down the center was meant to be followed, but instead of vast emptiness, shallow waters waited on either side with a stony floor only a few inches beneath.

Do not go near the shallows here...

This raised path was narrower than the first, but Dianna wasn't about to risk whatever trap was set in favor of running recklessly forward. She glanced up across the cavern and saw something gold shimmer from a doorway beyond it. Behind her, those who could also see it were excitedly murmuring to one another, jostling and pushing to get a better view.

"Stay out of the water," she warned, lifting her voice to be heard above the others. Then, taking a breath, she began the precarious task of crossing the narrow bridge.

"Stay on the path if ye like!" said one of Warren's men as he leaped off the path and began sloshing through the water. "I'm not letting ye take all th' best for yerself!"

Dianna held Richard back from doing the same. "Wait!"

A few more men clamored in agreement and eagerly followed the first, filling the cavern with the sound of splashing and rapacious shouts. The first man got about halfway across before he noticed something was off.

He lifted up his boot and smacked it, alarm written all over his face. "Somethin's in my boot!" He yanked it off and let out a strangled yell.

Half of his foot was missing.

The other men turned and rushed back to the path. Not one made it. The water churned and boiled up with sudden vicious activity, turning red with blood as the men were eaten from the bottom up. They barely had a chance to let out horrified screams before they fell into the shallow water and were completely devoured. After a few short moments, the water once again calmed. All that was left of the foolish men were their steam-powered, metallic limbs and enhancements. There weren't even bones.

After a long moment of silence, Dianna repeated, "Stay out of the water." This time, no one argued.

The closer they got to the room, the more the lanterns shone on gold and other glittering treasures; silver and gems twinkled and danced in the wavering light. Dianna didn't wait for the others when she reached safety. She continued onward, straight toward the room, and stopped just inside the very edge of the doorway. A vast island of treasure spread out before her. She barely heard the relieved shouts of pirates after they finally crossed to safe land. She didn't mind when they pushed her roughly out of the way to start hungrily gathering up everything they could put their grimy hands on. Wincing, Dianna rubbed her temples. The sound of singing in her head had become almost unbearably loud.

"And don't forsake your fate," she whispered to herself.

Maisy came to stand at Dianna's shoulder. "You okay?"

Her quiet voice broke the other's trance and Dianna jumped. Running a hand through her hair, she frowned. "There's something for me here. Once I find it…"

Maisy nodded. "Shall I tell the others?"

Dianna smiled grimly. "Please do, and help Sebastian get our wounded man back to the ship for medical assessment." The other woman nodded and slipped back through the doorway, disappearing as quietly as a mouse.

"What's the problem, darling?" Richard called down from where he had climbed up a pile of jewels. He was in the middle of decking himself out in an absurd amount of jewelry. "This is your inheritance! Aren't you going to take any of it?" Pulling a ring off his hand, he tossed it to her. "There, take that. It's almost as pretty as you."

Dianna caught the ring, barely glancing at it before she dropped it onto a nearby pile. She wasn't here for gold. Absently, she followed the edge of the cavern. About halfway around, she heard the sound of water and ducked past a corner where she found a boat rocking gently on the high tidal waters of a small cove. Light filtered in from the cave's mouth, and she could hear seagulls distantly calling to one another. Toeing the boat gently, Dianna wondered at its purpose. Then she pivoted and came face to face with a goddess.

A pack of stone hunting dogs eagerly crowded around the beautiful figure of Artemis, looking to her for direction. Stone clothing billowed around the statue in frozen movement as she drew back on a large bow. A necklace with an ornately set green pendant hung from the arrowhead. Upon closer inspection, Dianna noticed the pendant had a tiny clockwork mechanism, much like the one which had shattered. Carefully unraveling it from where it hung, she placed it around her neck.

The moment the stone rested against her skin, the singing ceased. Going back the way she had come, Dianna watched the pirates as they scooped up various treasures, trying to fit as much as possible on their persons and in ratty bags, heedless of the dangerous walk back, laughing and joking and fighting as they hoarded everything in sight. They were too busy with themselves to notice her slip silently away.

Dianna climbed onto the airship to find the last of Captain Warren's crew rounded up and trussed together. Ben stood before them, a grinning giant ready to take out anyone who attempted to wriggle free. The second Dianna was safely on deck, Rebecca and James pulled the gangplank back, then loosened the ropes holding the airship in place until only one secured them there. Dianna straightened her vest and braided her hair out of the way before thoughtfully eyeing the leftover crew.

"You have a choice. You can either join my crew, or I can have Ben throw you overboard, where you can take your chances with the waters below."

One of the pirates scoffed. "I won't follow a *woman!*"

She shrugged. "Well, there you go, Ben. A volunteer."

Grinning wickedly, Ben approached the prisoner and sliced through his ropes. Lifting him as easily as a feather pillow, the giant tossed the pirate over the rail. The scream disappeared in the distance and Ben turned back around to the other men, rubbing his hands together. "Anyone else?" Much to his disappointment, no one else offered themselves as fish bait.

"Captain!" James, perched on the lines, pointed to the cave.

Dianna leaned over the rail, beaming cheerfully. Captain Warren and Richard stood at the cave mouth, looking gloriously stunned. Their arms were full of gold and trinkets, while crew members behind them heaved bags of the treasure. Without dropping his armload, Warren casually walked to the edge of the outcropping and peered over. The ship was too far away for anyone to leap onto, and the only line holding them in place was far, far below. Black hair swirling in a sudden updraft of wind, he leaned back to look up at Dianna and laughed. Richard, on the other hand, dropped his treasure and started shouting. She was tempted to ignore his tantrum, but seeing him so riled up was too good to pass over.

"I need a pair of ears, please," she called over her shoulder.

Sebastian grinned and pulled out a set of mechanical ears. Strolling over, he leaned on the rail next to her and asked, "Want me to toss it?"

"Please do. To my husband, preferably." Dianna took one of the devices for herself.

Throwing the other device true, Sebastian struck Richard in the side of the head. The man stumbled and snatched it up. There was a brief sound of static before a string of curses filled the air. Dianna switched the volume off. When he finished, she turned it back on. "Sorry, did you want to repeat any of that? I didn't quite catch it."

Warren took the ear before Richard hurled it at the ground. "Well done!" He bowed to her in a flourish. Once he straightened, he added, "I do hope you don't think this is the last you'll see of me."

Dianna chuckled. "I didn't think it would be. Thanks for finding my inheritance, though! I never would've even *thought* about it without you two being greedy, pigeon-livered, miserable canker-blossoms. Unfortunately, there's *just* not enough space here for both of your egos and me, so I had to leave the less valuable things behind. I'm sure you understand." Even from where she stood, she could see Richard's face turn purple with anger. She cheerfully added, "Don't look so glum, darling. I left you a boat. You'll find it back in the cavern. You know how to row, right?" She began to turn away before changing her mind. "Oh, and Richard? I *had* come up with a very good reason to divorce you." She paused, smiling. "But, 'lost at sea' has a rather nice ring to it, don't you think?"

Rebecca stood next to Dianna, arms akimbo. "What now, Captain?"

The rest of the crew were behind her, waiting for orders.

Running her hand along the rail, Dianna admired the shine of her new ship. With the singing in her head stopped, she no longer felt a rush to run somewhere. There was plenty of time to use the new necklace and find what her mother had *really* left her. "Let's get Jonathan a proper stone. He deserves an honorable burial, even if we don't have his body." She was somber for a moment before brightening. "I think I'll have Richard pay for it!" At Rebecca's stare, Dianna grinned. "After all, we *are* still married."

More from E. A. Catania

Runaway Rails

Two runaways, one railroad, one big secret.

When their violent stepfather, Gael, threatens them, Kat reacts in a desperate attempt to keep her sister Annie safe. Unsure if she'd murdered him and terrified she hasn't, Kat convinces Annie to slip away in the night, fleeing together on a nearby railroad. Despite the ever-growing distance between herself and what she's done, peace and comfort elude Kat. When they're joined by two questionable but knowledgeable youths who know the ins and outs of traveling the rails, Kat realizes there's more to life than running in this adventurous 1940's historical fiction.

Find her books at:

https://www.goodreads.com/author/show/18150119.E_A_Catania

Also by Phoebe Darqueling: The Mistress of None Series

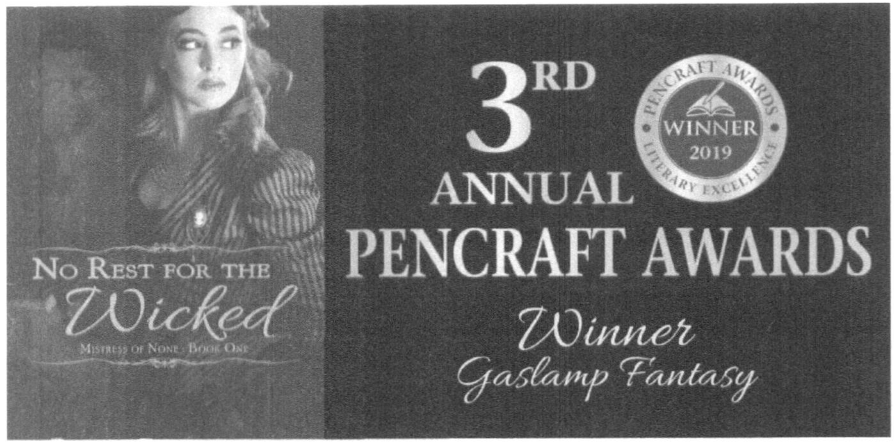

Other people just think they're "haunted by the past." In Vi's case, it's true. Clairvoyant Viola Thorne wants to forget about her days of grifting and running errands for ghosts. The problem? Playing it safe is dull. So when a dead stranger begs for her help, Vi jumps at the chance to dust off her hustling skills. The unlikely companions are soon tangling with bandits, cheating at cards, and loving every minute.

Then she finds out who referred him, and Vi has to face both a past and ex-partner that refuse to stay buried. Though she betrayed Peter, his spirit warns her of the plot that cost him his life. Vi's guilty conscience won't let her rest until she solves his murder. Though she's spent her whole life fighting the pull of the paranormal, it holds the key to atoning for the only deception she's ever regretted—breaking Peter's heart.

Available in print, e-book, and audio formats. Find them all at bit.ly/ViolaThorne

Nothing Ventured, Nothing Gained: Mistress of None Book 2 is coming Aug 2020.

Also by Phoebe Darqueling: Riftmaker

Save his boy, uncover a conspiracy, and master opposable thumbs—a dog's work is never done.

Buddy's favorite thing is curling up for a nap at the foot of Ethan's bed. Then he stumbles through a portal to a clockwork city plagued by chimeras, and everything changes… Well, not everything. Sure, his new human body comes with magic powers, but he'd still rather nap than face the people of Excelsior, who harbor both desire and fear when it comes to "the other side."

He discovers Ethan followed him through the portal and underwent his own transformation, and it becomes Buddy's doggone duty to save him. Buddy finds unlikely allies in an aristocrat with everything on the line, a mechanic with something to hide, and a musician willing to do anything to protect her. Using a ramshackle flying machine, the group follows the chimeras deep into the forest and uncovers a plot that could reshape the worlds on both sides of the rift.

Available in e-book and print formats. Find them at www.bit.ly/Riftmaker

Also by Phoebe Darqueling: The Steampunk Handbook

Get your e-book for FREE when you sign up to receive Phoebe's e-newsletter at bit.ly/SteampunkHandbook

The Steampunk Handbook is a collection of articles by Steampunk author and lecturer, Phoebe Darqueling. It covers topics such as the history of steam power, the philosophical roots of punk and punk literature as a whole, and the history and evolution of the Steampunk fandom. In addition, you will find information about the historical and cultural underpinnings behind twelve of the most popular tropes in Steampunk. Enjoy pages of recommendations for books, movies, and television shows that are perfect for fans of Steampunk both old and new.

Coming to print May 1, 2020.

Thank You

This book and it's companion, *Cogs, Crowns, and Carriages*, came to life thanks to the generous backers of a Kickstarter campaign. Our deepest gratitude goes to:

Aaron Turko
Abiran Raveenthiran
Alex Chapman
alicat
Allison Payne
Alyssa
Andi Newton
Andrew Parsons
Andy and Ali Prudom
Anna Kaling
Anonymous
Arielle Wasiak
Barb and Carl Kesner
Barbara O'Dell
Baronessa Arts
Beth Culp
Brandy A. Melville
Brittany Nock
Carol Gyzander
Cryptic Creative
Crysta Coburn
Cynthia Fry
D

Dale A Russell

detly

Dianne Nicholson

Donald

Emma & Simon Gelgoot

Engel Dreizehn

Erik T Johnson

Faye Ringel

Gaslamp Fancier

Gevera Bert Piedmont

Gordon Emrick

Grady Hess

Hel broisha

Hilary Anderson

Hisham Barazi

Ian Glover

Ian McFarlin

Ib Rasmussen

Irina Marinescu

James Jester

James Lucas

Javed Mawji

Jen Linton Carvahlo

Jennifer L. Pierce

Jess Gisler

JL Merrow

Joe Dubé

Joshua C. Chadd

Joshua Whitaker

Karen J Carlisle

Kathleen Burns

Kati Hamilton

Kevin Drew

King
Kirasha Urqhart
Kristi Fox
Kristin Anne Danko
Leigh Smith
Linda
Lisa Kruse
Madeleine Holly-Rosing
Mandy Burkhead
Mark Carter
Mark Featherston
Mark Lukens
Matthew Karpinski
Megan K. Ward
Melanie
Melissa Williams
Mercy J Meilunas
Michael the Horologist
Michelle Mishmash
Mike Bundt
Mitchell A Johnson
MoMo
Nathan Lueth
Nicholas Eng
Nicolas Aguirre
Olivia Montoya
Paul Hiscock
Rie Sheridan Rose
Robby T. Tatom, G.GiftGuru
Robin Komarica
Robinette Waterson
S and A Hudson
Saga Albright

Sarah Van Goethem
Shannon M.
Shannon O'Neill
Shawnee M
Sheldon Rock
Stephanie Gonzales
Steve Lemanski
Steven Peiper
SwordFire
thatraja
The Fryer Family
Tim "Buzz" Isakson
Tracy 'Rayhne' Fretwell
Zoltan Deathspawn